Above All Else

Sandy Cove Series Book Seven

Rosemary Hines

To Pastor Terry
and the multitude of pastors
worldwide
who faithfully teach the
love of the Father

See what great love the Father has lavished on us, that we should be called children of God!
And that is what we are!

1 John 3:1

CHAPTER ONE

"How am I going to make it through another year of him?" seventeen-year-old Caleb Baron muttered as he pulled out of the driveway and floored the car, leaving screech marks in his tracks. This was the third blow up with his dad that week, and all Caleb could think about was getting through his senior year and getting out of the house for good.

As he barreled toward his job at the Coffee Stop, he ignored the speed limit and squeaked through a four-way stop with barely a pause. Maybe he'd make it to work on time after all.

Then he saw it. The flashing lights in the rearview mirror. Great! Now I'll be late again, and this will give Dad one more opportunity to blast me. Pulling over to the side of the road, he tried to control his rage as the officer approached his window. After listening to the lecture and signing the ticket, he feigned repentance and got rid of the cop. This was going to cost him more than one day's work.

"I wonder what it would be like to have a father who wasn't always on me for everything. One who would help me out with things like this ticket," he mused to himself aloud. "Guess I don't have to worry about ever finding that out," he added, mumbling to himself.

When he got home later that night, he decided to just get it over with. Spotting his dad working in the study,

Caleb walked in and dropped the ticket on the desk. "Don't worry, I'll pay for it," he said.

At first, his dad looked baffled. "Pay for what?"

"This ticket," Caleb answered, pushing it toward him. "I was running late, remember? Because of the trash."

"Because you didn't take it out earlier when you were supposed to?" Steve said.

"Yeah. Whatever."

Steve took a deep breath. Shaking his head, he stood up and handed the ticket back to Caleb. "On top of paying for this, you'll be attending traffic school as well, or our insurance will go through the roof."

"Fine."

"What's with you these days?" his father asked, studying Caleb's face.

"Nothing," he replied, taking the ticket and walking out of the room. *Good old, Dad. Always knows how to make me feel like a jerk. I'll bet he regrets the day they adopted me. Well, he's not the only one.*

Billows of white satin swirled around Madison's feet as Michelle Baron helped her daughter step out of the second dress of the day. It was their third stop of the day, and she could see that Maddie was feeling discouraged.

"You'll find it, honey," Michelle said, lifting the discarded dress and handing it to the shopkeeper's assistant. "And when you do, you'll just know—this is it."

Madison smiled, but she didn't look convinced.

"Let's go get a bite to eat and then try Vintage Bridal," Michelle suggested. "It's near your dad's office. Maybe he'd like to join us."

Laughter escaped Madison's mouth. "You think? Dad in a bridal shop? He gets impatient at the grocery store."

She's right, Michelle mused silently. "You never know. He's buying the dress. Maybe he'd like a say."

Raised eyebrows told her Madison was skeptical. "Up to you, Mom," she replied as she slipped on her jeans and sweatshirt. "Maybe we should start by seeing if he wants to join us for lunch."

"Good idea! Then he can pay for that, too," Michelle agreed with a wink.

Madison checked her cell phone as they walked out the door. She'd texted Luke a picture of the front of the shop along with a "Look where I am!" message when they'd first arrived. She sighed when she confirmed there'd been no reply.

"Something wrong?" Michelle asked, reading her daughter's anxiety.

"Luke still hasn't replied to my text."

Michelle could hear the familiar insecurity in her daughter's voice. Although Madison had come a long way in the six years since high school, she still battled feelings of not being good enough, especially when it came to Luke.

Thankfully, nursing school had been so good for her. Madison was a natural and seemed like a different person when she was in her nurse's uniform. She'd graduated with honors and fulfilled her internship at the pediatrician's office and had an offer in the wings to work there part time.

But Michelle could sense a very vulnerable part in Madison's heart. It was likely she still hadn't forgiven herself for a bad relationship in high school, and it continued to lurk in the shadows of her mind with regards to Luke.

Michelle had seen Maddie's insecurity surface several times lately when her fiancé was mentioned. Now she hoped her daughter's anxiety wouldn't cloud the beginning of her upcoming marriage.

"I'm sure he'll get back to you soon, Maddie. He's got a lot going on right now with finishing up his finals and packing to come home."

"Yeah, I guess," her daughter replied, not sounding convinced.

They caught Steve between meetings at his law firm. "Lunch sounds great," he replied. Soon the three of them were settled into a booth at a nearby café perusing the menu.

"I think I'll just have a half order of the chef's salad," Madison said as she slid out of the booth to head for the ladies' room.

There was a time when this would have concerned Michelle and Steve—a season when Maddie was in high school and wrestling with her self-image. There'd been battles over her compulsive dieting and exercise as they'd watched her lose pound after pound.

Thankfully those days were over. Madison had just completed her nursing degree and was turning a page on a new chapter in her life. Soon she'd be marrying the boy of her dreams—Luke Johnson.

Michelle had so many fond memories of watching the two of them grow up side by side since Luke was the son of their pastor and close friend, Ben and his wife, Kelly. But it was hard to imagine that those two kids were now adults and about to embark on a whole new life together.

"So it's really happening." Steve's voice interrupted her thoughts.

Michelle reached over and placed her hand on his. "Yep. Our little girl is going to be a bride."

Steve took a deep breath and let it out. "And to think I could have stopped it," he said. "I could have just said no."

"What do you mean?" Michelle asked with a grin.

"I could have told Luke 'no' when he asked for her hand," he said with teasing seriousness.

"Right. I've got a big picture of that," Michelle replied, squeezing his hand as Madison approached the table.

"What are you guys talking about?" their daughter asked.

"About how your father could have told Luke no when he asked for your hand in marriage," Michelle replied.

"Daddy!"

"Just kidding, princess. You know we love Luke. He's a great guy." He paused and then added, "It's just going to be tough letting you go. We're kind of used to having you around," he added with a wink.

After lunch, Michelle and Madison convinced Steve to accompany them to their next stop—Vintage Bridal. She caught Maddie checking her phone again. From the way she tossed it back in her purse, Michelle could see that there was still no answer from Luke.

As Steve held open the door of the shop for them, Michelle's eyes swept the room. It was very different from the other bridal stores they'd been to that day.

Gowns from a variety of eras graced headless mannequins. Vintage photos of weddings of the past accented the walls and rested in tabletop frames, and fresh flowers sweetened the air as they sat poised on antique furniture pieces and stands along the walls and in the corners. Dark hardwood flooring and an elegant crystal chandelier transported the three of them to another time.

A chime from the open door brought the shopkeeper out to greet them. "Good afternoon," the middle aged woman said with a warm smile. "Welcome to my shop. I'm Amelia," she said, extending her hand to Steve and Michelle, who introduced themselves. Then, turning to

Madison, Amelia added, "And I'm guessing you are the bride."

Madison beamed and nodded. "I like your shop. Very retro."

"Why thank you," Amelia replied, clearly pleased by Madison's enthusiasm.

"So are these used gowns?" Steve asked, fingering one of the old fashioned styles from the mid nineteen hundreds.

"Many of them have graced brides of the past," Amelia confirmed. "But some are remakes of older styles with slight modifications such as changes in the neckline or lace."

Steve lifted the price tag on the gown he'd been looking at. His eyes told Michelle the price was not cheap. Michelle gave him a subtle shake of her head to send the message it wasn't time to talk about prices.

Amelia held her hand out to Madison. "May I show you around the shop?"

Nodding, Maddie took her hand and followed as the shopkeeper led them to a far wall of hanging gowns. The rack was divided into sections with black and white photos illustrating each division. Above the photos were framed newspaper headings showing a specific era and noting the headline with a snapshot in time.

"As you can see, our dresses go back to post World War II—the beginning of the baby-boomer generation, as soldiers came home and married their sweethearts."

Madison glanced over at Michelle. Her eyes were filled with delight, and Michelle could almost feel what it must be like to be her daughter at this moment. She flashed back to her wedding to Steve, and the one-stop shopping for her own bridal gown.

Of course, it had been a wonderful afternoon with her mother. But it was a quick trip, and she bought the third dress she tried on. Watching Madison soak in the ambiance of the shop and enjoy the stories of the owner made Michelle's heart sing with joy. Glancing back at Steve, she could see that he was momentarily caught up in their daughter's adventure as well.

Madison selected five dresses from various eras that she wanted to try on. While Amelia placed them in the fitting room, Madison looked at some necklaces in a glass case on the counter.

"Would you like to see our 'some day' dresses?" Amelia asked.

Madison's expression prompted the shopkeeper to continue.

"We have a small selection of contemporary gowns as well," Amelia explained, leading them to a corner in the back. "I call them our 'some day' dresses because in the not too distant future, they, too, will be vintage."

"I like that," Madison said, clearly taking to this woman.

Carefully shifting through the gowns, Amelia selected one and pulled it out. "This one would be lovely on you," she suggested, holding it up for Madison's approval.

"Yes. I'd like to try that one, too," Madison replied, nodding in agreement.

Before the three ladies headed for the dressing room, Amelia suggested that Steve help himself to some coffee and relax in the sitting area. "We'll let you know when she's in the first gown and you can come take a look," she promised.

"Are you okay for time?" Michelle asked.

Steve glanced at his watch. "Let me check in with the office," he replied pulling out his cell phone. "I should be fine for another half hour or so."

Madison decided to work her way from the past to the present. The first gown she tried was from the 1940's. It was a surprisingly sophisticated style, much sleeker than Michelle expected to see in a vintage dress. The three-quarter length cream colored satin gown had an off-the-shoulder shawl collar with a cluster of pink satin roses at heart level. A fitted bodice flared to a curve hugging, tulip style skirt and flutter hemline.

"The brides of this era had weathered a war. They'd seen the women on the home front take up the slack for the men overseas. There was a certain level of confidence and boldness these gals had developed. The notion of a traditional gown was seen as outdated and old fashioned to many of them," Amelia explained as she zipped up the dress and cinched it in the back with extra pins to show Madison the fit that could be achieved with some tailoring.

"What do you think, Mom?" Madison asked.

Michelle hesitated for a moment. "Honestly? It looks more like a bridesmaid's dress to me."

Maddie nodded. "Yeah."

"Do you want me to go get your father?" Amelia asked.

"No. Let's wait. I'll try on the one from the sixties," Madison replied, gesturing to the next dress on the rack.

Three gowns later, Madison slipped into a dress made just for her. As the chapel length train fell to the floor, Michelle's voice caught in her throat. "Let me get your father," she managed, before slipping out of the dressing room. Tears filled her eyes as she approached Steve.

His face dropped in response. "Is something wrong?" he asked, concern furrowing his brow.

Michelle shook her head and smiled as she dabbed at her tears. "Come on in," she said, taking his hand and giving it a squeeze.

Amelia had just finished pinning the dress in the back. Madison looked absolutely stunning.

"Wow," was all Steve could manage. Michelle nodded her head in agreement.

After the dress had been ordered, Steve headed back to work, and Michelle and Madison got into the car to drive home. Michelle could see Maddie digging through her purse for her phone. Pulling it out, she checked her texts.

"Anything from Luke?" Michelle asked hopefully.

"Nope," was Madison's reply.

Michelle watched some of the day's joy drain from her daughter's face as they pulled out of the parking lot. *Oh Lord, please help her get past these insecurities,* she prayed silently.

CHAPTER TWO

"So your dad told me about the ticket," Michelle said to Caleb.

"Yep. I messed up again. Your perfect son," he replied sarcastically.

"What's that supposed to mean?" she asked.

"It means Dad's right, I'm a loser," he answered, trying to sound nonchalant.

"No one ever said you're a loser, Caleb," his mother countered, an edge to her voice.

Caleb felt himself soften a little. After all, it wasn't his mom who was always after him. "Maybe not in those words, Mom, but you know how he is."

"He's just trying to help you be the best man you can be," she said, reaching out and putting her hand on his shoulder.

Pulling away, Caleb steeled himself against the emotions that were threatening to overtake him. He looked into her eyes for a minute then walked away.

Madison's heart leaped when Luke's face appeared on the screen of her cell phone. She immediately punched the accept button. "Hi stranger," she said lightly.

"Hey." Luke's voice sounded distant and tired.

"You didn't answer my text. What's wrong?" Madison asked, hoping for a reassuring explanation.

"Yeah. Sorry about that. I've had a lot on my mind."

"Anything we should talk about?" Madison's stomach tightened.

"Hold on a sec," he replied. Luke didn't sound very happy. Maybe he was having second thoughts about the wedding, or even about getting married.

She couldn't blame him. Not really. Sure, she'd pulled her life together after a disastrous stint in high school. If only she had known then what she knew now, she never would have gotten involved with Miles.

But there was no going back. She'd given herself away to a boy who was just looking for a good time.

Luke was different. They'd grown up loving each other. Not romantically, of course, until that brief stage when Madison was in junior high, and he was in high school. But it wasn't until after Madison's relationship with Miles that Luke confessed his true feelings for her, feelings Maddie had tried to bury in her own heart.

They'd thought about getting married while both were in college, but their parents had wisely steered them to focus on school first and then build their life together as a couple. It had been four long years of texting, phone calls, FaceTime, and vacations for courting. Now they were finished with college, Luke with a master's degree in theology and Madison with a bachelor's in nursing. In one more week, Luke would be home for good!

They'd been officially engaged since Christmas. When Luke had shown up that morning with a wrapped sweater box in hand, Madison's heart sank. She'd hoped it would be a ring that he'd be bearing. As her hand caressed the soft, raspberry colored cashmere sweater inside, she noticed a small bulge.

"What's this?" she asked, digging under the soft wool and retrieving a small satin pouch.

"Oh, that? Just a little something to go with the sweater," Luke replied casually.

As she pulled it out and opened the drawstring ribbon, he slipped off the couch and onto one knee. A sparkling diamond ring fell into her hand. Looking at Luke, her eyes filled to the brim.

"Madison Baron, would you do me the honor of being my wife?" Luke asked while the whole family sat on the edge of their seats.

"I will," she managed through her tears, reaching out to him and pulling him into an embrace as the family cheered.

Luke took the ring and slid it onto her finger then cupped her face in his hands as he kissed her right there in front of everyone.

"Way to go, dude!" Maddie's brother, seventeen-year-old Caleb, exclaimed. "Finally I'll have a brother around here."

"Maddie, are you there?" Luke's voice interrupted her thoughts.

"Yeah."

"Sorry, that was the resident director reminding us of when we need to have our stuff out of the room," he explained.

"Are you excited?"

"About?"

"About coming home?" she asked, suddenly feeling nervous. Why did he sound so short with her?

"Oh. Yeah. It'll be good to see everyone again."

Everyone? Really? She took a deep breath and tried to calm her racing heart. "I'll bet you've missed your family."

"Listen, Mad, I've gotta go. Pray for me this week, okay? My mind is going in a million directions."

"Okay. I will," she replied. "See you Sunday afternoon?"

"Yeah."

"Okay. Love you," she added.

"Love you, too."

"We should probably make an appointment with the florist to finalize our order," Michelle said to Madison the next day.

"Maybe we should wait, Mom."

"Why? It's one more thing we can cross off our list," Michelle said as she held up a clipboard.

"I'm not feeling that great," Madison replied, her voice a little shaky.

Michelle walked over and sat down on the bed beside her daughter. "What's up?"

"It's just…I don't know, Mom. Something's not right." Madison looked like she was about to cry.

"What is it, honey?" Michelle asked as she draped an arm over Maddie's shoulder. In an instant, Madison was in tears. Michelle drew her into her arms and held her close. "You aren't having second thoughts, are you? I mean about getting married."

Madison shook her head as she pulled herself away. "No, but I think Luke might be."

"Why do you say that?" Michelle could feel her heart begin to race. Surely Luke was not backing out of the relationship after all this time?

"He just sounded so distant when we talked yesterday. Like he barely had anything to say to me." She grabbed a tissue from the nightstand and blew her nose. "And when I sent him that text from the bridal shop, he never answered it."

"Oh, Maddie. He's got a lot on his mind right now. I'm sure he's eager to see you again. Everything will be fine when he's home. Trust me."

Madison studied her face but didn't respond.

"Maybe we should all go to a movie tonight," Michelle suggested. "We can take a break with the wedding planning. Pretty soon, you'll be out of the house, and we won't have any more family nights."

Madison gave her a sad smile. "Okay. Yeah. That sounds good."

"I'll go talk to your brother and see if he's up for a movie."

As Michelle stood, Madison grabbed her hand. "Thanks, Mom."

"You're welcome, honey. And I mean it. Everything's going to be fine."

Caleb's door was ajar as Michelle approached it. She knocked lightly and pushed it open. Caleb was at his desk on his laptop, which he promptly shut before turning nervously to face her.

Something didn't feel right. "Watcha doin', pal?" she asked.

"Nothing. What's up?" he replied hastily.

"Madison and I were thinking about catching a movie tonight."

"Okay."

"Would you want to go? I mean, like the whole family," she asked.

"Uh...sure...I guess," he answered, still feeling a little badly about how he'd talked to her earlier. "What movie?"

"You and Maddie pick. Dad and I will be fine with whatever you two decide."

"Okay. Just tell her I'm in here. We can look the shows up online."

Michelle nodded. "Nothing with torture, okay?"

"Okay, Mom. No torture. Got it," he replied with a smile.

After his mother had left the room, Caleb opened his laptop again. A list of agencies popped up on the screen—all designed to help find birth parents. Caleb knew his birthmother—a former student of his mother's who'd gotten pregnant with him while she was an eighth-grade student in Michelle's class.

Although he hadn't met her until he was six years old, Amber Gamble had been a part of his life ever since. She would come up to Oregon to their home in Sandy Cove every couple of years to see him. And he'd been to her place in Arizona when they'd gone on a vacation to see the Grand Canyon.

But Caleb wanted to meet his real father. And Amber was not cooperating with him. She refused to give him any information at all, other than saying the relationship was a big mistake and that the guy was older than her. Apparently, he'd been in high school at the time.

Caleb had been at the same campus for three years now andwould be a senior this fall—old enough to find out who his biological father was. Maybe the guy still lived in Sandy Cove. It was possible Caleb had even seen him around town.

Lately, it seemed like his other dad was always after him about something. "Cut your hair," "Get that grade in science up," "Better figure out what college you want to go to." His dad was full of directives. It wasn't that Caleb didn't love him or feel loved back. But he knew Steve wasn't his flesh and blood. And for some reason, that mattered right now.

Both of his parents had been great about Amber. They let him talk on the phone with her, write letters and emails, and hang out when she was in town. But whenever he mentioned anything about his birth father, everyone put up walls.

How bad could the guy be?

Caleb wanted to find out for himself. And nothing was going to stop him.

Glancing at the college brochures on his desk, he flashed back to a fight with his dad the day before. Steve had come in unannounced and handed him the flyers. "Time to start looking, bud," he'd said.

"I just got out for summer, Dad. Can I have a break here?" Caleb asked.

"Not if you want to get into a good school," his father retorted. "Competition's stiff, especially if you want to do something like pre-law."

"Pre-law? Really, Dad?"

"Would it be so bad to follow in your father's footsteps?" Steve asked, his voice tinged with impatience. "You could walk right into a junior partnership here with me."

"Great," Caleb replied.

"Just think about it, son," his dad added in a much softer tone.

"Yeah."

After Steve had left his room, Caleb had tossed the brochures off to the side of his desk. What was the big push about college? Maybe it would be good to take a year off. Allowing his mind to wander, he considered a road trip across the United States. *Or I could concentrate on learning to surf better and travel down the coast to hang out with Uncle Tim in Seal Beach. Yeah, that would be a blast.*

But first, he wanted to find his real father. And see just what kind of guy he was.

"Hey," Madison said as she walked into her brother's room. She noticed that he immediately shut his computer before turning to talk to her. "What are you doing on there?" she asked casually.

"Nothing."

"You shut it awfully quickly for 'nothing,'" she replied.

"It's nothing that concerns you," Caleb said. "So Mom wants us to have a movie night," he added, clearly wanting to change the subject.

"Listen, Caleb, if you're getting into something stupid on that computer, Mom and Dad will find out eventually, so you might as well come clean with me."

Her brother stared at her for a minute and then clapped his hands on his knees. "I'm just looking for someone, okay?"

"Okay. Like who?" Madison asked.

He hesitated before answering. "Promise you won't say anything?"

"Depends on who you're looking for," she teased.

"Come on, Mad. I'm serious."

"Okay, okay. I promise."

Caleb took a deep breath and turned back to his computer, opening it to reveal the screen.

"Finding a Birthparent" appeared in the search engine box. Madison walked over and skimmed the listing below. "You already know your birthmother," she said.

"Yeah. But not my father," he replied, shutting the computer again.

"Oh man, Caleb. Are you sure you want to do this?" Maddie asked. "I'm sure Amber would have told you if she thought you should know who he is."

"Amber doesn't get to decide everything for me. And she probably lost touch with him a long time ago," he said. "For all I know, he's still living in Sandy Cove. Maybe he wonders about me, too."

Madison could see the earnestness in her brother's eyes. Finding this guy was really important to Caleb. But it creeped her out to think of him approaching some stranger and claiming to be the guy's son.

"Listen, Cale. I know I promised not to tell," she began.

"And you'd better not," he jumped in, his tone warning her of his seriousness. "I mean it, Mad. I'll never trust you again."

"Okay. Fine. I won't say anything. But I need you to promise to keep me updated on your search. Please, whatever you do, do not go see anyone without letting me know. Deal?"

"Deal."

Feeling at least a little reassured, Madison remembered the reason she'd come into his room in the first place. "Mom wants us to pick a movie for tonight," she said.

"Yeah. Right." Caleb once again opened his laptop and navigated to the theater page. Soon they were perusing their choices.

CHAPTER THREE

The week had dragged by, and Madison was getting more and more nervous as Luke's return hastened. Every phone conversation between them seemed strained, and Luke often let over an hour go by before responding to her texts. The pediatrician's office had called twice to see about her interest in the part-time nursing position. She'd thought she should discuss it with Luke first in person, but maybe she should just go ahead and take it.

"What are you looking so serious about?" Madison's father asked one evening.

"Just stuff," she replied, standing to walk out of the room.

"Hey, hold on for a second. Can't you give your old man a few minutes?" he asked. "Soon you'll be married and out of here, and I won't have you around."

Madison relented. "Okay, Dad," she replied, walking over and sitting on the arm of his chair.

"So Luke comes home tomorrow, right?" Steve asked.

"Yep."

Her father looked at her intently. "You don't sound very excited about that."

"I guess I'm a little nervous," she admitted.

"Come here, princess," Steve replied, pulling her to her feet and then into his lap. "I still have room for you here," he added, shifting in his chair to accommodate her.

Madison rested in his arms, suddenly feeling very small.

"So why are you nervous, honey? Is it all the wedding stuff? I know you've been under pressure to make a lot of decisions lately."

She sighed. "No, it's not that." Hesitating, she finally added, "It's Luke. There's something different about him."

Steve shifted again, this time to make eye contact with her. "What do you mean?"

"I mean he's acting funny, Dad. Like something's bothering him," she began. "And he takes forever to answer my texts. It's almost like he's avoiding me."

"That doesn't sound like him," Steve replied. "He must have a lot on his mind, Maddie."

"I guess."

"Don't jump to any conclusions, sweetheart. Luke loves you. We all know it." Steve drew her close again. "There's a lot on a man's mind when he's about to get married," he added. "I remember suddenly feeling a new weight of responsibility on my shoulders about a month before your mother and I took the plunge."

"Really, Daddy?" she asked.

"Really. Even though I knew your mom wanted to become a teacher, I still felt like the role of breadwinner and provider was going to be on me." He paused for a moment and then said with a chuckle, "I guess it's wired into us males—to want to take care of our women."

Madison smiled. "So you think that's what's bothering Luke?"

"Maybe. It wouldn't surprise me."

"You don't think he's having second thoughts?" she asked.

"About marrying you?"

"Yeah."

Steve hugged her close. "I'm sure it's not that. Don't go down that rabbit hole."

She was quiet for a minute. Then she sat upright. "Thanks, Dad. Thanks for listening. I hope you're right." She stood up, kissed his cheek, and walked out of the room. "And, Dad?"

"Yes?"

"Do you think I should take the position at Dr. Kramer's office?"

"It sounds like a solid offer to me. When do you need to let him know?" he asked.

"The other nurse is going part time in a month and then she'll be off for maternity leave around Christmas."

"What does Luke say?"

"I haven't had a chance to discuss it with him yet," she replied. "Guess I should do that first."

"If you're asking me, I'd say yes, you should. You two need to start making your decisions and plans together now."

"Yeah," she replied with a nod. "Thanks, Dad." She gave him a hug and then started walking away.

Steve watched her go, saying a quick prayer for wisdom and confidence for his only daughter.

"I'm concerned about Madison," Michelle said tentatively, as she and Steve were getting ready for bed that night. She didn't want to worry him, but Madison's reluctance to press forward with the wedding arrangements had her stumped.

"Me, too," he replied. "We had a little talk this afternoon. I don't know where it's coming from, but she seems suddenly insecure about her relationship with Luke."

"I know. I just don't get it."

"Do you think I should talk to Luke?" Steve asked. "I mean man-to-man, and see if the signals Madison thinks she's picking up are valid? She says he's not responding to her texts, at least not in the timeframe she expects, and that he's been distant on the phone."

"She told me the same thing," Michelle replied. "I'm not sure about you talking to Luke, though. It seems like something Maddie has to do herself."

"Yeah. I guess. I just don't want her heart broken by him."

"By Luke? Really? He's crazy about her. And he's not the type to lead someone on."

"Yeah." Steve sank onto the bed beside her. "Maybe you should talk to her and remind her of that."

Michelle nodded. "Sometimes I think she never completely outgrew the insecurity she felt in high school. She's like two different people these days—self-assured and confident in her nursing skills, but still wavering in her footing as a future wife."

"Well, I didn't say this to her, but a guy doesn't want to be battling his wife's insecurities all his life. At some point, Madison needs to realize that Luke loves her and start resting in that truth. Otherwise, there could be problems."

Michelle felt her stomach clench. After all that Madison had worked through in her teens—her issues with her body image, her feelings of being unpopular, and her disastrous relationship with Miles—she deserved to be happy. "I'll try to talk to her," she promised, slipping her hand into his as they began their end-of-the-day prayers together.

Madison was on the other side of their door listening to what had been said. Anxiety surged through her body. Her father was right, of course. No man wanted a wife who was always needing reassurance and bolstering up. Maybe she should be the one to call off the marriage, so Luke wouldn't have to.

She could probably still return the dress. It hadn't been altered or anything. And her parents didn't seem to mind having her live here with them. She could take the job at Dr. Kramer's office and save up money to get her own place. Plus, she'd be around to keep an eye on her brother and his search for his birthfather.

Havoc could break loose when that happened. And she'd be here to be a buffer between her parents and Caleb.

Maybe this was God's will all along. Having a long distance relationship with Luke had helped her have the confidence to make it through nursing school. And he'd been able to focus on his studies, not on finding a wife or girlfriend.

Yeah. She'd talk to Luke and explain how it was better for both of them to hold off on getting married. Feeling sad, but somehow also relieved, she headed for bed. As she fell asleep, she drifted into a dream about her fiancé.

Luke arrived at their door, looking nervous. When Madison invited him inside, he turned and looked toward his car. Following his eyes, she could see a beautiful girl sitting in the passenger seat. The girl smiled and waved at Luke.

"Who's that?" Madison asked.

"We need to talk," he replied, pointing inside. "Can I come in?"

"*Sure, yeah.*" *Madison stepped aside, and he walked past her into the living room. It looked different. A large, cavernous room with heavy brocade drapes, dark paneling, and crystal chandeliers. The air was cool, and Madison felt a chill.* "*Here, sit down,*" *she said, gesturing to the stiff Victorian sofa facing the darkened window.*

"*I can't stay,*" *Luke replied, remaining standing just inside the room. His expression was so business-like. No familiar warmth at all.*

"*Okay. Just say what you came to say,*" *Madison began. But before he could reply, she said,* "*No wait. Let me talk first.*"

Luke glanced toward the front door and nodded.

"*So, I've been thinking that we rushed into the whole idea of getting married. And, well, I think I need more time to figure things out.*"

She could see his face relax. "*Okay.*"

"*So let's just call off the wedding for now,*" *she said.* "*I need to get a job and take care of my brother.*" *She'd suddenly become aware that only she and Caleb lived in this mansion.*

"*Yeah,*" *Luke replied.* "*That makes sense.*"

"*We can still be friends,*" *she offered.*

"*Okay. That's good,*" *he replied.*

The cool damp air hung heavy between them for a moment. Then Madison heard Caleb calling her name. "*I'd better go,*" *she said.*

"*Yeah. Me, too.*" *Luke walked over to the door, turning and lifting his hand to wave goodbye before he headed out.*

"Maddie, hey, wake up," Caleb's voice penetrated her sleep. Turning over in bed, she found herself in the comfort of her own room, her brother standing over her.

"What time is it?" she asked.

"It's one-thirty."

Madison struggled to focus. "In the morning?"

"What do you think, the middle of the afternoon?" he asked sarcastically.

30

She shook her head as if to shake off her dream. Then she sat up and leaned against the headboard. "What are you doing in here?"

"I think I found him," he replied.

"Who?"

"My real dad."

CHAPTER FOUR

"Check this out, Maddie," Caleb said.

Madison leaned over the laptop and looked. It was a picture of a younger Amber on the front lawn of Magnolia Middle School with a guy sitting beside her.

"I found it by searching for pictures from Magnolia. Someone had posted the whole yearbook online. Pretty cool, huh?" he said with a grin.

"How do you know that is the guy you're looking for?" Madison asked, peering closer at the photo.

"I just think it is. Doesn't he kind of look like me?"

She studied the photograph carefully. "Yeah. I guess."

"The bummer is that there's no name beside the picture. Not even Amber's. It was just a random photo to fill an empty spot," Caleb said.

"What are you two up to?" Michelle asked as she poked her head into the room.

Caleb quickly shut the computer. "Nothing, Mom." He looked over at Madison, shooting her a warning glance.

"Sorry we woke you up," Madison added.

Michelle hesitated for a moment, and then said, "You guys need to get to bed."

Maddie wandered through the house the next day, her stomach in knots. Luke would be arriving home anytime now, and she and her family were invited over for dinner to welcome him back.

"You're wearing a path in the carpet," her mother commented with a smile.

Madison glanced over and sighed. Sinking into the couch, she plopped her feet on the coffee table. "Why hasn't he called yet?" she asked herself aloud.

"He's probably not home," Michelle replied. "I'm sure you'll be the first one to hear."

Madison nodded reluctantly. "Do you think we're doing the right thing? I mean getting married right out of college like this?"

Michelle put down the catalog she'd been flipping through and looked Maddie in the eye. "Where did that come from?" she asked.

"What?"

"That question." Her mother leaned forward in her chair and seemed to be studying her.

Madison's heart began to pound. *Why did I have to go and open my big mouth?* She wondered. "Nothing."

Her mother didn't seem satisfied with her answer, eyebrows raised in a skeptical look.

Hedging, Madison added, "I was just thinking about how young we are and everything. Like maybe we should take a little more time to be sure."

"So are you questioning whether or not you want to marry Luke? Because I thought you were gung ho to jump into marriage right out of high school."

Madison sucked in the air around her. "I was. And I still am. It's just…I don't know…maybe it would be better if Luke had some time to kind of get settled into his career and everything…"

Michelle didn't respond right away. Her penetrating stare was making Madison nervous. "Quit it, Mom."

"Quit what?"

"Quit staring at me like that."

Her mother sat back into her chair, resting her elbows on the armrests and steepling her hands together at the fingertips. "Has Luke been saying something that makes you think he's not ready yet?" she asked.

Madison shifted uncomfortably. "No. Not really."

"Not really? But kind of?" Michelle probed.

"I don't know, Mom. He just seemed distant when I talked to him on the phone. And he said that we needed to talk." She paused and then added, "It sounded serious."

"Okay, well, let's not jump to conclusions, honey. I'm sure it's not about the wedding. He's probably just got a lot on his mind, trying to figure out plans for the future."

"Yeah. Maybe," she replied, wishing her voice sounded more convincing.

Just then Madison's cell phone rang. Glancing at the screen, she saw Luke's photo. "It's him," she said, standing up and walking out of the room.

"Madison? Are you ready?" she heard her mother call out from downstairs.

"Just a sec. Be right down," she called back.

Just then Caleb stuck his head in her room. "Come on, Mad. Let's go. Loverboy is waiting," he teased.

Madison picked up a shoe and threw it in his direction, watching it bounce off the door he'd closed just in time.

"Guess this is it, Lord,"she said softly, tossing her brush into her purse, making one final check in the mirror, and heading downstairs.

As their van pulled into the Johnson's driveway, Madison could see Luke sitting on the top step of the porch talking to his sister, Lucy. He looked up and stood as they parked the car.

Madison's insides were doing somersaults. She was excited to see him but suddenly felt overwhelmingly nervous at the same time.

Caleb bounded out of the car and gave Luke a high five. "Welcome home!" he said with a grin. "Hey, Luce, where's Logan?"

"He's out back helping Dad with the barbecue," she replied as she pushed up from the stairs and waved at Madison.

Michelle and Steve both greeted Luke. Then Maddie saw her mother elbow her dad and point to the house. "We'll be inside," she said to no one in particular as she took hold of Steve's hand and started toward the front steps.

Luke came up to Madison and putting one hand on her shoulder, bent down and brushed his lips over hers. "Hi."

"Hi," she replied.

Lucy laughed from the porch. "I'll see you two inside," she said.

"So how was your flight?" Madison asked.

"Too long. It's good to be home." After a kiss, he draped his arm over her shoulders and gave her a little squeeze. "We should go inside. I think the dinner's about ready."

Madison felt nervous throughout the meal. It seemed like all Luke's parents could talk about was the wedding plans. Every once in a while, Madison caught Luke staring at her. He looked so serious, although he would flash a smile when they made eye contact.

After dinner, Luke stood up and helped his sister clear the table. Then he came over, rested his hands on the back of Maddie's chair, and leaned down close to her ear. "Let's go for a walk," he said softly.

She nodded and rose from the table.

"We'll be back in a little while," Luke said as he took her hand and led her to the front door.

"Everything okay?" Luke asked as they walked down the front porch steps.

"Yeah. Why?"

"I don't know. You just seemed kind of quiet during dinner."

"I did? I guess it's all the wedding talk." She hesitated, not sure how to put it, and then added, "It feels kind of surreal. Know what I mean?"

He laughed softly. "Yeah."

They were almost to the street when Luke asked, "Wanna go down to the shore?"

Something about the beach always gave Madison a feeling of peace, like everything would be all right. "Sure. Sounds good."

"Be right back!" Luke dropped her hand and sprinted toward the house, returning a minute later with keys in hand. "We'll take Dad's beater," he said, pointing to an older truck parked at the curb.

Madison tried to picture her attorney father driving a vehicle like that. What a contrast to Pastor Ben. Both men were hardworking, but Luke's dad's rewards were definitely not monetary.

Ben seemed perfectly happy driving an old pickup with faded paint and evidence of having traveled a ton of miles, while her father zipped around in a sleek new BMW. She didn't think the worse of her dad, but it made her realize her life with Luke would be very different from the one she'd had growing up. Not that she minded.

As she was about to slip into the passenger seat, she noticed a stack of papers on the seat, along with one of Lucy's sweatshirts and a pair of tennis shoes on the floor.

"Dad doesn't travel light," Luke said apologetically, leaning over and grabbing the shoes and sweatshirt and tossing them into the back. He picked up the stack of papers. "Looks like some sermon notes," he added, shaking his head. "Mom keeps telling him to get a briefcase or something." Opening the back door, he placed them on the seat.

Then he gestured to the empty spot. "Okay, it's all yours."

She slipped in, and they took off.

Pulling away from the curb, he patted the middle seat. "Scoot over, you," he said. "There's a perk to this old tank."

Maddie smiled and slid across the bench seat. Luke's body felt warm next to hers, and her heart soared as he draped his arm around her and pulled her close, kissing her head.

"I've missed you, Maddie."

"I missed you, too," she replied, leaning her head on his shoulder. For a few moments, she was at peace. It felt so right being with him. Maybe everything would be okay. She really did want to marry him. "So have you decided about asking Caleb to be one of your groomsmen?" she asked.

"Let's not talk about the wedding anymore tonight, okay?" he said, seeming to stiffen a little.

Madison's heart sank. Fears and doubts rushed in to replace her brief moment of peace.

Caleb and Logan were shooting baskets out back. "So what are you doing this summer?" he asked Luke's brother, who was two years older than Caleb.

"Work as many hours as I can get at the Coffee Stop. How 'bout you?"

Although Caleb's parents paid for Maddie's college and would also pay for his, he knew the Johnsons couldn't afford to foot the bill for all six of theirs. That meant full-time summer jobs. Seemed a shame to waste an entire vacation like that. Part time was one thing. But full-time ate up the entire summer. On the other hand, Caleb respected Luke and Logan for how hard they worked.

Before he answered Logan's question, Caleb weighed how much he should share. "Don't know. I might go out to Arizona to see Amber," he replied, wondering how his parents would respond to him visiting his birthmother.

As if reading his thoughts, Logan asked, "So does that freak out your mom and dad?"

"Nah. They're cool about it," he hedged. Taking careful aim, he lobbed the perfect swish into the basket.

"Nice one," Logan said. "So your parents are totally cool with you visiting Amber?"

Caleb hesitated. *Should I tell him what I'm doing?* He paused and thought about it. *What the heck. I can trust him.* "Yeah. They let me stay in touch with her, and they said I could go out there sometime. But they'd probably freak if they knew why I want to go now."

Logan stopped bouncing the ball and turned to look at him. "Why? What's up?"

"You can't tell anyone, okay?"

"Fine. But I hope you aren't planning to move out there or something dumb like that."

"No. It's nothing like that." He knocked the ball out of Logan's hand and bounced it over to the hoop, easily making another basket. "I'm trying to find my dad," he said.

"Whoa. Seriously? I'm guessing that really would freak them out."

"Yeah. So that's why you can't say anything. I mean it, Logan. Not to anyone."

"No one else knows?"

"Only Mad. She promised she wouldn't tell them."

"Are you sure this is such a smart thing to do?" his friend asked.

"I need to know."

"But why? You already have a great dad."

Caleb shrugged. "Yeah, but it's not the same. And lately, things haven't been so great between us. I mean sometimes it seems like he's never satisfied with me."

"I know what you mean. Dads are like that sometimes. They want their sons to be better than they were."

Nodding, Caleb added, "Plus, it's totally possible my real dad is still in Sandy Cove somewhere. It seems weird that I might see him at the beach or somewhere and not even know he's my dad."

"Yeah. That's kinda weird," Logan agreed. "But I don't know…I'd think about this seriously, Caleb. You might never find him, and you could really hurt your parents by trying."

Madison and Luke stood at the edge of the water hand in hand. The full moon lit the beach and reflected off the liquid horizon. "It's a beautiful night," Luke observed.

"Yeah." Madison shivered slightly.

"Are you cold?"

"A little."

Luke dropped her hand and wrapped his arms around her. As she pressed her head against his chest, she could hear his heart beating and a muffled, "I love you, Maddie." She held him tight, suddenly feeling like she was going to cry. *What's the matter with me?*

They stood clinging to each other for a few minutes, the sound of the waves breaking on the nearby rocks filling the air.

Then Luke pulled back and looked into her eyes. Without saying a word, he bent down and kissed her.

Madison melted, and she felt a yearning that almost scared her. As Luke's kiss deepened, she found herself pushing away.

The hurt in his eyes was clear. "What's wrong?"

"I can't do this," she replied, a tear escaping her eye.

CHAPTER FIVE

Luke stared at her like he couldn't believe his ears. "What do you mean you can't do this?"

"I'm scared, Luke."

"Of me?" he asked incredulously.

"Of us." She looked like she was groping for words.

"Do you still love me?" he asked. She could see the muscles in his jaw tighten.

Madison sighed. "Yes."

"Then what's the problem?"

"It's just that when we're together like this, I get scared."

He searched her face. "You know I'd never do anything to jeopardize our relationship, right? I'm not like Miles, Madison. You get that, right?"

Madison flashed back to Miles, her high school fling that had ended with her losing her virginity to a guy who had no problem taking off as soon as she put the brakes on their physical relationship. Ever since then, she'd wrestled with feelings of shame and regret.

Then on a short-term mission trip, Luke had surprised her with his own confession—his realization that he'd loved her for years. And that had started what Madison thought would be the fairytale ending to her story.

But now...now that it was actually about to come to pass, Madison's concerns had begun to consume her. She doubted she could ever be the kind of wife Luke deserved.

"Maddie? Did you hear me?" he asked gently, drawing her focus back to the moment.

"Yeah. I know. Believe me, I know, Luke. You are definitely not like him."

"Do you still want to marry me? Because you're freaking me out right now."

"I'm sorry, Luke. I don't know what's wrong with me. It's not you. It's probably just all the pressures of the wedding and stuff," she said, looking down at the sand.

He cupped her face in his hands and lifted it, so they were looking into each other's eyes. "So we're good? You and me?"

She nodded.

"Because I really love you, Madison Baron," he said, his expression serious.

"I love you, too, Luke Johnson," she replied, trying to sound lighthearted.

"We're not kidding around here, Maddie."

"I know," she said.

He pulled her close again, and as she listened to the steady beat of his heart, she felt herself relaxing again. Maybe things would be okay after all.

On the drive back to Luke's house, Madison remembered he'd said something on the phone about needing to talk. Once again she felt her anxiety beginning to surface as she asked, "What was it you wanted to talk about?"

He looked puzzled. "When?"

"When we were talking on the phone before you came home. You said there was something you wanted to talk to me about. You sounded serious. Like something was wrong."

"Oh, that. It's about an offer my dad made me."

"What kind of an offer?"

Luke pulled over to the curb and shut off the engine. "Before I tell you, I just want you to know that our marriage is going to be a total partnership, okay?"

"What does that mean?"

"It means we make all the big decisions together, you and me. I'm not going to go off and decide anything about our future without you having an equal say," he explained.

"Okay."

"So, here's the deal." He reached over and took her hand. "I know we both were thinking we'd like to be on the mission field together some day. But I also know we talked about staying here in Sandy Cove for a few years first."

"Right. We were going to both work and save up. You know I got that offer from my internship—the job at the pediatrician's office. It's only part time, though, so I'd probably supplement at the hospital or something. They're always looking for nurses, especially in pediatrics."

"Yeah. About that—let me explain what my dad and I discussed."

"Okay, tell me. Did he offer you a position at church?"

"Well, not exactly. He offered to have the church sponsor us on the mission field in the orphanage in China. The couple who have been running it would like to come back to the states for a few years."

"Wow. Really?"

"Yeah. I know. It's a lot to think about," he replied.

"So we'd go right after the wedding?" she asked, trying to process this news.

"Right after the honeymoon," he replied, searching her face for a response.

"I don't know what to say."

"You don't need to say anything right now. Just think about it. I wasn't planning on springing this on you my first night back. And remember what I said, about us deciding everything together. This is huge. We won't go if you're not ready. But just think, babe—what a great opportunity to use your nursing skills with kids."

Madison flashed back to images from the orphanage on their short-term trip a few years back. So many sweet children, and many of them with medical needs. "It does sound like a great opportunity," she said, while her stomach flip-flopped nervously. "Let's both pray about it."

Luke pulled her close, and as the waves crashed on the shore, Madison tried to reassure herself that she was up to getting married and taking on the new challenges that life would hold.

As Madison got dressed the next morning, she could hear the loud voices of her brother and father in another one of their heated exchanges.

"I want you out there cleaning the garage in the next ten minutes," Steve said. "It's going to take you most of the day, and you won't get it done sleeping in until noon."

"I'll get it done," Caleb barked in response. "Get off my back. I told you yesterday I'd have it cleaned out by dinner time, and I will."

"You'd better believe you will. Just because it's summer, doesn't give you the license to shirk your responsibilities around here," their father said.

Madison shook her head. *Those two! I'll be glad when I'm not living under the same roof with them.*

By the time she got downstairs, her father had gone, and Caleb was eating breakfast. "Dad sounded pretty upset," she commented.

"Nothing new, there," her brother replied, picking up his bagel and heading out to the garage.

Sighing, Madison grabbed a banana and headed out to her car. She had an important visit to make today. Praying silently for God's guidance through what she was about to do, she drove in the direction of her great grandmother's apartment.

Pulling her car into the parking lot of the Shoreline Manor Retirement Community, Madison thought through her plan one more time. *Maybe it wasn't such a good idea to ask Grams about her feelings before she married Gramps. Would it stir up her grief over his death again? That was the last thing Maddie wanted to do.*

But something inside her nudged her forward. Besides, she hadn't been here for three weeks, and she knew Grams loved her visits. She'd keep it brief about her concerns regarding Luke, and spend most of their time together talking about her great grandmother's new project. Nodding to herself in agreement, she climbed out of the car and headed for the apartment.

As usual, the front door was unlocked. Madison pushed it open and found Joan dozing in her rocker recliner, Bible open on her lap. The small round table by the kitchen still had remnants of toast on a plate and a half-empty coffee cup. Beside the breakfast dishes were piles of papers—Grandpa Phil's sermon notes that Joan was compiling into a devotional book.

Madison closed the door softly so as not to startle her great grandmother. Carrying the breakfast dishes to the kitchen, she gently placed them in the sink, checking the stove to be sure the burners were all off.

"Maddie, is that you?" Joan said, dropping the leg rest and sitting upright.

"Hi, Grams. Hope I didn't wake you up," she replied.

"Nonsense. I was just resting my eyes for a minute," Joan said. "Did I know you were coming over?"

Madison smiled. "Nope. I wanted to surprise you." She pointed to the front door and added, "You should lock your door, Grams. Anyone could walk right in here."

Joan waved her hand dismissively. "Nobody around here but us old folks. I never was much for locking doors. Your Grandpa Phil harped on me about that all the time. But I guess that's just how I was raised."

"Well, Gramps was right. You should lock the door."

"Enough about my door, sweetheart. Let me fix you a cup of tea," she offered, rocking herself slightly back and forth in the chair to get up enough momentum to stand.

"I'm fine, Grams. Really. You just relax. I can put the tea kettle on if you'd like."

"The day I can't make tea for my guests is the day I'm going home to be with Phil," she replied with a wink, brushing past Madison and into the kitchen. As she filled the kettle, she asked, "So how are the wedding plans coming along? I heard your young fellow is home."

"He is. We were over there last night."

"Must have been quite a reunion," Grams said as she placed the kettle on the stove and turned to get two teacups from the cupboard. "How long's it been since you saw him last?"

"Three months," Maddie replied.

"That can feel like a lifetime," Joan said as she walked out of the kitchen with the cups in hand.

Madison noticed the burner was not on under the kettle, and why was Grams bringing empty cups into the living room? "Here, let me take those," she said, reaching for the cups. "Why don't we make the tea in the kitchen first? It'll be easier than carrying the kettle in here."

"Silly me!" Joan exclaimed. "I don't know what I was thinking."

Maddie could see the confusion clouding Joan's eyes. "No worries, Grams." Changing the subject, she gestured to the table. "Looks like you've been busy with your project." She slipped back into the kitchen, set the cups on the counter by the stove, and turned on the burner. "Are you finding lots of great material for your book?"

Joan's face brightened. "Yep. It's a lot of work. But I think Phil would be pleased."

"For sure. It's great that you're taking the time to do this. It'll be a treasure for all of us, including my own kids someday," Madison said.

"Your own kids," Joan mused. "That someday is probably around the corner, Maddie," she said with a smile. "It seems unbelievable that I may be a great great grandmother soon." Her countenance changed as she stared off into space.

Maybe this was the time to ask her, Madison thought. "Let's not rush things, Grams. I'm not even married yet."

"Hmmm?" Joan seemed a bit lost.

"I was saying I'm not even married yet, so there won't be kids coming anytime soon."

Joan nodded, but her eyes were still a bit vacant. The teakettle began to whistle, and she shuffled into the tiny kitchen. "I have your favorite cinnamon tea," she said.

"That sounds great. Want any help?" Madison offered, right on her tail.

Together they made their tea and got some shortbread cookies from the cookie jar. *I'll always remember*

Grams when I eat these for the rest of my life, Madison mused to herself.

"What a mess," Joan said as she surveyed the table.

"Let's drink our tea in the front room," Maddie offered, carrying their cups.

They settled into the cozy chairs by the window. After a moment of silence, Joan asked, "Now what were we talking about?"

"About how it will be awhile before I have kids."

"Oh yes. The wedding and your handsome suitor," Joan replied. "Now tell me again when the wedding is. I'd better get it on my calendar."

Madison smiled to herself. Gram's life revolved around that calendar. Most of the entries were medical appointments or something related to her little Bible study group. But lately, she'd taken to adding deadlines about her new project. *Finish two more entries* was scrolled across the bottom of each weekday. It was cute how she took Saturdays and Sundays off. Old habits died hard.

"The wedding is set for August 21st," Madison said.

"Uh huh," Joan agreed as she studied her calendar. "Yep. That's what it says here."

Madison took a deep breath and rallied her courage. "Grams?"

"Yes?"

"Can I ask you a personal question?"

Joan looked surprised. "Sure, darling. What is it?"

"Did you ever feel like maybe you shouldn't marry Grandpa?" Madison asked.

"Why, no," she replied. "You know I was smitten with him long before we courted."

Madison nodded.

"Come to think of it, we were a smidge like you and your Luke. It seems I recall you two making eyes at each other way back when you were at your mother's school."

Madison smiled, flashing back to the crush she'd had on Luke when she was in middle school.

"Do you remember how you two used to sit out on the bench with those thinga-ma-bobs in your ears?" Joan asked.

"Yep. We used to listen to music on my iPod together."

"Is *that* what you were doing?" she asked with a wink.

"What did you think we were doing?"

She chuckled. "Never you mind." She took another bite of cookie and looked right into Madison's eyes. "What's troubling you, Madison?"

Her great grandmother could cut from confused to complete clarity in a moment's time. "I'm just wondering…"

"About?"

"About whether or not I'm the right one for Luke." The words came tumbling out leaving Madison completely open and vulnerable.

"Oh, my. That old devil's been messing with your mind, honey. Luke is head over heels for you."

"But, Grams, he's going to be a pastor someday. I just know it. And the church has offered to sponsor us on the mission field right after we get married."

"Well, that's wonderful! You'll spend a lifetime serving our Lord together," Joan said enthusiastically.

Madison nodded.

"You don't look happy, honey. What is it?"

Tears started to well up. Maddie stood and carried their empty cups into the kitchen, trying to regain her composure. When she returned to her seat, Joan was scratching something down on a pad of paper. Hoping to change the subject, Madison asked, "What's that?"

"It's my prayer list for our meetings of the Silver Sisters," she replied.

Madison smiled. Her great grandmother had started her own sisterhood of believers shortly after moving to the Shoreline Manor. They met once a week right here in this tiny apartment. The Silver Sisters of the Sword.

"I'm so glad you pray for us, Grams." Her emotions started to build again. "So you never felt like Grandpa Phil was way ahead of you spiritually speaking? Or that you might not be up to being a pastor's wife?"

"Well, now, I didn't say that, young lady," Joan replied. "My, oh my. I fretted myself silly at times about all that."

Madison sat on the edge of her chair. "You did?"

"Why, yes. Your great-grandfather was an exceptional man. He knew God like no one else I'd ever met." She paused and gazed off into space for a moment then returned her focus to Madison. "He never made me feel as though I was lacking, though."

Madison nodded.

"Phil said the good Lord knew just what He was doing putting us together like that."

"That's sweet, Grams. I can just picture him saying that," Maddie replied. "Did you ever feel over your head, though, as a pastor's wife? I mean, what was it like?"

"Well, it's a lot of long days and some long nights, too. And I'll warn you, sweetheart; it can be lonely sometimes. Oh, I'm not saying Phil ever neglected me, or anything like that. But his flock, those folks were like family to us. And when they needed him, he tried to go."

"Yeah. I get that. Hanging out at the Johnsons' house, I've seen how Ben gets calls after work and ends up at a hospital or someone's home."

"But there's something else bothering you, isn't there?" Joan asked.

"I guess it's just that I wonder how I will do in *my* role," she confided. "I have no doubts about Luke. He'll be great."

"Just what exactly do you think a pastor's wife's role is, Maddie?"

"I guess they run all the women's ministry stuff, act as a role model for all the rest of the church, keep a spotless home, and help in Sunday school. All that stuff. Plus be supportive of their husband and his role."

"Whew wee! No wonder you're feeling a little scared!" Smiling, Joan reached over and patted her on the knee. "God will show you what He wants you to do. You just focus on Him and on loving and taking care of your young man, and the rest will come."

"Really, Grams?"

"I promise," she said reassuringly. "Now, is there anything else?"

Madison just couldn't bring herself to share her feelings of shame and unworthiness as a wife. "No. That's all, Grams."

CHAPTER SIX

Caleb logged into his computer and pulled up his email account. He could hear his mom in the laundry room down the hall. Before he entered his password, he walked over and quietly closed the door, pushing the lock button on the handle.

After checking his inbox, he clicked the compose button. A new message screen popped up, and he began typing Amber's name into the address slot. Immediately his email server recognized her name and filled in the rest of her address.

Caleb sat back in his chair for a moment. How should he begin? Rubbing his hands together, he stared at the picture of his birthmother on the bulletin board over his desk. It always felt a little awkward to type 'Amber,' but he'd never called her 'Mom' or anything along those lines.

Opting for a simple greeting instead, he typed "Hey!" and then hit the return button. Now what? How should he invite himself out for a visit? Leaning back again, he thought about his options. "Come on, dummy," he said under his breath. "Just tell her it's summer, and you want to come out."

Taking a deep breath, he plunged in.

So, school's finally out for summer. Logan's probably going to be working most of the time. Not sure what I'll do for the next three months. If I hang around here, Dad will probably find plenty of stuff that he wants me to do. You know, fun stuff like cleaning out the garage.

I was thinking maybe I could come out to see you. We could go to that water park we went to last time I was there. Plus, I could help you paint that office room you've been wanting to paint.

Everything around here is just wedding stuff. Mom spends all her time with Mad, and Dad's working like crazy as usual. I could come anytime.

A knock on the door interrupted his typing. "Caleb? Got any dirty clothes in there? I'm throwing in a load of jeans."

"No. I'm good," he replied, glancing over at the mess of clothes on the floor by his closet. He still had at least one pair of clean jeans hanging up in there. The rest could wait.

"Okay," his mother's voice came back through the door. "I'm heading out to the photographer with Maddie in about twenty minutes."

"Cool," he replied. "I'll be here."

After she had walked away, he returned his attention to the email. With a quick, "Hope it works out," he signed off and clicked 'send.'

Amber Gamble flipped open her laptop and clicked on the email tab. Scrolling through some junk mail, her eyes stopped on the subject box that read, 'Hey.' An email from Caleb!

She quickly opened it and read through his message. Every time she heard from her son, it made her day. She sat back and smiled. It would be great to see him again.

Caleb was the one good thing from a messed up past she often wished she could erase.

At age thirty-one, it was hard to believe it had been seventeen years since she'd given birth to him. Looking back, she could clearly remember the day she'd discovered she was pregnant.

And only fourteen years old.

After bouncing around to a number of foster homes and finally ending up separated from her younger brother, Jack, she'd latched onto her boyfriend, Adam, as the one hope for finding love and a place to belong.

But Adam was only a kid himself. Granted he was older than her. And a high school guy, who seemed to like her. Until she got pregnant, that is. And then all he could talk about was how she had to have an abortion and, he wasn't interested in commitment.

Amber cringed as she thought back to how she'd believed he would marry her, and they'd be a family—her, Adam, the baby, and Jack.

Ha! What a dreamer she was.

Thankfully she'd confided in her favorite teacher— Mrs. Baron—the only person who genuinely cared what happened to her. Michelle was great. She'd helped Amber through it all and had agreed to adopt her baby boy, even going along with Amber's choice of names.

"What are you thinking about so seriously," Will asked, leaning over and giving her a kiss.

Amber closed the laptop and smiled up at him. "Nothing. I just got an email from Caleb."

"Everything okay?"

"Yeah. He's just already getting bored with summer."

"Kids. Wish I had time to be bored," he added wistfully. "I've gotta run, babe. Top will blow a gasket if I don't have that Benz ready today."

Amber smiled thinking about Will's boss, gruff old Hank Topper. The guy could be pretty intimidating, but

Amber suspected he was actually a softie underneath that tough exterior.

He owned anauto repair shop for high-end automobiles, where her husband worked as a mechanic. That's where she'd met Will, the day her car quit on her right at the corner where the shop was located. Although it was definitely not a 'high-end' vehicle by any stretch of the imagination, Will had spotted her stuck in the intersection while other motorists blasted their horns at her.

She grimaced at the memory. It was her second day on the job as a teacher's aide, and she was in tears by the time he'd tapped on her window.

"Need a hand?" he asked with that winsome smile of his.

Soon he'd pushed her car into the lot at the shop and was offering her a lift to school. One thing led to another, and soon they were dating. A year later, they married, with Caleb and his whole family in attendance. This month would be their fifth anniversary, and Will still made her heart race. Her only regret was that they'd never be able to have kids together. Caleb had been her one and only. The scar tissue from all the bleeding caused by her placenta previa and the subsequent emergency c-section had caused irreparable damage to her uterus.

Amber stood and gave her husband another kiss. This one lingered as she melted into him.

"Whoa, girl," Will said with a grin. "Careful or I'll forget all about that Benz."

She laughed. "Go to work, dufus."

"Okay, but we'll pick up where we left off tonight." He grabbed his water bottle off the counter and headed for the garage.

As the door closed behind him, Amber sat back down to answer Caleb's email. Then she remembered she hadn't asked Will what he thought about her son coming out to visit them. Maybe she'd better wait until later to reply.

Lucy sat on Madison's bed flipping through one of her bridal magazines. "This dress is amazing," she said, pointing to a full-page portrait of a bride and groom. "The guy's not bad looking either," she added.

Madison leaned over and looked at the photo. "You'd look good in that," she told her best friend, soon to be her sister-in-law.

"Ha!" Lucy exclaimed. "Right!"

"I'm serious, Luce. You should go for a gown like that when you get married."

"If, you mean," Lucy replied. "My prospects aren't so hot these days."

"Just because you and Spence are taking a break, doesn't mean you won't get married."

Lucy shrugged. "Let's change the subject," she suggested. "Are you getting nervous about the big day?"

"Maybe, a little," Madison admitted.

"You should see Luke. He's having all kinds of secret talks with Dad. I've never seen him so serious."

I wonder what that's about? Madison thought to herself, but all she said was, "Really?"

"Yeah. They go into Dad's man cave, so I don't know what they're talking about. Probably stuff like bills and birth control."

Madison blushed. "Lucy!"

"What?"

"Sometimes you crack me up."

Lucy laughed. "Luke's such a perfectionist. He'll want to do everything just right."

"Well, he's sure not getting a perfect wife," Madison mumbled under her breath.

"What?" Lucy asked.

"Nothing."

Lucy's phone beeped, and she pulled it out of her pocket. "Gotta go. Mom made me promise to be home in time to go to the store with her before dinner." She stood up and handed Madison the bridal magazine. "Have fun dreaming about your prince charming," she added with a grin.

Madison swatted her on the shoulder with it. "You, too."

"Wanna shoot some hoops with me?" Caleb asked Madison as he poked his head into her room.

Looking up from her email, she replied, "I'm kind of busy."

"Doing what?"

"Email, dummy. Can't you see?"

"Come on, Mad. You can do that anytime."

"Like I can't shoot hoops with you anytime?" she asked, glancing his way.

"Not for long. Pretty soon you'll be an old married lady living with Luke." He paused and then added, "Just fifteen minutes. And I promise I won't ask Luke when he comes over tonight."

"Okay, okay. If you promise not to try to snag him into a game, I guess I can shoot a few hoops with you. But just fifteen minutes. Then I've got to get some stuff done."

"Fine," he agreed with a grin.

As they bantered back and forth on the court out back, Caleb said, "So can you believe you're getting married?"

She paused before answering. "Yeah, I guess."

"You don't sound very excited. Should I tell Luke you're changing your mind?" he teased.

Madison hit the ball out of his hand and bounded to the basket, sinking the first shot.

"Nice!" Caleb exclaimed. "Seriously, though, Mad, is there something wrong? Just tell your little brother."

She laughed. Caleb might be five years younger than her, but at six foot one, he towered over her.

"I can deal with Luke if he's giving you any grief," he added.

"Oh really?" Madison said with a smile.

"Sure. Just let me know."

"I'll be sure to do that," she replied, and then added, "So what's new on your secret search?"

Caleb shot her a look and then glanced over at the house.

"Mom's gone," Madison reassured him. "She's going over to see Grams."

"Okay. That's good. Don't forget—you promised not to say anything," he reminded her.

"Yeah, yeah. Your secret's safe with me," she said reassuringly. "So have you done anything else?"

"I emailed Amber to find out about going out there."

"And?"

"She hasn't answered yet. Probably needs to check with Will."

Madison nodded. "When would you go?"

"As soon as I can."

"Did you mention this to Mom or Dad?" she asked.

"No. Not until I hear back," he replied. "And don't you go saying anything either," he warned.

Madison held up both hands in surrender. "Okay, okay. Mum's the word." Her cell phone rang, and she pulled it out. Looking back at her brother, she said, "It's Luke." Then she tapped the accept button and started walking to the house as she answered.

Michelle headed over to pick up her mother on the way to her grandmother's house. With all the busyness of wrapping up another school year of teaching, as well as working on planning Madison's wedding, she hadn't been able to spend much time with either her mom or her grandmother. It would be nice to have an hour or two to catch up.

Sheila was waiting on the front porch when Michelle pulled into the driveway. "Hi, Mom," she said as her mother settled into the front seat beside her. Sheila looked a little flustered. "Everything okay?" Michelle asked.

Sighing, Sheila nodded. "I guess. Rick's pretty upset. The dean asked him to teach a different course next term. Apparently, his curriculum has been too pro-Christian for the board. They'd like to have him move away from the religion subdivision of anthropology and shift to more of an evolutionary angle on culture."

Sheila's husband, Rick, was Michelle's anthropology professor back when she was pursuing her teaching credential. He'd been very antagonistic to Christianity at the time, but now he was passionate about his faith. Although he and Sheila had only been together for about ten years, a second chance at love for Michelle's mom after her first husband's death, the entire family had embraced Rick. Now Michelle had grown to love him as a father figure and the grandfather of her two kids.

"What did he tell the dean?" she asked.

"He hasn't said anything yet, but I think he's going to consider leaving the university."

"Really? Like retiring?" Michelle asked.

"Possibly. Or he may also look into positions at Christian universities or high schools." Sheila turned to Michelle. "He loves teaching. You know how that is," she added with a smile. "It would be a shame to give it up."

"Yeah. He'd probably love teaching in a Christian school. It's too bad, though, because he was reaching some kids that weren't hearing about God from anyone else."

As they pulled up to Shoreline Manor, Michelle asked, "Mom, have you noticed Grandma's starting to struggle more with her memory? She repeats herself quite a bit when I talk to her on the phone."

Sheila nodded. "Yep, the phone is the worst. She does better in person."

They walked along the paved path from the parking lot to Joan's apartment, the cool breeze overriding the warmth of the sun. It was a clear day—the first in weeks. And Michelle took a moment to pause and look out over the ocean. "Grandma's very blessed to live here," she remarked as they approached her front door.

Sheila pulled out the key to her mother's door and inserted it into the bolt. It was already unlocked. Peeking inside, they saw Joan asleep in her rocking chair. "Mom," Sheila said softly, reaching over and placing her hand on her mother's shoulder.

Joan opened her eyes and looked up with a confused stare. "Sheila?"

"Yeah. Michelle and I are here. Remember, we made plans yesterday to come by."

Joan nodded, but her face revealed no memory of them. Turning to Michelle, she said, "Hi, dear. It's good to see your face."

"Good to see you, too, Grandma," Michelle replied, leaning over and giving her a quick kiss.

"Well, goodness me," Joan piped up, gathering her wits about her. "Let me put the teakettle on. And I think I still have some of those shortbread cookies we picked up at the market last time."

"Let me do that, Mom," Sheila said. "You and Michelle can visit while I get us a little snack and some tea."

"That would be lovely," Joan replied, sitting forward in her rocker and gesturing to the overstuffed chair near her. "Relax a spell and catch me up on your sweet family."

Michelle sank into the soft cushions, suddenly realizing how bone tired she was. "Everyone's fine, Grams."

"And are the wedding plans coming along?"

"Yep. We met with the photographer this week. We need to finalize the flowers and get the invitations out."

"Woo wee!" Grandma Joan exclaimed. "Such a to-do these days! When your grandfather and I got hitched, we just had a small ceremony in the chapel with our families, and then a little punch and cake in the fellowship hall."

Michelle smiled. "That sounds nice, Grams. I'll bet you were relaxed and able to enjoy the day."

"Well, I don't know about relaxed, sweetheart. After all, I was starting a whole new life." She rested her head back and gazed off into space. "Oh, your grandfather was such a handsome fellow! I can still see him in that blue suit of his, lanky frame and all, watching me walk up the aisle on my papa's arm to meet him."

They sat in silence for a few moments, Michelle not wanting to break the spell.

"Mom, do you have any more of that cinnamon tea?" Sheila's voice came from the kitchen.

"I don't think so, dear. Madison and I had some the other day, and I think I finished off the last of it yesterday morning," Joan called back.

"Madison was here?" Michelle asked.

"Yes. We had a lovely visit. I'm surprised you didn't know," Joan replied. "She was full of questions, that one was."

"Really? About what?"

"She wanted to know if I ever had second thoughts about marrying your grandfather," Joan said.

"Probably just pre-wedding jitters," Michelle said, but she made a mental note to talk to Madison. They hadn't had much of a chance to just talk lately. Everything was about wedding plans.

"She asked me if I ever wondered if I was the right one for Phil or he was the right one for me." Joan laughed softly, shaking her head. "That one's always second guessing herself," she mumbled.

CHAPTER SEVEN

Finally, Caleb thought as he opened his email account and spotted a reply from Amber.

Hi, Caleb! I was so happy to get an email from you! But I admit I was a little surprised that you'd want to come out here to the heat. It's been over a hundred and five degrees daily all week. Wish I could go there instead!

Will and I discussed it, and you're welcome to visit for a week or so. Money's a little tight these days, so I can't send you a ticket or anything. But if you can work out the flight on your end, just let me know when you'll be coming, and I'll be at the airport to pick you up.

You talked to your parents about this, right?

Love,

Amber

Caleb sat back in his chair and smiled. He was good to go to Arizona. Now he just had to convince his mom and dad to let him go. There was enough money in his savings from his part-time job at the Coffee Stop to pay for the ticket.

Leaning forward again, he began his online search for a non-stop flight. Sweet! There was a special on for the next two weeks, but he'd need to fly out within the following five days. He could stay for up to five days. Less time than he wanted, but the price was hard to pass up.

Tonight he'd talk to his mom about it. Dad would drill him about missing work, like his part-time job was such a big deal. But Mom—she had a soft spot for Amber, so if he played his cards right, he could make it sound like Amber got the idea of him coming out.

Just then Madison stuck her head in the door. "What're you doing?"

Without thinking, he snapped, "None of your business."

"Whoa. Sorry I asked," she replied.

Caleb turned around in his chair. "Wait a sec," he said. "I didn't mean to snap at you. Come on in." As she walked in, he added, "Close the door."

"Uh oh. What is it?" she asked, sitting on the edge of his bed.

"I got an email from Amber."

"And?"

"And she said it's fine to go out there for a week."

Madison looked at him with her eyebrows raised.

"What?" he asked.

"You know how I feel about this. You're only going out there to try to get information on that guy."

"If by that guy you mean my father, then yes that's the main reason. But I also want to see Amber and Will."

"Right." She stared at him, and Caleb started wishing he'd never confided in her at all. Before he could say another word, she said, "Your *father* is right here in Sandy Cove. He's the man we call 'Dad.'"

Turning back to his computer, he muttered under his breath, "Whatever."

"You are really selfish. You know that, right?" She shot back, starting to leave. "All you're going to accomplish by this is to upset Dad." Walking out, she slammed the door behind her.

"What was that about?" Steve asked as Madison nearly collided with him in the hallway outside of Caleb's room.

"Caleb's being a jerk, as usual."

Steve put out his hand and gently took hold of her arm. "Hold on," he said. "Tell me what's happening."

Madison balked. She didn't want to be the one to tell her dad about Caleb's crazy notion of finding that loser of a father from the past. "Why don't you ask your son?" she said, pulling away.

"Okay, I will. But is everything alright with you, honey?" he asked. "You seem edgy lately."

She took a deep breath. "I guess it's just all the wedding stuff."

"Mom told me you had a talk with your great grandmother," he said.

"Really? I was kind of hoping that conversation was confidential between me and Grams," she replied, feeling her defenses rising.

Her dad must have heard the emotion in her voice because his softened as he put his hand back on her shoulder. "Maddie?"

Looking up into his eyes, she crumbled. As her tears flowed, he took her into an embrace. "Oh, Daddy," she managed. "What if I'm not good enough for Luke?"

Holding her close, he sighed. "Honey, any man would be blessed to have you for his wife."

She sniffled back her tears and looked up at him. "You're just saying that because you're my dad."

"Maybe," he teased with a wink. Then his expression changed as he held her at arms distance with both hands. "Seriously, Madison, Luke loves you very much. I have no doubt about that. None at all. If I did, this wedding would not go forward."

I hope he's right. I can't live my whole life wondering.

Once Madison had gone downstairs, Steve turned to Caleb's room. "Hey," he said as he pushed the door open. "Can I come in?"

"Sure. Why not," his son replied, closing his laptop.

Steve walked in and sat on the edge of the bed. "What's up with you and your sister?"

"Nothing."

"She seemed pretty upset when she left your room," Steve commented.

"She was just getting into my business," Caleb replied.

"And what business is that?"

"Nothing."

Steve studied his son. Caleb seemed so preoccupied lately. Something was definitely up. "Madison's just edgy because of the wedding," he offered, hoping to break ground and get to the root of what was going on.

Caleb stood up. "Right."

"Son?" Steve said, immediately noticing Caleb's wince. "Is something bothering you lately?"

"No, why?"

"You just seem to be spending a lot of time on your computer instead of outside shooting hoops or something."

"I'm not a kid anymore. And last time I checked, there wasn't anything illegal about being on the computer," he snapped.

"Hey," Steve replied. "I don't like your tone."

"And I don't like getting the third degree from everyone," Caleb said, brushing past him and walking out of the room.

"What just happened here?" Steve thought aloud. He was tempted to flip open Caleb's computer and see what he'd been doing. Searching the room for other clues, he began to praysilently for wisdom. And for his son.

"Madison, have you and Luke decided when you're going to register for wedding gifts?" Michelle asked. "Grandma was wondering."

Madison felt her stomach tighten. Why did everything about this wedding seem to make her edgy? "No. I'll talk to him tonight."

"Are you guys going out to dinner? Or will you be here?"

"We're going out. He should be here anytime," Madison replied, checking her phone for messages.

"Who should be here anytime?" Luke asked as he snuck up behind her and put his arms around her waist.

Madison's heart jumped. "You startled me!"

"Sorry about that," he replied, releasing her and greeting her mother. "Caleb was out front and let me in."

He bent down and gave her a quick kiss. "Ready to go?"

"Yeah." She grabbed her purse off the counter and gave her mom a hug. "I won't be out late."

Once they were outside, he took her hand. "Where to?"

"Wherever you want is fine with me," she replied. Her appetite was marginal these days. The closer the wedding got, the more nervous she felt.

"You okay?" he asked.

"Yeah. Why?"

"I don't know. You just seem kind of quiet."

She turned and gave him her best smile, determined to push down her anxiety. "I'm fine. Really."

"Okay. Whatever you say." He stopped and turned to face her. "Can I have a kiss?"

"I thought you got one in the kitchen," she said.

"I mean a real one," he replied with a smile. Leaning down, he brushed his lips on hers gently at first, and then with a deepening kiss.

Madison felt herself tingle a little. She melted against him, willing all her doubts and fears to disappear.

Suddenly Luke pulled away. "We'd better go," he said.

And the anxieties rushed right back into her heart.

Over dinner, their conversation was surface, until Madison brought up what Lucy had said. "She told me you're having lots of serious talks with your dad."

He nodded.

"Anything we should talk about?" she asked.

"Not yet."

What does that mean? She wondered. "So are you having second thoughts?" The words slipped out of her mouth before she could catch them.

Luke looked at her stunned. "Why would you ask that?"

Hedging, she replied, "No reason. It's just…well…I'd understand if you were."

"You would?"

"Yeah."

Luke stared at her, and she felt like he was looking right into her soul. "Are you having second thoughts?" he asked.

"I don't know. Maybe." *Why am I saying all this?* She asked herself.

He looked at her with a fear that mirrored her own. "Did I do something to upset you?" he asked.

"No. Nothing like that."

"Then what is it?"

"It's not you, Luke. It's just the wedding...getting married...all that stuff. Sometimes I wonder if I'm ready." *Why am I lying to him like this? What is the matter with me?* It was like her fears had taken on a personality of their own.

Luke looked really hurt. Great. Now she was hurting the person she loved most in the world. And why? Suddenly an unexpected surge of courage welled up in her. "I don't want to disappoint you," she said.

"What's that supposed to mean?"

"I don't know. I just feel like I'm maybe not ready."

He stared at her again and then shook his head. "So are you breaking off our engagement?" he asked, clearly bewildered.

Madison's eyes blurred with tears. How could she explain to him about her fears and doubts? Maybe it would just be best to let him go. Then he could find someone who wasn't so insecure. Someone who was ready to be missionary wife.

"I love you, Maddie," he said, his own eyes filling with tears.

"Do you? Do you really love me?" she asked, her voice shaking. "Because I'm not sure why you would." An avalanche of emotions swept over her.

Scrubbing his face with his hands, he took a deep breath and looked her in the eye. "What do you mean, why? You are a wonderful and beautiful person. And you've accomplished an amazing goal with your nursing school program."

She smiled slightly. "Thanks," she replied softly.

Luke's tone dropped a notch. "You've got to get over this, Madison. When are you going to quit beating yourself up? I love you. I do. But I can't make this okay for you. Only God can."

He looked away for a moment and then back into her eyes. "You are the one I want to marry. You are the one I want to spend the rest of my life with. Okay?"

"Okay," she replied.

That night, as Madison was getting ready for bed, she thought about her conversation with Luke. Pulling open the bottom drawer of her desk, she rifled through the contents until she found a fabric colored journal.

Before opening it, Madison caressed the cover and thought back to the first time she'd pressed open its lined pages. She'd just begun seeing a Christian counselor named Taylor James. During their first meeting, Taylor had suggested journaling as a way to help Madison process her thoughts and feelings.

Maddie smiled, thinking about Taylor with her big smile and broad face framed in curls. Together they'd spent a summer exploring Madison's issues of self-doubt and shame. It had helped propel her out of a destructive mindset and into her degree program. Now she realized she hadn't completely conquered her fears.

Opening the familiar book, she began reading her entries and remembering the insights she'd gleaned from their sessions coupled with scripture and some pretty intense times in prayer. God had shown up for her in a big way back then. But somehow she'd let her time and passion wane.

"I guess I just got busy," she said aloud to herself. But in her heart, she knew that was no excuse. Luke was right. He couldn't fix this for her. Only God could. And He'd used Taylor to help her in that process before. Maybe it was time to check back in with her again.

Flipping to the back of the journal, she found Taylor's business card. Her cell phone number was written in ink at the bottom. She'd told Madison she could call or text if she ever needed to reach her again.

Taking a deep breath to steady herself, Madison reached for her phone. *Please, Lord. Help me find the confidence I need to be a good wife for Luke.*

She opened her text messaging and began typing.

Hi Taylor. It's me, Madison Baron. I was thinking about you tonight and wondered if we could get together this week. I've got some stuff to sort through, and I could use your help.

Fifteen minutes later, her phone beeped, signaling a reply.

Madison! Great to hear from you! I'll be in my office all week. How about tomorrow at 4:30?

Madison smiled. "Perfect!" she typed in response.

As she climbed into bed, she opened the journal once again, reading her notes and reflecting on scriptures that had helped her so much in the past. She drifted off to the words of Zephaniah 3:17 filling her spirit with peace.

The LORD your God is in your midst, a mighty one who will save; he will rejoice over you with gladness; he will quiet you by his love; he will exult over you with loud singing.

CHAPTER EIGHT

"Where are you heading off to?" Michelle asked Madison the next afternoon.

"To see Taylor," she replied casually, hoping to avoid a big conversation with her mother.

Michelle stopped what she was doing. "Really? Is everything okay?"

"Yeah. Fine." Madison gave her a quick peck on the cheek. "I'll be back before dinner."

As she parked her car in front of the counseling office, she paused for a moment to pray. Lord, help me move past my doubts and fears about marrying Luke. I don't want to blow this.

Entering the waiting room, she noticed an updated décor. The new paint and furniture, along with a single serving coffee maker well-stocked with a variety of flavor brews, was attractive and continued to communicate an ambiance of comfort and safety.

Madison smiled. It had been several years since she'd been in this place. But it felt good to be back. She remembered the many times she'd walked through this door feeling distressed and had left with a renewed hope for the future.

"Madison?" A familiar voice from the hallway drew her back into the moment.

"Yeah, it's me," she replied with a grin.

"You look great! And I love the new haircut," Taylor said.

Fingering the tips of her now shorter hair, Madison smiled. "Thanks!"

"Well, come on back, and let's get caught up," her counselor suggested.

Soon they were settled into her private office. The same comfortable couch and pillows drew Madison into its arms as she sat back and kicked off her shoes, slipping one foot under her in a casual position. Talking to Taylor was like talking to a best friend. No pretenses. Just a safe zone for truth.

But with Taylor, unlike her best friend Lucy, Madison didn't have to worry about anyone finding out what she shared—including her doubts about her upcoming wedding. Lucy would never purposefully reveal a confidence, but she was as tied to Luke as she was to Madison. Plus, life for Lucy was pretty cut and dry. 'You love the guy so what's the problem. Just get married, and it will all work out fine,' would likely be her response.

Taylor, on the other hand, had no vested interest in what Madison decided to do. And she could hear beneath the words on the surface the issues that Madison struggled with in deeper places of her soul.

"So, did you finish your nursing program?" she asked, as she took a seat herself.

"Yep. All done," Madison replied.

"That's great! Are you starting work soon?"

"Well, I'm not sure yet. Lots of things are happening right now," she added, absentmindedly twisting her engagement ring with the other hand.

"Is that what I think it is?" Taylor asked, pointing the end of her pen toward Madison's hand.

Immediately Madison stopped her twisting and smiled. Lifting her left hand and turning the back of it toward Taylor, she showed off her ring. "Yeah. Luke and I are engaged."

"That's wonderful," her counselor replied enthusiastically.

"I guess," Madison responded.

"You don't sound very excited." Taylor's observation hung in the air for a moment.

Taking a deep breath and then letting it out, Madison nodded. "That's why I'm here."

"I see." Taylor studied her in anticipation. "Shall we pray before we get into this?" she asked.

Madison nodded again. "Yeah, I'd like that." Although she respected Taylor's degree in psychology, she appreciated her faithful walk with Christ even more. At this point, Madison was pretty sure she'd never go to a secular counselor.

Leaning forward in her seat and bowing her head, Taylor prayed for God to give both of them wisdom and insight as they shared with each other. Then, sitting back, she smiled compassionately at Madison. "So tell me why the hesitation about marrying Luke."

Madison paused for a moment, trying to figure out how to begin. "I guess it's mostly just that I'm not sure I'm cut out to be a pastor's wife."

Taylor nodded. "And Luke has decided he's called to be a pastor?"

"Well, not exactly. Not yet. He wants to start on the mission field. And his father, who is the pastor of our church, has offered us a position at an orphanage overseas."

"Seems like I recall you and Luke serving together on a short-term mission trip before he went off to college."

"Yeah. We did," Madison replied.

"Wasn't that part of what drew you to nursing? That you felt you would be able to use that skill as a missionary someday?"

Madison nodded. "Luke and I were really impacted by that trip. It's when we decided we both wanted to serve overseas."

"And now you have that opportunity."

"Yes."

"But you're hesitating to marry Luke and dive into this because…"

Madison smiled. Taylor made it seem so simple. "It's not the missionary work I'm concerned about. I think we'd be good at that. Good together, I mean."

"Okay. It's the pastor's wife role you mentioned earlier that has you scared?"

She nodded. "I look at Luke's mom, and I see someone who is so strong and sure of herself. She's sacrificial and loving and patient. But most of all, she's strong."

"And you don't see yourself that way?"

"Not really," Madison replied.

"Has Luke told you he plans to become a pastor?" Taylor asked.

"He hasn't talked about it lately."

"But?"

"But he sure has the heart of a pastor. I think it's pretty inevitable that he'll become one in the future," Madison said.

"And if he does, then you'd become a pastor's wife."

She nodded.

"But that doesn't feel okay to you."

Madison thought about it for a moment. "It scares me a little."

Taylor nodded. "Change can be scary. And so can responsibility. Which of those scares you most?"

Madison laughed nervously. "Both, I guess."

"What is the scariest thing about being a pastor's wife, in your mind?"

She hesitated, considering the question carefully. "I guess being in charge of so much at church."

"Like?"

"Like the women's ministry. The children's ministry. The helps ministry. All of it."

"That's what Luke's mom does?"

"I think so."

"And that's what Luke would expect of you?"

She nodded, beginning to twist her engagement ring again.

"Correct me if I'm wrong here, Madison, but it seems like you might be borrowing trouble from tomorrow. Trouble that might not ever come."

Madison looked her in the eye. "What do you mean?"

"Well, first, Luke's not even talking about becoming a pastor right now."

Madison nodded.

"And it doesn't sound like you've ever discussed with him what your role would look like if he did step into that role. Right?"

"Right," Madison admitted.

"Okay, so although I'm sure you know that scripture tells us not to borrow trouble from tomorrow, let's just do a little soul searching here."

"Okay."

Taylor looked her in the eye and said, "Let's imagine you and Luke have just returned from the mission field."

Madison nodded.

"And let's say Luke sits you down and shares that he's feeling called to assume the role of a pastor in a church."

"Okay."

"Tell me what he would say to you."

She studied her counselor. "What do you mean?"

"Pretend he's sitting across from you right now. He's just told you he's feeling called to move into pastoring a church. What else would he say?"

"Like about me?"

"About anything."

She thought for a moment. "He'd ask me what I thought."

"Okay, good. So he wouldn't just announce a decision?"

Madison shook her head. "No, I'm pretty sure he'd ask me for my input first."

Taylor smiled and nodded. "And what would you say?"

Madison took a deep breath and thought. "I guess I'd tell him what a great pastor he'd be."

"Anything else?"

She smiled. "And how scared I was to be a pastor's wife."

"Good, Madison. I'm glad to hear that," Taylor responded with encouragement. "Now, tell me what Luke would say about your fears."

"I guess he'd ask me why I was afraid, and that he thought I'd be fine."

"Would you feel comfortable telling him what you thought you could and could not do in that role?"

Madison thought about it. Then she smiled and nodded. "Yeah. I think I could."

"So, let's say, for example, you told him you weren't comfortable leading the women's ministry. What do you think he would say?"

"Hmmm…I guess he'd say that I wouldn't have to do anything I wasn't comfortable doing…but that he thought I'd be a great leader if I let myself do it."

Taylor nodded. "I'd have to agree with him on that one," she replied with a smile. "But what I hope you're getting from this little exercise is that you are marrying a man, not a ministry. And you know him, Madison. You know his heart for you. My guess is that he puts you above ministry. That only God holds a dearer place in his heart than you."

Madison felt a weight lift from her spirit. Taylor was right. Luke would never place demands on her or push her into something she feared. He just wasn't like that.

"Why do you suppose I keep getting tripped up like this?" Madison asked.

"Because you really care. And you want to do things right," Taylor said. "But also because the enemy found a foothold he can use to manipulate you. My guess is that he's used the same ploy on your mother and maybe her mother, too. That's how he works. Strongholds are often generational."

Madison nodded.

"Maybe if the opportunity presents itself, you can ask your mom if she's ever felt like she's not good enough. You might be surprised at her answer."

Madison nodded. "So how do you break a generational stronghold?" Madison asked.

"By doing what we're doing here today. Breaking it apart with the truth," Taylor replied. "It's a process, Madison. For some, that process lasts a lifetime. But hopefully, we each keep growing stronger in Christ and more effective in disarming the principalities that seek to derail us."

"Yeah," Madison agreed. She was really glad she'd decided to come talk to Taylor. It always seemed to make things clearer in her mind and to lift any dark cloud that was trying to drag her down.

"I've decided I'm going out to Arizona to see Amber," Caleb announced at dinner.

"Whoa. What?" Steve asked, looking up from buttering his potato.

"I'm going to see Amber."

"When did you decide this?" Michelle asked.

Madison cleared her throat, and Caleb quickly shot her a look. "What? I didn't say anything," she fired back.

"What's going on here?" Steve looked from one of them to the other.

Madison just shrugged. "Ask your son," she said pointedly.

Caleb felt himself wince inwardly. "I just thought it would be good to go see her and Will. It's been a while."

"I think they're going to try to come out for the wedding," Michelle offered.

"Yeah, but everyone will be busy then, and they probably won't stay long," he replied. "Besides, Will was going to teach me about transmissions," he added. "I like going to his shop with him and learning new stuff, so I can fix my own car when I get one. And speaking of that, you said we'd talk about getting me one for next year, so Mom doesn't have to shuttle me to sports practices."

"Let's tackle one subject at a time, kid," Steve replied.

"You know it's annoying when you call me that, right?" Caleb said, feeling his irritation rise.

"What?"

"Kid. When you call me 'kid' like I'm still in elementary school or something," Caleb retorted.

"Sorry," Steve replied, raising his hands in surrender.

Madison rolled her eyes, and that just made Caleb more irritated. "What's your problem?" he asked.

"Nothing. Nothing at all."

Ever the peacemaker, Michelle redirected them by asking, "So when was it you thought you'd go? To Arizona, I mean."

"Like in a couple of weeks. I've already checked with Amber, and she said it was fine. Plus, I've saved up enough money to cover the flight."

"What about work?" Steve asked.

"I'm only going for a week. I'll clear it with the manager, so he doesn't put me on the schedule."

"Okay. It sounds like you've covered all your bases," his father replied.

"So I can go?"

Steve nodded. "Sure. Just for a week, though."

Caleb felt his spirits rise. "Cool. Thanks!" He turned to Madison and smiled smugly. She just shook her head and looked away.

CHAPTER NINE

"You seem like you're a million miles away," Luke said to Madison as they drove to the beach to watch the sun go down. Luke had spent the day with his father discussing the orphanage where he and Madison were praying about serving as missionaries. He was eager to talk to her about the things he'd learned. But her mind was definitely preoccupied.

Glancing over, he could see she was still staring out the window. "Maddie?"

She roused herself and turned to look at him. "Yeah?"

"What are you thinking about?"

"My brother," she replied.

"Caleb? Why?"

She shook her head. "He's got some ridiculous notion about finding his biological father."

"Wow. When did that start?" Luke never thought about Caleb being adopted. Even when Amber was in town, she seemed like she was just a friend of the family's. Caleb never referred to her as 'Mom' or anything like that.

"I guess he's probably been thinking about it for a while," she answered. "But he's getting serious about it now. He's even decided to go to Arizona to talk to Amber about it."

"Do your parents know?" he asked as he pulled the car into a parking spot facing the shoreline.

"They know he's going to see her. But they don't know why."

"Oh." Luke turned off the ignition and reached for her hand. "You seem pretty worried."

She nodded. "I have a bad feeling about it." She paused and then added, "I get that he's curious. And I know lots of adopted kids go looking for their biological parents..."

"But?"

"But, like Caleb said to me himself, his other father might still be living right here in Sandy Cove."

"I hadn't thought of that," Luke said. "That is a little weird, huh?"

"Yeah. He was saying to me that maybe we see the guy around town and don't even know it's him."

"I wonder how that would be for Cale after he discovered who the guy was. I mean seeing him from time to time. Is he actually planning to try to meet him?"

"I think so."

"It's hard to imagine what that would be like," Luke said.

"What if the guy is a druggie or something and tries to get Caleb into that?" she said, a worried look on her face.

"Do you really think your brother would fall for something like that, babe? He's a pretty smart kid, you know."

"Yeah, I guess," she admitted. "But I'm also worried about how this will affect Dad and their relationship. Caleb pushes his buttons sometimes. Especially lately. I've noticed how they set each other off. It just seems like this could drive such a wedge between them."

Luke nodded. "Maybe you should see if your brother would consider talking to my dad about this before he tries to meet this guy."

Madison looked skeptical but nodded. "I guess I can suggest that." Glancing out the windshield, she squeezed his hand. "Look at that sunset," she said. "Let's walk down to the water."

As they walked, Luke wondered if he should bring up the orphanage. Maybe it would be good to just start by talking about the wedding. Maddie seemed so emotional when he first got home from college, especially about getting married.

Before he could say anything, she turned to him and put her hands on his face. "I love you, Luke," she said, as she looked him squarely in the eye.

That felt good. Really good. "I love you, too, babe," he replied with a smile. Leaning down, he kissed her, gently at first and then with abandon, the water swirling at their feet.

Luke felt his body responding, and he ached to hold her in his arms. Pulling back, he took a deep breath. "Whoa. Wish we were already married," he mumbled softly.

"Me, too," Madison replied, giving him a tight hug.

They both turned toward the sea, watching the sun disappear behind the horizon as the sky was bathed in orange and purple.

Madison took his hand and pulled him up the beach a bit, away from the water. Then she sank onto the sand, drawing him down to sit beside her. Fingering her engagement ring, she smiled. "Soon I'll be Mrs. Johnson," she said with a grin.

"Not soon enough for me," he replied, still aching to fully express his love for her.

"We could go elope tonight," she suggested coyly.

He looked over at her. "You're not serious, are you?"

"I don't know. Should I be?"

It was tempting, to be sure. But Luke wanted to see his bride dressed in white before all their family and friends. He wanted her to have that moment when all eyes turned to her. And then they shared their love for each other and their promise of a lifetime before God. Draping his arm over her shoulder, he pulled her close to his side.

"You are going to be the most beautiful bride the world has ever seen," he said as he breathed in the fragrance of her hair.

"Thanks!" she replied, snuggling close.

Luke's heart swelled with joy. A week ago, Madison had seemed distant and afraid. He'd prayed diligently for her, and tonight he could see the answer. "You seem different," he said softly.

"I do?"

"Yeah. More at peace. More confident."

Madison shifted her body and turned to sit facing him in the sand. "God's been working on me," she began.

Luke took both her hands in his and nodded, listening intently.

"Do you remember Taylor?"

He searched his memory. The name sounded familiar. Before he could recall who she was, Madison filled in the gaps. "She was my counselor awhile back."

Oh yeah. He remembered now. Maddie had sought counseling her first year in college. "Yeah, she works at the center beside the Calvary Chapel downtown."

Madison nodded. "Yep. So, I went to see her after we talked the last time we were down here at the beach."

Luke could vividly remember that conversation and how frustrated he'd felt. Like he might never be able to convince Maddie of how much he loved her.

"My head was pretty messed up," she continued. "I guess it's just kind of hard for me to picture myself as a missionary or as a pastor's wife." She paused and looked him in the eye. "I mean, after my past and everything." Her voice shook a little, and her vulnerability pierced his heart.

"Oh, babe," he began, reaching over and stroking her arm.

She smiled a sad kind of smile. "Let me finish."

He nodded, letting his hand slip down and take hers.

"So anyway, Taylor's helped me look at us from a different perspective. She helped me see that I'm not marrying a ministry. I'm marrying a man. A man I love very much." She leaned forward and placed a gentle kiss on his lips. "I may not be the perfect wife, but I'm pretty sure I'm getting a perfect husband," she added with a smile, tears filling her eyes.

"I think you've got that backwards, babe." He pulled her up to standing and held her close. "I couldn't imagine a more perfect wife for me."

CHAPTER TEN

Caleb grabbed his carry-on bag and headed downstairs. "Dad? Are you ready?" he called toward the kitchen.

A moment later Steve appeared with his travel mug in hand. "Okay, let's go."

The drive to Portland Airport was a quiet one. Caleb was thinking about his mission to get information from Amber, and he could tell his dad wasn't thrilled about him going to Arizona. *If he knew why I was going, he'd be even more upset,* Caleb thought to himself.

As they pulled up to the departure area, Steve began to move toward the parking lot. "No need to park, Dad," Caleb said. "You can drop me off here at the curb. I'll be fine."

Steve glanced over at him. Before he could say anything, Caleb added, "I've done this before. I know the ropes." He could see his dad's jaw tightening as he pulled to the curb. "Relax, Dad. I've got this." Caleb threw open his door and hopped out, retrieving his carry-on from the back seat. He liked to travel light. No need for a bunch of luggage. Amber had a washer and dryer if he needed it.

Leaning back into the passenger seat, he smiled at his father. "Bye. See you in a week." Then he headed into the terminal, excited about seeing Amber again and nervous about the main reason for his trip.

Steve watched his son disappear into the airport. The kid was taller than him now. In another year, he'd be out of high school. Amazing.

A rap on the window got Steve's attention, and he looked over to see an airport security guard waving him to pull away from the curb. Steve smiled, waved, and drove off.

On his way from the airport to his office, he thought about his son. Caleb had been such an unexpected addition to the family. He could still remember when Michelle had approached him and told him about the pregnant student in her class that wanted her and Steve to adopt the baby boy she'd soon be having.

It had been a tough decision. After a failed adoption attempt in the past, both Steve and Michelle were leery. And Steve wasn't about to watch his wife go into another season of heartbreak. The teen girl who had selected them for adoptive parents the first time around had also been having a boy. At the last minute, she changed her mind and decided to keep the baby. But not before Michelle had decorated the nursery and the two of them had selected the name Caleb for their little boy.

Caleb. It was a name God used to confirm this second attempt to adopt. Michelle's student, Amber, had asked for one favor in return for relinquishing her son— that they would name him Caleb. She liked the name because she'd heard the Bible story about the spies Moses had sent into the Promised Land. Only two had come back with a good report—Joshua and Caleb.

Amber had no idea at the time that they'd already lost a Caleb.

Steve sighed. He flashed back to their son in an isolette in the hospital the day after his premature birth. He'd been so tiny and helpless. It was hard to believe that little guy was the same person as the tall, lanky son, who was on his way to see Amber right now.

As he replayed history in his mind, Steve recalled the early days of Caleb's childhood—his innocence and sweet spirit, and all the fun times they'd shared throwing the baseball or football, shooting hoops in the backyard, and all the other 'guy stuff' as Michelle called it. Steve and Caleb had been best buds.

But things were different now. More strained somehow. Steve could feel Caleb pulling away more and more.

Sighing again, he shot up a silent prayer for his son's safe travels and for God to work in their relationship. Hopefully, this was just a phase when Caleb was trying to break free of childhood and become his own man.

Amber was waiting when Caleb arrived at the airport. He could see her standing just outside the door of the arrival area. Rolling his carry-on behind him, he quickly walked through the automatic doors and headed in her direction.

"Caleb!" she exclaimed. "Wow, you're as tall as Will now."

He smiled and walked into her open arms. "Hey."

"Hey, yourself," she replied, stepping back and looking him over again. "Okay, so I don't want to sound like one of those old people, but you really have grown a lot, Caleb."

He laughed. "Now that we've got that over with, how about lunch? I'm starved."

"Lunch it is," Amber said, leading him to her car. "Tacos or burgers?"

"I could go for a big, juicy burger with bacon and avocado," he replied, almost tasting it as he spoke.

"You're on. Off to Bill's Burgers."

Amber peppered him with questions about Michelle and about Madison's wedding as they drove to Bill's. "You're in the wedding, right?" she asked.

"Yep. Monkey suit and all."

"And you approve of Luke?"

"Yeah. He's cool," Caleb replied.

As he ate his burger and Amber drank her shake, Caleb asked about Will. "Everything good with you guys?"

She nodded with a smile. "I'm so glad I found him. For a while, I was wondering if there'd ever be anyone for me. Seemed like fate was against it," she added.

Caleb thought about her two former boyfriends—his biological father and then the guy she'd been dating after she first moved to Arizona.He'd died in a car accident when they were visiting Caleb and his family in Sandy Cove. That had been horrible. He could still remember how devastated Amber had been.

But Will was a great guy. And who knew? Maybe Caleb's biological father wasn't such a loser anymore, either. After all, he'd been younger than Caleb was now when Amber had gotten pregnant. Caleb couldn't imagine what that must have been like.

"I'm glad you and Will are together," was all he said. He'd give it a day or two before he brought up his biological father.

As it turned out, he wouldn't have to wait that long.

Will picked up Caleb mid afternoon and took him to his shop. While they were gone, Amber set about preparing Caleb's favorite dinner ~ spaghetti and meatballs. Although she wasn't the best cook in the world, she'd learned how to make the sauce from scratch and let it simmer for over an hour to let the seasonings work their magic.

Once it was in the pot cooking, she mixed and formed the meatballs. Soon the house smelled like an Italian restaurant. With her iPod playing a mix of oldies, she danced around the kitchen celebrating Caleb's visit. He'd grown into such a handsome young man. Smart, too. Although she'd messed up her life back then, she had no regrets about bringing him into the world. It was the best thing she'd ever done.

Her mind drifted to the day she'd placed him in Michelle's arms. Tears welled up in her eyes as she remembered how heart-wrenching that moment had been. He'd been so tiny and fragile. And she'd been a blubbering mess.

Now she was proud of herself. She'd given Caleb wonderful parents and a great family. And she'd been able to follow his life and keep in touch. God had truly blessed her.

She thought about Adam and how she could see his eyes in Caleb's. Leaving the kitchen, she wandered into her bedroom and pulled a box out from under the bed. Opening it, she pulled out a photo of her old boyfriend and studied his face. It was the eyebrows more than the eyes themselves that seemed to match Caleb's. And his forehead, too. Both Adam and Caleb had high hairlines in front. It was as if they were cut from the same pattern.

Her heart caught in her throat when she heard Caleb's voice at the bedroom door. "Dinner smells great," he said.

She froze for a moment, trying to decide what to do with the picture in her hands. Before she could do anything, he walked over and sat down beside her. "What're you looking at?" he asked.

She quickly flipped the photo over and dropped it into the box. "Just an old photo," she replied, standing to put the box back under the bed.

"Can I see it?" he asked. "I love old photos."

Will stood at the doorway watching them. Amber looked at him, and he nodded. Taking a deep breath, she sat back down beside her son. Keeping her hand on the lid of the box, she began to explain. "So, I was looking at a picture of my old boyfriend."

He shot her a questioning look. "My father?"

Amber nodded. "Adam. He was my boyfriend when I got pregnant with you."

"Can I see?" he asked, gesturing toward the box.

Will came over and sat on the other side of her. He didn't say anything, but his presence gave her courage. She opened the lid of the box and pulled out the photo, handing it to Caleb.

He studied it intently. "Wow. He was just a kid like me," he said.

"Yeah," she agreed. "You have his eyebrows and forehead," she added with a sad smile.

Caleb lifted the photo closer and nodded.

"Did you ever talk to him after I was born?" he asked.

"No. It was over between us long before then." She tried to sound casual, but she could feel herself shaking a little with the memory of how badly it had gone the last time she'd seen Adam.

Will draped an arm over her shoulders and gave her a squeeze. She'd never been so thankful he was at her side.

As she reached to take the picture back, Caleb asked, "Do you have any others? Photos, I mean?"

Amber shook her head. "No. Just that one. I hope you won't take this wrong, but he was a loser, Caleb. You're so much better off with the parents who raised you."

He nodded. "Yeah. But sometimes I wonder about him," he added, glancing at the photo one more time before handing it back. "Do you think he might still be in Sandy Cove?"

"I have no idea," she replied, a sense of uneasiness settling over her. "Why?"

Caleb hesitated. "So, I was thinking about maybe trying to find him," he admitted.

Fear and anger rose up in Amber. Not with regard to Caleb. But she didn't want Adam to have anything to do with her son. Not now. Not ever. Then she glanced over at Caleb and saw such earnestness in his face. And then she felt torn. How would she feel if she knew she was adopted? Would she want to find her birth parents, too?

She glanced over at Will, hoping her eyes communicated her plea for help.

"What do you say we go eat that spaghetti feast and then talk about this later," he suggested.

Caleb nodded. "Sounds good to me!"

CHAPTER ELEVEN

The following morning, Caleb got up early and left with Will to head for the auto shop. While they hung out together, and Will gave him some pointers on car repairs, the conversation about Adam came up again.

"So, what does Amber think about me looking for Adam?" Caleb asked.

Will was bent over a car's engine, but he stood up to answer. Wiping his greasy hands on a rag, he looked Caleb in the eye. "Amber gets that you're curious about him," he began. "But she's pretty freaked out about you trying to find him."

"Why? I wouldn't involve her or anything," Caleb replied.

"It's not that. She's just concerned about how Adam might react," Will explained. "And about your parents."

Caleb nodded. "Yeah. They're going to freak, too."

"So you haven't told them?"

"No. I kind of wanted to do this on my own," he said. "And who knows? I might never find him anyway. So all their fretting would be for nothing."

"But what if you do?" Will asked. "Find him, I mean. What then?"

"I guess I'll just have to play that by ear," Caleb replied. "I mean, I'd like to get to know him, if he's open to that."

Will nodded. "You know Adam might not want to have anything to do with you, though, right?"

"Yeah."

"So you're not wanting Amber to help you try to find him?" Will asked.

"Not really. But it would be great if I got some basic information from her, like his last name, his age, and where he lived when she knew him." Caleb paused, watching Will's response, but he couldn't read much there. "What do you think? Would she give me that stuff?"

"Maybe. I'll talk to her and see how she reacts."

"Thanks!"

"You bet. Now let's get back to work here." Will retrieved a wrench and leaned back down over the exposed engine.

"So Caleb's pretty serious about finding Adam," Will said to Amber that night as they were getting into bed.

"What do you think I should do?" she asked.

"I think at some point he's going to figure out a way to find Adam. And like Caleb said, Adam might still be living in Sandy Cove."

Amber shook her head, dreading the whole idea. "I think the whole thing is a bad idea."

"Well, be prepared. Because Caleb's going to ask you for information to help him."

"Like what?"

"Like Adam's full name, his age, his old address in Sandy Cove."

Amber's heart sped up a notch. "Do you think I can refuse him?"

"Of course. But I'm not sure how that would affect your future relationship with Caleb."

"Yeah. That's what I was afraid of." Amber sank back against the pillows at the headboard. "I love that kid so much. And I don't want to be cut out of his life. But I hate the thought of helping him find Adam. The guy was such a loser. He could really hurt Caleb. Not physically or anything. I'm not worried about that. But I'm betting he'd pretty much deny he ever knew me or that he had any part in Caleb's life."

"Why don't we just see how things go tomorrow? You'll figure out what to say," Will offered, snuggling close to her.

As Amber flipped off the light, she prayed he was right.

Madison sat across from her counselor as they discussed some of her anxieties. "I just really don't want to let Luke down when we are serving in the orphanage. It's going to be a ton of work and responsibility, and I want to do it just right—for him and for the kids."

Taylor smiled. "You are gifted with love and compassion, Madison. I know that is part of all this. My goal is to help you embrace those gifts without the snare of perfectionism, which you have wrestled with in the past."

Madison nodded. "That's for sure."

"So let's look at that for a few minutes. What do you think motivates the drive to be perfect? Other than the desire to do well," Taylor asked.

Madison considered the question carefully before answering. "Fear, I guess. Yeah, fear."

Taylor nodded. "Fear of…?"

"Of letting people down?"

"Maybe." Taylor paused as if waiting for more.

Madison searched the ceiling for answers. Sighing, she finally added, "Fear of rejection?"

"Ahhh. Okay, so we've already addressed the rejection issue concerning Luke and you."

Madison nodded.

"So, rejection from who else?" Taylor asked.

Maddie pictured the orphanage in her mind. She knew the kids would not reject her. They happily accepted anyone who would give them a little time and affection. Was she concerned about the director's approval or that of the hired staff? She certainly shouldn't be worried about rejection from the young volunteer interns she'd be overseeing with Luke.

"I honestly don't know," she finally admitted.

"Would it be accurate to say that you've lived most of your life in the mode of people-pleasing?" Taylor asked.

Madison nodded. "Yeah."

Taylor leaned in. "Perfectionism and people-pleasing often go hand-in-hand. How do they make you feel inside?"

Her stomach tightened, and so did her throat. "Like I'm tied up in knots," Maddie admitted.

"Tell me how God sees you, Madison."

Maddie looked down at the floor. She knew God loved her. And she knew the Bible taught that she was precious in His sight—that she was His valued child. It was what she'd learned since she was a toddler. Lifting her head, she began to explain all of that to her counselor.

When she finished, Taylor said, "So whose opinion matters more than God's?"

Without missing a beat, Madison replied, "No one's."

"So now, it seems to me that the most important thing is to move what you already know in your head down into your heart," Taylor suggested.

"Yep," Maddie agreed. "How do we do that?"

"We start by understanding that *we* do not orchestrate the goodness within us. God does." She reached over onto her desk and picked up an index card. Handing it to Madison, she said, "Read this to me."

"The fruit of the Spirit is love, joy, peace, patience, kindness, goodness, faithfulness, gentleness, and self-control. Galatians 5:22-23," Maddie said, reading the familiar passage aloud. "This is what I want," she added. "All of this."

Taylor nodded. "Me, too." She sat back and smiled warmly. "Now read the first six words again."

"The fruit of the Spirit is," Madison said.

"The fruit of the what?" Taylor asked.

"The Spirit," Maddie replied.

"Ahhh…Are you sure that's what it says?"

Madison looked at the card again. "Yeah."

"Is it possible you've been thinking that phrase said, 'The fruit of a good Christian is'?" Taylor asked.

A light went on in Madison's head. "Wow, I guess I kind of have been seeing it that way."

Taylor smiled. "I think many of us do, Maddie. We receive God's grace and salvation then turn around and try to live out the Christian life in our own flesh and strength."

"And that leads to people-pleasing and perfectionism?"

"Yep."

"So, if it's the fruit of the Spirit, how do I get it?" Madison asked.

"Let's start by you spending the next week just contemplating that fact. Love, joy, peace, patience, kindness, goodness, faithfulness, gentleness, and self-control are not of *us*. We don't stir them up inside. They are fruits of the *Spirit*—evidence of *God* working in us.

"So, whenever you catch yourself exhibiting any of these fruits, pause for a moment and thank God.

"And when you find yourself falling short in these areas, realize that you are on a lifelong journey here, and fruit growing takes time. You wouldn't plant a seed in your garden and then stand there and berate it for not growing fast enough, right?"

Madison smiled at the analogy. "Right."

"I've got to run over to the shop and meet a guy who's picking up his car," Will said after dinner the following night. "Wanna come?" he asked Caleb.

"No, but thanks. I'll just hang here," Caleb replied.

Will nodded. "Okay. Be back soon." He pushed away from the table and headed out the door.

Guess this is as good a time as any, Caleb thought. Following Amber into the kitchen, his dirty dishes in hand, he said, "So can I ask you a few questions about Adam?"

"I guess," she replied over her shoulder.

"Great! So first, what's his last name?"

She turned and gave him a serious look. "You're intent on finding him, aren't you?" she observed.

"Yeah."

"You know he left me high and dry when he found out I was pregnant with you."

"Yeah," Caleb replied. "But he was just a kid. Younger than me."

Amber nodded, her eyes looking sad. "You're right. He was. But I was even younger than him. And I couldn't just run away from everything."

"So what are you saying? That you won't tell me?" he asked.

She paused, and he could feel her looking into his soul. "I just want you to understand why I'm concerned about you finding him. When I needed Adam the most, he turned his back on me."

Caleb nodded, wishing she wouldn't stare at him like that. "I get it. I really do. But you need to understand how I feel. I've never even met the guy whose blood runs through my veins. And he might still be in Sandy Cove. Maybe I even see him around town and don't know it's him." He paused to let that sink in. Then he added, "Besides, maybe he's changed."

Amber gave a sad laugh. "Maybe. But don't count on it, Caleb. The last thing I want is for you to get hurt."

Suddenly she looked so vulnerable and small. Caleb reached out and pulled her into a hug. "I promise I won't get my hopes up. Just please help me."

She nodded. "Okay. His last name is Wilson."

Caleb's spirit soared. Now he had a full name to begin searching. Next, he plied her for Adam's old address, the one he had when they were dating.

"I don't remember his actual address, but he lived on Fourth in a two-story white and gray house," she said. "It was on the corner of Magnolia."

"Fourth and Magnolia. Got it," Caleb replied, as he punched the information into the memo pad on his phone. Then he looked at Amber again. "He was a couple of years older than you? Is that right?"

"Yeah. So he'd be about thirty-three or thirty-four now." She paused and stared off into space. "Wow. It's hard to picture him not as a teenager."

Caleb nodded. "Yeah. I can see how that would be weird for you. But he's still going to seem pretty young to me. Compared to my mom and dad, that is."

Amber smiled. "Yeah. So you said your parents are doing well?" she asked. "But they don't know about this search of yours, right?"

"Yeah. They're both fine. Like I said, they're really busy with Madison and the wedding. Plus, dad's work, of course. He's pretty booked as usual." Caleb thought for a moment about how he and his father had drifted apart the past year. Another reason why he wanted to find Adam.

Then he turned back to Amber. "And you're right. They don't know about me looking for my other dad, unless Madison's said something. But she promised she wouldn't."

Amber winced.

"What?" he asked.

"It just kind of bugs me when you call Adam your other dad."

"Oh. Sorry about that. You know what I mean, though, right? Like, he is my biological father. That's all I meant."

She nodded. "Just remember, that's not what makes a person a dad, okay?"

"Right." He helped her rinse the dishes and load them into the dishwasher. Then he said, "Think I'll go for a run." Heading back to the guest room, he retrieved his shoes and grabbed his water bottle off the dresser before taking off.

CHAPTER TWELVE

Amber couldn't sleep that night. She kept imagining Adam—what he must look like now, and how he would respond to Caleb if and when they met. Then her thoughts would turn to Michelle and Steve. They'd been so good to her at a time when she desperately needed help.

How could she have given that information to Caleb? Now he'd probably have no problem finding Adam.

She thought about what Michelle would say to her if she knew she'd helped Caleb in his search but hadn't told Michelle about it.

Oh, God. What should I do? She prayed silently in the darkness.

But all she could hear was the taunts of the enemy. You should have known better than to get mixed up with a guy like Adam. If you'd used your brain back then, none of this would be happening.

She cringed at the thought. If she could take it all back, would she? That would have meant no Caleb. Of course, it would have been easier on her. Much easier. But as she finally drifted off to sleep, an image of her son filled her mind, and she knew she had no regrets.

The next morning, after Will and Caleb left for the shop, Amber's phone rang. It was Michelle.

"Hey, there," Amber answered, hoping her voice sounded light and cheerful.

She and Michelle exchanged pleasantries, and then Michelle asked about Caleb. "So how's he been acting?" she asked, quickly adding, "Seems like he's had something on his mind for a while now. He hasn't been himself at home lately. Hope he's not causing you and Will any problems."

"Oh, no. Nothing like that," Amber replied.

"Good. Has he shared anything about his plans for the summer?" Michelle asked.

"He mentioned a job," Amber hedged.

"Anything else? I just can't kick this feeling that he's up to something."

Amber paced the kitchen floor, trying to decide what to say. She hadn't promised Caleb she wouldn't say anything to Michelle. But she knew he probably assumed she wouldn't. On the other hand, maybe it would be best if Michelle knew in advance so that she could prepare herself and Steve.

Besides, she couldn't help but think that Caleb would need his parents more than ever once he met Adam.

"There is one thing," she began. "He has a lot of questions about Adam."

"Adam?"

"Yeah. You know, his biological father."

There was a pause at the other end. Then Michelle said, "Okay, so now it's coming together for me. The secretive persona he's been giving off lately, like spending more time in his room on his computer than he usually would and flipping it shut whenever we walk in the room."

"He's pretty set on finding him," Amber said.

"Why wouldn't he tell us?" Michelle asked. "I just don't understand. We've been so open with him about you and about letting him have a relationship with you."

"Yeah. I think this is different, though. He's known about me from the start. He's not sure how you and Steve would react to the Adam thing," Amber explained.

"I guess. So what did he want to know?"

"Adam's last name, his age, and his old address when I knew him."

"Wow. Okay, I'm glad I called," Michelle said. "I'll talk to Steve about this."

Amber felt a sense of dread. "Do you think Caleb will hate me for telling you?"

Michelle laughed. "No. He might be mad, but he won't hate you. Don't spoil your visit with him by telling him I called. Steve and I will handle all this on our end. And I promise I'll defend you to Caleb."

Relief replacing her dread, Amber thanked Michelle and said she'd be praying for wisdom for her and Steve as they approached Caleb about his search.

"So I talked to Amber today," Michelle began as she and Steve sat down for dinner.

"No Maddie tonight?" he asked, glancing at their daughter's empty chair.

"She and Luke are meeting with Ben tonight. They're going to discuss the orphanage and what the job would entail if they take it."

"Hmmm. Okay." Steve gazed off into space as if deep in thought.

"What are you thinking?"

It took a moment for her husband's attention to return to the present before he replied, "Just wondering about how Maddie would do. It's a lot to bite off at one time—marriage and a big overseas move to start something completely new."

Michelle nodded. "Yeah. I've been wondering the same thing. She does seem to be getting stronger though. I think it's good that she's seeing Taylor again."

"Hmmm. Yeah, maybe. I'm not big on counselors. Other than pastors, I mean," he added quickly.

"I know, Steve. But Taylor's really helped her in the past. And I'm seeing that Maddie's getting more confident again since she started going back to her."

"Well, Taylor won't be in China with her," he remarked.

Michelle could feel exasperation creeping into her emotions. *Please, Lord, let's not make this into a big deal. I need to talk to Steve about Caleb tonight.* Hesitating for a moment, she decided to take the path of least resistance. "You're right, honey. Taylor won't be there."

Standing to go refill her water glass, she attempted to draw the conversation back to Caleb. "So, like I was saying, I talked to Amber today."

"Oh, yeah. How's everything going out there?" he asked.

"Fine, I guess. But we need to talk about Caleb."

Steve looked up. "What about him?"

Michelle paused, searching for the right words. "So, apparently Caleb had more than just a visit in mind," she began.

"What? He's not thinking he's going to move out there and live with Amber, is he?" Steve's voice was filled with alarm.

"No, no. Nothing like that," Michelle replied, hoping to sound reassuring.

"So what do you mean by 'more than a visit'?" he asked.

Michelle reached over and took Steve's hand. "It seems he's on a search."

"For what?"

"For Adam," she replied.

"Adam who?" Steve asked, his face drawing a complete blank.

"Adam, Amber's old boyfriend."

Steve still looked puzzled.

"Caleb's biological father," Michelle said softly, searching Steve's face for his response.

He looked shell-shocked. "You're kidding me."

"No. He's been asking Amber questions," Michelle continued.

"Like what?"

"Like Adam's last name, his age, and his address in Sandy Cove when he and Amber were dating."

Steve shook his head. "I didn't see this one coming," he remarked, looking distressed.

"Me neither."

Sinking back into his chair, Steve pulled his hand away from hers, staring off into space for a minute. "I suppose it's inevitable that we would face eventually," he said, without looking her way. Then he tipped his head back and to each side, a habit Michelle recognized immediately.

"Here, let me help," she said, standing up and stepping behind him to rub his neck and shoulders. They were hard as rocks. Steve always did carry his tension there. He'd have a headache all night if she couldn't get those muscles loosened a bit.

Closing his eyes, he leaned into her hands and sighed. "Thanks, babe. You've got the magic fingers."

Michelle leaned forward and kissed the top of his head. "Happy to help."

A few minutes later, Steve reached up and put his hand over hers. "Better," he said. Gently guiding her back to her seat, he asked, "So what do you think we should do? Does Caleb know Amber told you?"

"No. She's not going to tell him that she talked to me."

"Okay, that's probably for the best. He'd just blow up at her. His fuse has been pretty short lately."

Michelle nodded. "I think that might have something to do with this search of his. I'm sure he's feeling pretty torn, wanting to find his birth father but not wanting to upset us in the process."

"Yeah. I wonder if Maddie knows anything about this?" Steve commented.

"Maybe. I don't see any reason we can't ask her. She's bound to find out when he gets home, anyway, whether she already knows or not."

Nodding, Steve said, "I'm glad we have a few days to think about this before he comes back."

"Me, too," she agreed.

Steve stood to begin clearing the table, but Michelle stopped him. "I'll take care of the dishes," she said. "Do you think we could maybe pray about this right now?"

Steve smiled. "Sure." He sat down and took her hand, bowing his head as he began. "Lord, we're not sure how to handle this new situation with Caleb. But I know it's not coming as any surprise to You. Would You please give us wisdom? And help us be sensitive to Caleb's needs, while guarding him from unnecessary pain or problems. We ask this in Jesus' name. Amen."

"Amen," Michelle echoed.

Madison and Luke sat side by side on the sofa in Ben's church office. Spread out on the coffee table before them were brochures and photographs from the orphanage the church helped to support in China. Eager

106

faces of young children smiled up at Madison as she perused the documents.

"They're cute, aren't they?" Ben asked as he watched her.

For a moment, Madison flashed back in her mind to the short-term mission trip she'd taken to another orphanage with Luke before college. Much of it was a blur now. That had been such a pivotal time for her. It was when she and Luke had finally admitted their feelings for each other. Most of her memories revolved around their relationship as well as their time with the kids. Forcing herself back to the moment, she replied, "Yes. I can hardly wait to meet them."

"Me, too," Luke added, giving her hand a squeeze.

"And you'll have plenty of interactions with them," Ben continued. "But, Luke, your main role will be as a supervisor of their caregivers and the correspondence manager of all the incoming emails and calls. Madison will be assisting in the infirmary."

Luke looked at her and smiled. "You'll be great in that role."

Ben nodded in agreement. "And you'll both be instrumental in assisting the director with coordinating short-term mission teams, like the one you were both on a few years ago. Now you'll be on the other side, helping those teams connect with the kids and staff."

Madison tried to imagine what all of it would be like. Life in a different country. Married. Working side-by-side with Luke as they managed such an important ministry. It was exciting but also a bit terrifying. Turning to Luke, she asked, "So, do you think we're up for this?"

"I am if you are," he replied with a grin.

"You two talk all of this over," Ben interjected. "And we'll go into more detail next time we meet."

"Sounds good," Luke replied, giving Madison's hand a reassuring squeeze.

The three of them stood up. "Let's pray before you leave," Ben said, stretching his hands out to take theirs. As they stood in a circle of three, he asked Luke to lead their prayer.

Madison felt her heart swell as she listened to her fiancé commit their future and their orphanage into God's hands. His calm voice and steady hand slowed her racing heart. *Thank you, Lord,* she prayed silently in gratitude.

CHAPTER THIRTEEN

"When's Caleb's flight arriving?" Madison asked her mother the next morning.

"Tonight at eight. Your dad's working late and going straight to the airport to pick him up," Michelle replied.

"Oh," Madison replied, thinking of the reason for her brother's trip. She couldn't help feeling a little worried about what would unfold in the coming weeks.

"So, I had an interesting phone conversation with Amber," her mother added.

"Really?" Maddie could feel defenses rise.

"Yeah. Apparently, Caleb is on a quest," Michelle replied.

Madison glanced out the window, feeling her mother's eyes on her. What should she say? Should she tell her everything she knew or wait to see what Amber had said.

Michelle took care of Maddie's dilemma by asking point blank, "Did you know he was looking for his birth father?"

Madison turned and looked her mother in the eye. "Yeah, I did. I'm sorry I couldn't tell you, but he swore me to secrecy."

Michelle nodded. "I figured that was the case. So how serious do you think he is about all this?"

"Pretty serious," Maddie replied. "He'd been searching the internet for a couple of weeks before he left."

"I'm really surprised he didn't say anything to us. Surely he knew we'd learn about this eventually."

"Yeah. I guess he just wanted to see if he could find the guy before he told you," Madison explained. "He doesn't want to hurt you and Dad," she added, "and I think he wasn't sure how to explain how important this is to him."

"It kind of hurts me more that he hid it from us," Michelle replied. "I understand his curiosity, but I'm concerned about your father. He and Caleb have had a strained relationship lately."

Madison nodded. "He thinks Dad doesn't support him and his choices."

"Really?" Michelle looked surprised. "I know they've had a few exchanges about Caleb not wanting to work full-time this summer. Is that what you mean?"

Madison paused. "That's only part of it, Mom. He also feels like Dad is already riding him about his career and college. Like he wants Caleb to follow in his footsteps and be an attorney, which doesn't interest Caleb at all. Right now he just wants to relax and enjoy being a teenager and not think about careers."

Michelle tipped her head to the side and studied Madison. "What do you think? Does your father come across that way to you?"

She sighed. "Kind of. With Caleb, at least. It's like he's got some vested interest in his son following in his footsteps or something."

"Wow. I mean, I knew he'd mentioned the law firm to Caleb and that he'd welcome him in as a junior partner if he decided to take that career path, but I never thought Caleb was feeling pressured about it."

"Well, you might want to tell Dad to back off a little. 'Cause that's how Caleb sees it right now, whether or not Dad means to come off that way." Madison opened the refrigerator door and searched the contents. Changing the subject, she asked, "Want me to make you a salad for lunch? I think I'm gonna have one."

Her mother looked distracted as she gazed out the window. But she murmured a reply. "Sure, honey. That sounds good."

Caleb was itching to get home and press on with his search. Now that he had a last name and an old address, he felt certain he'd soon find his real father. Walking through the airport with his carry-on bag at his heels, he searched the faces, spottinghis dad before Steve saw him. Then heading in his direction, Caleb waved to catch his eye.

"Hey there," Steve said as they met. "Your flight was a little late."

"Yeah. Some problem with the plane. We had to sit there on the tarmac for thirty minutes before we were cleared for take off," Caleb explained.

"Let's go. You must be starved. We can pick up dinner on the way back."

"Cool. All they gave us was pretzels and a drink."

Soon they were driving out of the airport. Steve spotted a burger drive-through, and Caleb got a double cheeseburger, fries, and a shake. "Wish I could still eat like that and be as fit as you," his dad remarked.

Caleb laughed. "Sorry, pops." Pulling back the wrapper on the burger, he dove into his dinner.

"So what's new with Amber?" Steve asked.

"Not much. She's sticking with the idea of college and getting a credential. Will and I hung out at the shop a lot," Caleb replied between bites.

"They seem happy? I mean as a couple."

"Yeah. They're good." Caleb licked some ketchup off his finger. "Want some fries?" he asked, holding out the overflowing box.

"You eat what you want, and I'll finish off the rest," his father replied.

They rode in silence for a while as Caleb finished his meal, passing a handful of fries to Steve at the end. "So, Amber said they're coming out a few days early for the wedding. I guess they're making it a little vacation, too."

Steve nodded. "Your mom said something about that."

"Really? I thought they just decided while I was there."

His father kept his eyes on the road as he replied, "Maybe. Your mom talked to Amber a few days ago."

Uh oh. Hopefully Amber didn't say anything about Adam, Caleb thought. "I didn't know that. Amber never mentioned it," he said. "Must have been when I was at the shop one day."

"Probably."

Caleb could see the muscles in his father's jaws clenching. Not good. "Is everything okay?" he asked.

Steve glanced over. "I don't know. Is it?"

"What's that supposed to mean?" Caleb asked.

"I mean, is everything okay with you? Why don't you tell me what's been going on and why you were so eager to visit Amber?"

Caleb looked away and began fiddling with the armrest on his door. "Sounds like you already know," he replied.

Steve took a deep breath and let it out. "I wish you would have come to us, Son. Your mom and I were caught off guard. We had no idea you were even thinking about something like this."

Caleb noticed his dad couldn't even say the words. A combination of guilt and anger battled within him. He could tell his father was hurt, and he'd never intended that. But he was really ticked with Amber. Why did she have to say anything? Groping for the right words of reassurance, he began saying, "I know it's probably hard for you to understand, and I'm sorry I didn't tell you guys. It's just that I wasn't sure I'd even be able to find him—Adam, I mean—and I didn't see any point in freaking you and Mom out."

Steve nodded, his eyes fixed on the road.

"Are you mad?"

His dad paused before answering. "What exactly is it you're hoping to find in this search?"

"Adam."

"I get that part. But what does that mean for you?"

"I'm just curious, you know? I'd like to meet my real dad." As soon as the words were out of his mouth, he wished he could take them back.

Before he could say anything else, Steve said, "So that's who Adam represents to you? A real father?"

Caleb could hear the edge in his voice. Trying to figure out the right way to put it, he replied, "I know he bailed on Amber when she got pregnant with me. And I'm really thankful you and Mom adopted me. But there's someone out there who is part of me. I can't explain it, Dad. But I need to find him."

"And what do you hope to accomplish when you do?"

Caleb slumped back in his seat and thought for a moment. "I'm not sure. I guess I'll figure all that out when the time comes."

"I see." After a pause, Steve added, "I don't suppose I could persuade you to hold off on all of this until after your sister's wedding?"

Caleb shook his head in frustration. "Why would I do that?"

"Because you're putting her before yourself. After the wedding, and she and Luke are settled, we can talk about this again. And maybe your mother and I can help you think this through more carefully."

"Right. And convince me to back off," Caleb said angrily.

"I didn't say that. I just thought maybe it would be good for us to make this decision together," Steve replied.

"It's not about you and Mom," Caleb retorted. "I get that you want to have control over this like you want to control everything about my life. But it's not going to work this time. I'm doing this, Dad. So you guys need to either support me on it or at least stay off my back."

"How'd it go?" Michelle asked Steve after she gave Caleb a welcome home hug and he disappeared upstairs.

"Apparently, I'm trying to control him like always," Steve replied, throwing up his hands. "I tried to talk some sense into him and to ask him to at least wait until after the wedding. But he's got it in his mind that he's barreling forward with or without our approval."

Michelle winced. She could imagine her two men going at it in the car. "I'll try talking to him," she said softly, putting her hand on Steve's shoulder.

"Good luck," he said with a grimace.

Michelle found Caleb unpacking his carry-on. He was throwing the dirty clothes into the hamper in his closet as if playing basketball against a fierce foe. "Hey, bud," she said.

"Hey," he replied without looking her way.

Michelle cringed inwardly. Her heart was breaking for their son. Yes, Caleb was adopted. But he was truly their son. "Everything okay?" she asked, knowing it wasn't.

"Sure. Fine."

"I heard about your conversation with your father," she said.

"I'm sure you did. Seems like everyone's been talking about me lately," he added, his voice edged with sarcasm.

Michelle took a deep breath. *Don't let this become a battle of words*, she warned herself silently. "I know you're upset about Amber telling me, Caleb. But she was only looking out for your best interests." She paused and then added, "We all are. We're on your side, bud."

Caleb spun to face her. "Really? Because it's not feeling like that to me. All Dad cares about is Madison's wedding and keeping me from upsetting her day. Of course, that makes perfect sense. She is his princess, after all. And I'm just some kid who lives with you guys."

"Hey, wait a minute," Michelle warned. "You know that's not fair. We've never shown favoritism with either of you two. We love you both the same, Caleb, whether you can accept that or not."

"Whatever," he replied, shrugging his shoulders and turning back to his unpacking.

"You need to look at this from Dad's side, too," Michelle interjected.

Caleb tossed her a look over his shoulder. "Why do you think I kept this to myself?" he asked. "I'm not doing this to upset Dad or to ruin Mad's wedding. I just want to know who my biological father is. Is that such a crime?"

Michelle shook her head. "No. It's not a crime, honey. And to be honest, I don't blame you. Neither does your dad. We've tried to be open with you from the beginning. That's why we let you know Amber and spend time with her. We knew she really cared about you, too." She paused and then added, "None of us, including Amber, know anything about Adam—where he is, what kind of person he's become, or how he would react to you finding him. That's what we're all concerned about." She paused and then parroted his words. "Is that such a crime?"

Caleb turned back around to face her. His face reminded her of the little boy he once was. So vulnerable and with such a good heart. Michelle rose to her feet and walked over, pulling him into her arms. That little boy had somehow morphed into a young man that was several inches taller than her. But at that moment, heart to heart, she hoped the little boy inside could feel how very much she loved him. The love of a mother for her only son.

"I get it, Mom," he admitted softly. As he gently pulled back, he added, "but I need to do this. I really do."

She looked him in the eye and nodded. "Okay."

CHAPTER FOURTEEN

It was a beautiful day for a bridal shower. The sun came out early after a night of light rainfall. "Sweet!" Michelle proclaimed as she opened the curtains in her bedroom. She'd been praying for sun for this special event.

Slipping into her jeans and a tee shirt, she hurried downstairs to make coffee. Steve was already out for a morning run, and Michelle was supposed to meet her mother to set up the decorations.

The shower was being held at Michelle's grandmother's retirement community. Shoreline Manor had a cozy recreation room that overlooked the ocean. It was available for the residents to reserve for events like this. They'd put in a request a couple of months ago, and the afternoon was free. Grandma Joan was delighted, feeling like she was hosting the event.

Michelle smiled as she thought of her elderly grandmother. Joan was such a wonderful example of growing old gracefully. Although she hobbled around now because of her arthritic knees, and her memory was not very sharp, Grams had a friendly smile and a warm welcome whenever Michelle visited.

Today would be a special treat for Joan since her group of prayer gals would be attending the shower. They'd named themselves the Silver Sisters of the Sword and had become a close-knit group of friends who prayed for each other and their families. Michelle knew they'd prayed Madison through her turbulent adolescent years, and they'd all adopted her into their hearts as their granddaughter.

Luke and Maddie's friends from church were hosting a co-ed shower for them in another week, but today was ladies only. 'The Old Lady' shower was how Michelle fondly referred to it.

"You're not old, Mom!" Madison would reply whenever it was mentioned.

Sipping her coffee, Michelle smiled. She'd miss having Maddie around. Not only was her daughter getting married, but she was also going to a far away land for at least a year. Michelle gazed out the kitchen window and tried to imagine what the year would be like back here in Sandy Cove without Madison.

Her heart was torn. She was excited for her daughter and the new adventure she faced ahead. But a lonely ache deep inside revealed how difficult it would be to let her go. "Where did the years go?" she asked herself quietly.

Stirring a bit more cream into her cup, she glanced at the clock on the wall. 8:30. She'd better get going. She still needed to pick up the flowers and balloons and then meet her mom in an hour. They wanted a couple of hours to set up the banners and decorations, as well as the food which Luke's mom Kelly was picking up on her way over at eleven-thirty.

When Michelle drove into the lot at the Manor, she spotted her mother's car parked near the walkway. Pulling into an adjacent stall, she unloaded the first box, which was full of flowers, and headed up the path.

Sheila must have stopped to see her mother on the way in because she was not there when Michelle walked in. Setting the box of floral arrangements on the counter, she headed back to the car, retrieved the helium balloons with one hand and the bag of tablecloths, banners, and other miscellaneous decor with the other before retracing her steps.

Still no sign of her mother in the room.

Michelle looked around and began replaying the plan of their set up in her mind. She needed to move a few tables first. Setting to work, she rearranged the furniture to suit her before beginning to set out the tablecloths.

She'd just set up the last table when Sheila walked in with Joan on her heels. "Grandma wanted to come supervise," she explained with a wink.

"Great!" Michelle replied, giving her grandmother a hug and then turning and giving one to her mother.

Joan began peppering them with questions about the decorations. She pooh-poohed the location of the big banner, suggesting it needed to go directly above where Madison would sit to open her gifts. "That way it will be in all the pictures," she said firmly.

Michelle glanced over at her mother and smiled. Grandma Joan was sweet, but she was also outspoken and opinionated at times. "Whatever you think," Michelle replied. After all, it was a rare occasion that Joan 'hosted' anything these days. And Michelle knew she'd been looking forward to it for weeks.

"Are all the Silver Sisters coming?" Sheila asked her mom.

"All but Sylvia. She's down with a nasty cold again," Joan replied. "We've been praying for her all week, hoping she'd be well. But the good Lord must know she needs a rest instead."

"That reminds me," Michelle said. "I've got to give Madison a wake-up call. She and Luke were out late last night with some friends, and I encouraged her to sleep in this morning so she'd be fresh for the shower."

Madison picked up on the third ring. "Hi, Mom. I'm up. Caleb had some music blasting in his room about fifteen minutes ago. I guess he went out somewhere because it's quiet now."

Michelle shook her head. Oh well. At least Maddie'd gotten to sleep in a little. "Sorry about that, honey," she said.

"No worries. How are things going over there?"

"We're getting set up. Grams is here helping us," Michelle said.

"Uh oh. Well, good luck. I'll see you at noon," Madison replied, and Michelle could hear the laughter in her words.

As soon as she hung up, the three ladies set to work transforming the room into a bridal shower of pinks and lavenders, the ocean sparkling in the distance through the open windows.

"You aren't wearing those jeans to the shower, are you?" Sheila asked Michelle as they finished their work.

"No, Mom. I've got a dress in the car. I figured I'd change here at Grams." She headed out to retrieve it, along with her makeup bag and curling iron, meeting her mother and grandmother back at the apartment. By eleven thirty, she was ready to meet up with Kelly and help her arrange the lunch spread along the buffet counter.

Sheila pulled out the beverages they'd stored in the refrigerator earlier that week and loaded the coffee maker as well. Soon everything was ready. Madison arrived right on time, dressed in a skirt and tee shirt. She looked pretty, but so young to Michelle. How could it be that Maddie was about to be a bride?

Thankfully, there was little time to ponder that thought. As Madison began perusing the buffet, three teacher friends from Magnolia Middle School, where Michelle taught English, arrived together. Right behind them were two of the Silver Sisters followed by some neighbor gals who had watched Madison grow up.

The other three of Joan's prayer group friends arrived a few minutes later, and soon the room was teaming with friendly faces and voices as introductions were exchanged and the gifts were stacked on a corner table next to the desserts.

Michelle watched Madison graciously greeting the guests. She was the only one in the room who was younger than forty, but even in her natural shyness, she was mixing and mingling with the multitude.

Soon Joan rang a little bell she'd brought. "Attention please," she said.

The chatter died down, and all eyes were on Madison's great grandmother.

"If we could all just gather close, I'd like to say a little prayer for our luncheon and shower," she began. With all heads bowed, Joan clasped her hands in front of her heart and prayed a blessing over the meal and over Madison's new life as a wife and missionary. Michelle could hear her grandmother's voice crack as she prayed, and she couldn't help wondering if Joan would still be around when Maddie and Luke returned from China.

After a delicious lunch of croissant sandwiches, salad, and fruit, the ladies showered Madison with gifts, many of which Michelle and Steve would store for the couple until they moved back to Sandy Cove. That was the silver lining of them leaving. Both had reassured them they'd eventually be settling there.

Many of the ladies lingered after the shower was over, enjoying the peaceful view and fellowship while Michelle, Sheila, and Joan put up their feet and relaxed for the first time all day. Madison bowed out after about twenty minutes, explaining that she and Luke had another meeting with Ben that evening.

By the time Michelle got home at five, she was ready for a nap. Steve walked in on her settling down on the couch with her feet propped up on the arm. "Tired, babe?" he asked.

"Yeah. It was a great afternoon, but I'm beat."

He leaned down and placed his hand on her leg as he gently kissed her. "Sweet dreams, princess."

Michelle smiled. "Thanks."

When she woke up an hour later, she could smell pizza. "Steve?"

Her husband appeared from the kitchen. "You're awake. Just in time for dinner. Be right there."

Carrying out two paper plates with pizza on them, he set them down on the coffee table beside the couch. Then patting her leg, he said, "Sit up, babe. Let's eat."

"What about Caleb?" she asked.

"He's hanging out with Logan. They're grabbing burgers, I guess."

"He'll be bummed he missed pizza."

"I got extra large. There'll be plenty left for him when he gets back. You know how he loves to raid the fridge at midnight," Steve replied with a smirk.

Michelle nodded.

Caleb and Logan sat in the car eating their burgers. "So, your parents are pretty bummed about this whole Adam thing?" Logan asked.

"You could say that," Caleb replied. "Get this—my dad asked if I could wait until after the wedding. Like I might invite Adam or something, right?" he asked sarcastically.

Logan shook his head. "Are you going to hold off?"

"No way," he replied. "I'm so close now. It's not like I can just forget about it for a month."

"Yeah. Well, let me know if I can help, bro."

Caleb nodded. "I will."

CHAPTER FIFTEEN

Caleb pulled the car out of the burger joint and headed toward the outskirts of Sandy Cove.

"Where're we going?" Logan asked casually.

"To drive by the house where Adam lived when he and Amber were dating."

Logan just nodded. "Whatever you say. But we're not stopping, right?"

"Right."

As Caleb turned onto Fourth, his hands tightened on the steering wheel. He'd been on this street a million times. Especially when he was going to Magnolia Middle School. It was part of his route home on his bike.

The street was lined with trees and parked cars. The houses were old—among the first built in Sandy Cove. Once stately and impressive with manicured front yards, they were now sagging under the weight of age with weathered siding, faded paint, and a hodgepodge of landscaping. Although it was clear that some residents still took pride in their homes, many had let their places deteriorate with time.

Caleb remembered peddling down the sidewalk his first bike ride home from school, enjoying bouncing over the cracked and raised parts where tree roots had lifted and broken the concrete. Wow. He'd never even imagined that he might be peddling past his biological father's house.

As they approached the intersection of Magnolia Street, Caleb looked both right and left, searching for the two-story gray and white building Amber had described. He spotted it across the intersection on the far side of the street. Crossing over and then pulling off to the right, he pointed it out to Logan. "That's the place," he said.

A weed-infested lawn with a couple of overgrown rose bushes flanked the stairway up to the front porch. Caleb could see that the screen door had a large tear in the bottom half with the netting hanging loose. Looking around the property, he was a bit disappointed there were no cars in the driveway. Not that he would have gone to the door or anything. Not today, at least. He still had to figure out exactly what he was going to say when he did.

"Looks pretty old," Logan observed.

"Yeah. It could use a paint job," Caleb replied.

"So what now?"

Caleb thought for a moment. "I guess I'll just write down the address." He took out a scrap of paper from the console and copied the faded numbers from the curb.

They were just about to pull away when a woman came out of the front door. She looked to be about Amber's age and was followed by another woman, who was older. Caleb swung the car around onto their side of the street and pulled up, as they were about to get into a car parked at the corner.

"Excuse me," he said as he leaned over and called out through Logan's open window.

The younger lady looked his way. "Can I help you?" she asked.

"I'm looking for someone who lives on this street," he replied. "His name is Adam."

"Adam Wilson?" she asked. "Are you one of his martial arts students?"

"Yeah," Caleb lied. He could explain the truth later.

"Adam's at the gym," she said. "He should be home by five. Can I give him a message?"

"No, thanks. I'll just catch him at the gym," Caleb replied, waving as he pulled away and headed down Fourth toward home.

Ben looked his son in the eye. Luke had grown to be such a fine young man—one any father would be proud to call his own. The two of them were sitting together in Ben's office at the church for a meeting that was suddenly feeling a bit awkward to Ben.

Since he would be officiating at their wedding, he wanted to cover all the bases he usually did with a couple in premarital counseling. As invested as he felt in every engaged couple at their church, the future of this one was even more important to him.

The young man facing him would likely one day be the father of Ben's grandchildren. And he would soon be the husband of Ben's best friend's daughter. But most importantly of all, this was Ben's son, his firstborn, and someone who had taught him so much about being a father. He didn't want to blow it now.

Why did it always seem toughest to discuss important matters with family? Why was it so much easier to guide and counsel his parishioners than it was those closest to him? He supposed it was the depth of love he felt for them—a love that helped Ben grasp the love of God Himself for His children.

Clearing his throat, he stood from his desk and walked around to the other side where Luke sat waiting. "Let's move over here," Ben suggested, gesturing to the easy chairs in the corner of the room.

As they got settled, he sat forward in his chair and began to pray. "Heavenly Father, You have given us Your plan for marriage. It boggles my mind to think that Luke here, one of my most precious gifts from You, is ready to embark on that adventure now. You knew from the beginning of time that he and Madison would one day join their lives together as a couple. Please guide me tonight as I share some very special concepts with Luke about what it means to be a leader in his home.

"Help him to turn this next page of the book of his life with grace and humility, completely relying on You as his role model of sacrificial living. Prepare both Luke and Madison for the unknown future that awaits them—a future You have already visited and prepared for them.

"Give them patience with each other and themselves as they learn their new roles as husband and wife. And please give my son wisdom and strength and unconditional love. Help him to keep his eyes on You and to let You be his anchor through every storm that comes.

"And now, I ask for a special measure of your grace, as I share with Luke the things You have taught me about being a godly husband. Help me to be transparent and open with him as we talk man-to-man about the most important ministry he will ever have. In Jesus' precious name, Amen."

"Amen," Luke echoed.

"So are you feeling a little nervous about getting married? It's a big step, son."

Luke smiled broadly, his grin lighting up his eyes, too. "I'm actually really happy, Dad. Marrying Madison feels so right."

Ben nodded, his heart lifting with his son's contagious joy. "That's exactly how you should feel. It blesses me to hear you say it." He patted his chest at his heart. "So tonight we're going to go over the role of a husband. I know a lot of what I'm going to share with you is stuff you already know. But I don't want to leave any stone unturned in our premarital counseling, and I always like to have one session that is man-to-man with the groom."

"Understood," Luke replied, rubbing his palms on his jeans.

Ben recognized the gesture. He'd done it himself a million times—wiping the sweat off when he suddenly felt a little nervous. "So, I'm guessing it's a bit awkward to have your dad doing your premarital counseling."

"A little," Luke admitted. "But here's the thing, Dad. You've spent my whole life showing me what it means to lead a family, and what it looks like to be a godly husband—at least from what us kids could see. I figure I've already got an edge over the other grooms you counsel."

Ben's heart swelled, but he chuckled to keep things light. "I had to learn as I went, so I'm sure you can probably remember a slew of fumbles as well."

Luke shrugged. "You're human, Dad. Just like the rest of us. But you're a great father, and I'm pretty sure Mom would give you a good rating as a husband."

"Well, thanks for that, Luke." Ben paused and allowed himself to feel the mantle of pastor being placed on his shoulder from above. "We're going to talk about a number of things tonight—getting off to a good start from your first night together, to learning to listen to a woman's heart, and to navigating the unexpected bumps in life's path. In each of these areas, I'm going to challenge you to accept responsibility for not only setting the tone in your marriage, but also for being the compass that keeps pointing Madison back to God."

Luke leaned forward in his seat, resting his elbows on his knees. "Okay. I'm ready."

As Ben began sharing the importance of sensitivity and reading a woman's signals on their honeymoon, his anxiety evaporated and he found himself feeling great respect for the young man he was counseling. Luke didn't pull any immature stunts of making jokes or feigning embarrassment of delicate matters in a marriage. Instead, he listened attentively, asked questions that showed his deep love and concern for Madison's needs, and willingly shared his fears about Madison's past relationship with Miles infecting their times of intimacy.

By the end of the evening, they had covered a myriad of topics including ways of expressing respect, being a good listener, understanding the natural ebb and flow of relationships, and leading from a place of God's strength and personal humility. They examined the passage on love in 1 Corinthians 13 from the perspective of a man's role as husband and father, and Ben emphasized the importance of love being a commitment and an action verb.

"The world would have you view it as a feeling, Luke. And that is why so many marriages fail," Ben explained. "These days people are relying on feelings over faith."

Luke nodded.

"Right now, your feelings for Madison are strong and powerful. But those feelings are not your compass. As the years unfold, you will find yourself sometimes experiencing lulls in those feelings. That's natural. It happens in all long-lasting marriages."

Luke leaned in, showing he was listening carefully.

"Here's the thing, Luke. When you remain steadfast to loving Madison, no matter what you feel or don't feel, you'll find that those powerful feelings of love, that you thought had slipped away, keep coming back. And each time they do, they'll be deeper and more profound than they were before. You'll have more layers of history together. Good times and bad, which you've weathered as a couple. Things about each other that only the two of you know. And a deeper and deeper understanding of why God put the two of you together." Ben paused to let that sink in.

"Like you and Mom," Luke observed.

"Yep."

"Just so you know, we can see it, Dad. All of us kids do. We see the deep love and respect you guys have for each other."

Ben let that blessing wash over him. "Thanks for telling me, Son. Your mom's a special woman. I wouldn't be who I am without her in my life."

"I'm sure she feels the same," Luke replied. "So any other advice on how to keep the spark in a lifelong relationship?" he asked.

"Don't forget about having fun together. Keep dating and surprising her with adventures and gifts. It's easy to get caught up in the busyness of life, especially after you start a family. There are bills to pay, a home to maintain, and kids to raise. But Madison is always your first priority after God. She needs to know that you still treasure her when she doesn't have a twenty-two-year-old face and body. That she's still your bride to the very end."

Luke nodded. "She will be, Dad. I promise."

CHAPTER SIXTEEN

Madison sat across from Taylor in the counseling office. She'd had a nightmare the night before about Luke breaking their engagement, so she knew she still had some issues to resolve.

"Do you think I'll ever be able to forget my past and feel worthy of Luke's love?" she asked Taylor.

"I don't think forgetting the past is the answer," Taylor replied. "You've learned some things from the past that are valuable, Madison. On the other hand, I do believe that you will come to terms with your past, learn to forgive yourself, and allow yourself to be loved by Luke."

"How do I do that?" she asked.

"Let me ask you something. Tell me about your prayers. I mean, what is the typical content of your conversation with God?"

Madison hesitated, searching her mind for an accurate description. "I guess it's mostly a combination of thanking God and asking Him to watch over people I care about." She looked up at Taylor, who was nodding.

"When you first came to see me again, you talked about not feeling good enough for Luke."

"Right. I mean he's such a great guy, and he saved himself for marriage. I sort of feel like I'm ripping him off by the fact that I was with Miles in high school."

Taylor's face was full of compassion. "I'm going to propose something to you, Madison, that may sound very counter-intuitive at first."

Madison sat forward. "Okay, I'm listening."

"As you know, God's ways are not our ways. Secular psychology would focus on the good within you and make statements of affirmation to build your self-esteem. But that's not God's way."

Madison nodded. "I've tried that," she admitted. "But I still feel the same."

Taylor tipped her head to the side and smiled empathetically. "So, I'm going to suggest you quit trying to fight this feeling and give yourself a chance to own it before God."

Madison felt confused, but something inside nudged her forward. "Okay. How do I do that?"

"You do that through the biblical practices of humbling yourself and confessing. You didn't mention that, so I'm assuming that's not a regular part of your prayer life, right?"

Madison cringed a little. "Right. I guess it just scares me too much. Like if I let myself be totally open with God about what a mess I've made of my past, He'll turn away from me." Her voice began to shake as the tears welled up. "I mean, it's not like I wasn't raised in a Christian home. I knew what I was doing was wrong. But I did it anyway. And now I have to live with the consequences of feeling like I'll never be good enough for Luke or anyone else." She tried to hold back the tears, but she finally gave in.

Taylor reached over and placed her hand on Madison's, allowing the emotions to take their course.

After the storm, Taylor spoke. "There's a lot of fear inside of you, Madison. God wants to set you free."

Madison nodded.

"Here's the paradox of confession. What we think will be the undoing of our sense of self-worth, actually becomes the key to open the prison of self-condemnation and set us free. I know this because I have experienced it first hand."

"You have?"

"Yep." Taylor's smile moved to her eyes as she recounted the day she'd realized she was running from the one thing that could set her free. "I can still remember sitting in my rocking chair feeling very unloved and unlovable. I thought about all the mistakes I'd made in relationships. The words I'd said that I shouldn't have. And the ones I should have said that I didn't."

Madison cracked a smile of her own. "I certainly get that," she admitted.

"Finally, I just started praying and told God what a wretched sinner I was."

Madison sat on the edge of her seat. "And?"

"And a complete peace washed over me as I realized that God was still there, still loving me, still wanting me as His daughter and as the bride of Christ." She looked Madison in the eye. "It gave me a new depth of understanding of the cross and what it meant for all of us believers."

Madison nodded.

"I realized that God wasn't expecting me to drum up my own righteousness to be worthy of Him and His love. He'd already purchased my white robes of righteousness Himself, but I'd been refusing to wear them."

"Wow." Madison had never considered that confession could hold such freedom.

"Here's my assignment for you this week," Taylor said. "I want you to get alone with God somewhere and be completely open and transparent with Him about your sins. You know He already knows them, but speak your pain and regret with complete humility."

"Okay, I'll try," Madison replied.

"And then I want you to close your eyes and imagine God scrubbing out all the dark stains of sin within you. Picture a white robe of righteousness—a beautiful, sparkling gown made just for you—that you slip into." And here is a scripture for you to meditate on all week. She handed Madison a piece of paper.

I _____ delight greatly in the Lord; my soul rejoices in my God. For He has clothed me with garments of salvation and arrayed me in a robe of righteousness, as a bridegroom adorns his head like a priest and as a bride adorns herself with jewels. ~ Isaiah 61:10.

"Write your name on the blank line. Read this scripture aloud to yourself every day, imagining the robe of righteousness that only He can give you. It's a free gift, Madison, but you can't wear it as long as you are trying to be righteous on your own strength. Let Him do it through you as you openly confess." She studied Madison's face. "Don't be afraid. He's going to finish the good work He began in you. I promise."

"Okay. I'll do it," Maddie replied with a nod of affirmation.

Caleb turned onto Fourth Street. This time he was alone. No Logan to put any damper on what he was about to do. Peering out his side window as he approached Adam's house, he nearly clipped the open door of a car parked at the curb on his right. He wouldn't have known, except the man in the driver's seat honked his horn and flashed an obscene gesture.

Adrenaline surged through Caleb's body as he drove away. No way was he going to stop and risk an altercation with that man. He'd have to come back another time.

Steve cradled the phone to his ear as he rifled through the papers on his desk to find a notepad. *I've gotta get this mess straightened out,* he thought to himself as he waited for Jeff Jontry to pick up the other line. Jeff and Steve were in a men's group at church. The five of them met for breakfast on Wednesday mornings, sharing prayer requests and supporting each other in their walks of faith.

Jeff worked as a detective at the Sandy Cove Police Department. A few years older than Steve, his kids were all grown and married, and he had his first grandchild on the way. As a police officer in their community for the past thirty years, Jeff knew many of the locals, especially those who had had brushes with the law. Steve hoped to find out what Jeff might be able to tell him about Adam Wilson. Was he still living in Sandy Cove? Did he have a criminal record?

Between Michelle's midnight worrying and Steve's undercurrent of concern, he felt that he needed to do something before Caleb got himself in over his head.

"Steve," Jeff's voice greeted him. "What's up?"

"I'm trying to get some information about someone," Steve replied. "I was hoping you might be able to help."

"Sure, buddy. Happy to help if I can. What kind of information are you looking for? And who's the someone?"

"You knew that Caleb was adopted, right?" Steve asked.

"Uh, yeah. Now that you mention it, I remember you saying something about that. Is everything okay with him?"

"Yes and no. He's got it in his head to find his biological father."

"Oh. And that's the someone we're talking about here, I assume," Jeff said.

"Yeah."

"So what do you know about this guy?" he asked Steve.

"I know his name—Adam Wilson—and his approximate age—about thirty-three or thirty-four—and that he used to live in Sandy Cove on Fourth Street."

"That's quite a bit," Jeff replied. "Where'd you get all that information?"

"Caleb's biological mother. We've stayed in touch with her over the years. It was an open adoption."

"But the father's been out of the loop?"

"Yeah. He never even saw Caleb after he was born. He bailed on the biological mother as soon as he found out she was pregnant."

"Figures," Jeff replied, his voice tinged with cynicism. "So, how can I help you?"

"I'd like to find out if he's still in the area and if he's got a criminal record," Steve replied.

"Let me ask around and see what I can come up with. Because of the tightening of regulations, I can't run a formal search without cause. But I can drop his name to some of the guys here and see what responses I get. In the meantime, why don't you run a criminal check on him through one of the employers' search sites? I'm not sure how much information they require up front, but you could give it a try," he suggested.

"Good idea. I don't know why I didn't think of that myself," Steve replied, mentally kicking himself.

"I'm guessing you don't do much hiring over there," Jeff said.

"Nope. We've kept the same office manager and paralegal for twenty years. I don't think they had those employer background checks back then."

"Right. So I'll poke around here, and you see what you can find online. Then let's talk tomorrow after the breakfast. In the meantime, I'll be praying for your situation with Caleb."

"Thanks, man. I appreciate that," Steve replied.

That evening as they were doing the dishes together, Steve told Michelle about his conversation with Jeff.

"What the heck?" Caleb asked angrily as he burst into the room.

"Whoa there, bud. Lower your voice," Steve said, trying to remain composed on the heels of his son's unexpected entrance.

"Why are you butting into this?" Caleb demanded, his face red with anger.

"I'm just trying to protect you," Steve replied, feeling his defenses rising along with his voice.

"From what? You think Adam's some kind of serial killer or something?"

"I have no idea what or who Adam Wilson is at this point, Caleb, and neither do you."

"I wouldn't even exist if it weren't for him," Caleb lashed back.

Steve took a deep breath, trying to calm himself and give a rational reply. But before he could say anything, Caleb stormed out of the room, throwing a threat over his shoulder. "I'm going to do this, Dad. So accept it. And back off."

Glancing over at Michelle, his eyes met hers. "I've got a really bad feeling about this," he said.

"Me, too," she replied softly.

CHAPTER SEVENTEEN

With heads bowed, Steve, Jeff, and the three other men in their group prayed for the requests they'd shared throughout their breakfast. After their amens, three of them stood to leave. "We're hanging back for a few minutes," Jeff explained as the others waited for them to walk out to the parking lot together.

Once they were alone, Steve asked, "So did you find out anything?" His insides twisted a little as he considered the altercation with Caleb the night before. In one way he felt that he was betraying his son's trust, but on the flip side, he was determined to protect him.

"I asked around, and it sounds like this Adam guy is still in the area," Jeff confirmed. "I mentioned your concerns to my partner, and he suggested the U.S. People Search website to get more information. Apparently, if you pay for an advanced search, you can get criminal records."

"Okay, I'll try that site. You said, 'U.S. People Search,' right? That's the name?"

"Yeah."

"Got it. And thanks, Jeff." Steve rose from the table, tossing a tip into the pile of bills the men had left for the waitress.

"Wish I could have been of more help," his friend replied, resting his hand on the back of Steve's shoulder as they began to walk toward the door. "I'll be praying for you."

"Thanks, man," Steve replied.

The two men grasped hands in a firm handshake and then pulled into a quick hug. "See you Sunday," Jeff added as he walked across the parking lot.

"See ya."

When Steve got to his office, he unloaded some files from his briefcase, listened to his messages, and then powered up his computer. After checking his email, he immediately searched the Internet for the site Jeff had given him.

It was pretty user-friendly, and he had soon typed into the form all the information he had on Adam Wilson, including the street he'd lived on when Amber knew him and his approximate age. The site asked for Steve's email address for sending the report, and he entered his work email.

"Okay. Done," he said to himself. Now he'd just have to wait for the email. Before he turned to the pile of work that awaited him, he paused for a moment to pray for their son. *Please bring to light anything I need to know, God, and give me wisdom on how to handle all this with Caleb.*

Luke walked up the concrete path to the front door of Madison's house. The two of them had an appointment with the videographer for their ceremony, and he wanted to leave a little early to have extra time to find the place. He was about to ring the doorbell when Caleb burst out, nearly running into him.

"Oh, sorry," Caleb said. "I didn't know you were out here."

"No problem. I'm just picking up Madison for the videographer appointment we have in Portland," Luke replied. "Where are you going in such a hurry?"

"Just running an errand," Caleb muttered.

Luke studied him. Something wasn't right. Caleb was usually so friendly and easy going, but today he was wound up tight. "Something wrong?" he asked.

"No. Everything's fine." Caleb's voice was curt as he glanced down at his phone.

"You seem kind of edgy."

Caleb pulled the car keys out of his pocket. "Really? Sorry."

"Nothing to be sorry about. I'm just wondering if there's something on your mind. Something you might want to talk about," he added. Both Caleb and Logan had been acting kind of distant lately. Luke couldn't help but wonder if there was a connection. Was this about Caleb's search for his biological father? Logan hadn't said anything to him, and he wasn't sure if Madison had mentioned the idea to Caleb about talking to Luke's dad.

"So, Madison mentioned that you're trying to find your biological father," he said.

Caleb looked surprised. "Yeah. I didn't know she told you."

"Hope that's okay," Luke replied.

"Sure. No problem."

"Any luck so far?" Luke asked.

"Maybe. I found the house where he used to live," Caleb offered.

"And?"

"And I talked to some lady there who told me he was at the gym."

"Wow. So he still lives there," Luke said.

"Apparently."

"How are your parents taking all of this? Do they know you think you've found where he lives?"

"Mom's pretty quiet about it, but Dad blew a gasket. He's freaked out that Adam is dangerous or something."

Luke nodded. "He probably just wants to protect you, Cale."

"Like I need protection," Caleb replied sarcastically.

His attitude surprised Luke. Usually, Caleb was so down to earth and easy going. He wondered how all of this was affecting Madison, too. Hopefully, there wouldn't be some big family blow up right before the wedding.

"Is that where you were just headed?" Luke asked. "I mean to track down this Adam guy?"

Caleb shrugged. "I was thinking of driving by his house to see if he's still home. Maybe I could catch him on the way out."

Luke glanced at his watch. He'd like to offer to go along, but then they'd definitely be late for their appointment. "Wish I could go with you," he said, adding, "I'm free later in the day."

"That's okay. Thanks, though," Caleb replied, as he turned and headed for the car. "Have fun at the videographer," he added.

Luke waved and then peeked into the open front door. "Madison?" he called out.

As Caleb pulled up to the curb across the street from Adam's house, he heard loud voices from that direction.

"You jerk!" a lady yelled.

The front door opened and out stormed a guy yelling obscenities back over his shoulder. As the man came down the steps and toward a car parked out front, Caleb recognized him. It was the same man who had flipped him off the last time Caleb was on this street. The guy from the car Caleb had almost clipped. Sure enough, he was getting into the same car, which was now parked in the driveway.

Was that Adam? He looked like he could be about the right age.

Caleb decided to follow and see where he went. Once the guy's car was out of the driveway and part way down the block, Caleb swung out from the curb, made a u-turn and followed at a distance.

They wove through town, with Caleb almost losing him once at a light. Luckily he was able to catch up and see the man turn into a parking lot at the local martial arts studio in a strip mall near the Coffee Stop. Caleb watched him park, grab a duffle bag from his trunk, and walk into the studio.

Steve was surprised at how quickly he received his report on Adam Wilson. He'd just pushed aside a brief to take a short break when he heard a chime notifying him of a new email. There it was at the top of his inbox.

He sat forward and clicked on the email. A brief message thanking him for trying the service was followed by a link to a PDF document. Opening it up, he quickly began perusing the information.

The search engine had found an Adam Wilson living on Fourth Street in Sandy Cove. He was listed as thirty-three years old, single, with one known living relative—a sister in Portland. Other than one DUI from a few years back and a misdemeanor charge of drug possession, there were no other criminal convictions. It didn't seem to be enough of a record for Jeff's co-workers to be aware that he was still in town.

"I wonder what other charges might not have stuck," Steve wondered aloud. He knew the report would only show convictions, not other arrests or complaints.

At least the guy was not a sex offender or anything like that. Still, the DUI and the possession charge showed he was far from a model citizen.

Steve sat back in his chair, clasping his hands together in his lap as he thought about Caleb. Maybe finding Adam would be a good thing in some ways. It might help Caleb realize how being a biological father was not the same as being a dad. And from the way this guy sounded to Steve, he was pretty sure Caleb would recognize that Adam Wilson was not the kind of man he'd ever want for a father.

Still, Steve didn't like the idea of Caleb going over there by himself. How could he convince his son to let him go along?

"Excuse me," Caleb called out the window of his car.

The man turned and looked his way.

"Are you an instructor here?" Caleb asked, pointing to the studio. His heart was pounding as he made eye contact with this man who might very well be his father.

The man nodded. "Yeah, I am. Are you thinking of joining a class?" The hard lines of his frown softened somewhat.

"Maybe," Caleb replied.

"Why don't you park the car and come on in. You can watch my next class. It's starting in a few minutes."

Caleb nodded. "Okay."

"See you inside," the man said.

Caleb watched him disappear into the studio. It seemed surreal that he might have just had his first conversation with his real father. Pulling into a parking spot, he turned off the motor, took a deep breath, and stepped out of the car.

CHAPTER EIGHTEEN

As Caleb walked into the martial arts studio, he saw framed photos of the instructors on the wall above the front desk. There it was—the photo of Adam Wilson.

He stared at it for a moment, looking for similarities to himself. Maybe the eyebrows and forehead? And similar cheekbones. But for the most part, he could see much more resemblance with Amber than he could with this man.

"Can I help you?" a woman at the counter asked.

"Uh, I'm just here to check out the studio. I was thinking of watching the next class," he replied.

"Of course. No problem. Adam's class is about to begin. It's an intermediate Tae Kwon Do class," she said. "Follow me."

Caleb trailed her into the large open classroom with mirrors along the front wall. The students were seated on a mat that covered most of the wood floor, and Adam was entering from a door that must have been to a dressing area. He was wearing a ghee with a black belt cinched at his waist.

Adam didn't even glance at Caleb, who was now seated with several adults and a couple of young children, on a bench in the low bleachers at the back of the room.

Taking immediate command of the class, he had his students on their feet and returning his bow. Then he drilled them on several moves they'd been learning before moving into the day's lesson.

Caleb's focus remained on the instructor for the entire thirty minutes. He could see the athleticism in Adam that he also possessed, as well as the youthful vigor missing in his adoptive dad, who was at least fifteen years older. There was something very appealing about a father who was younger and had such a cool job. Maybe as they got to know each other, they'd be good friends. Caleb nodded to himself at the thought.

After the class was over, he walked up to the front of the room and introduced himself to Adam.

"So what did you think of the class?" Adam asked.

"Cool," Caleb replied with a smile.

"Ever taken martial arts before?"

"No. But I'm definitely interested. I've been more into team sports like basketball and baseball," he added.

Adam nodded. "Cindy at the front counter can give you a schedule of classes. Most of the students in the beginner classes are a lot younger than you," he said. "But I do have one adult beginner class starting in a couple of weeks on Tuesday evenings."

"Okay, sounds good," Caleb said.

Adam started walking away, but Caleb stopped him. "Hey, I have a random question for you."

Turning back to face him, Adam replied, "Fire away."

"You lived in Sandy Cove long?" Caleb asked.

Adam's expression changed to guarded. "Yeah. I grew up here. Why?"

"No reason," Caleb replied. He could tell Adam had put up his defenses. No point in taking it any further today. He'd sign up for the class and get to know Adam first. Then he'd let him know that they were actually related.

"Logan, I found him," Caleb said as he pressed his cell phone to his ear. "And I just signed up for the beginning karate class he teaches on Tuesday nights."

"What? Why did you go without me?" Logan asked.

"I just decided I needed to do it on my own," he replied. "But hey, if you want to take the class with me…"

"I work Tuesday nights," Logan reminded him.

"Oh yeah. Which reminds me, I'd better make sure my manager knows not to schedule me for that time," Caleb said.

"So what was he like?"

"He was pretty upset when I saw him coming out of his house. He was having a fight with some lady there. But after I followed him to the martial arts studio and met him, he seemed okay," Caleb replied. Then he added, "He invited me to watch his Tae Kwon Do class."

Caleb had told Logan about the guy who flipped him off, but he purposely omitted telling him that Adam was the same guy. No point in giving Logan preconceived ideas about him. Sure, Adam seemed to have a temper, and Caleb was pretty certain the guy was nowhere with God, but maybe that was why their paths were finally crossing—so Caleb could help his biological father find a better life, and maybe even become a Christian. He could only hope.

"So when does the class start?" Logan asked.

"Two weeks from Tuesday."

"You didn't tell him anything, right? I mean he doesn't know who you are or anything like that."

"No. I want to get to know him first," Caleb replied.

"Smart move."

Michelle picked up the phone on the second ring. *I wonder why Steve's calling me in the middle of the day,* she thought.

"Hey, babe," he said. "So I found him."

"You found him?" she asked, momentarily confused.

"Adam Wilson. I found his profile online," he explained.

Michelle sank into the sofa. "And?"

"And he's definitely still in Sandy Cove."

She sighed. "Anything else?"

"Well, he's still single, so no other family that I know of other than his father and a sister in Portland."

"Does he have a criminal record?" She asked.

"One DUI and a misdemeanor drug possession," he replied.

"So what do you think? Should we tell Caleb?"

"I don't know. I'll think about it," Steve said. "Maybe."

"I wish he'd just drop this whole idea," she murmured, mostly to herself.

"What was that?"

"Nothing. I just don't have a good feeling about this," she said.

"Me neither."

Madison studied her calendar. There was so much to do over the next two weeks. The wedding was coming up fast. Her excitement mingled with a twinge of anxiety. Was it all going to come together? And was she ready?

"Better remind Caleb about his tux fitting tomorrow," she said aloud to herself. Carrying her calendar into his room, she found him on the computer in his email. "Busy?" she asked.

"No. What's up?" He turned to face her.

"You have your fitting for your tux tomorrow," she said.

"Right. Three o'clock."

"Yeah. Luke and Logan will swing by to pick you up around quarter 'til."

He nodded. "Cool."

She turned to leave but was stopped by her brother's voice. "Mad?" he asked, using his favorite nickname for her. That used to really bug her. Now she didn't give it a second thought.

"Yeah?"

"Something happened today. But if I tell you, you can't tell Mom and Dad."

She studied him. What did he do? "Okay, spill."

He walked over and closed the bedroom door. "I met him—my father, I mean," he said under his breath.

She could see that he was serious. Taking a seat on the edge of his bed, she said, "So tell me everything."

Continuing to keep his voice low, he explained how he'd found Adam, followed him to the studio, and introduced himself.

"But he doesn't know who you are, right?" she asked.

"Right."

"Is he married?"

"I don't know. He was having a fight with some lady as he was leaving his house," Caleb explained.

"But no wedding ring?" she asked.

"I don't think so. None that I noticed," he replied. "I'll check when I start my first class."

"What class?"

"I'm going to take his beginner class for adults on Tuesday nights."

"When does that start?" she asked.

"Two weeks."

"That's the week of the wedding," she said. "It's going to be busy around here. Couldn't you wait on this?"

"Don't worry. I'll be here for the rehearsal dinner and all that stuff," he replied.

She felt a sense of dread creep into her spirit as she looked at her brother.

"Why are you staring at me like that?" he asked.

"I don't have a good feeling about this, Cale. I wish you'd reconsider."

"Now you sound like Dad," he replied, accusingly. "You'd better not say anything to him," he added. "You promised."

"Whatever. But I think you're making a big mistake," she warned as she stood up and walked out of the room.

"I'm going to hold off on saying anything to Caleb," Steve told Michelle that night as they took an evening walk. "With Maddie's wedding coming up so soon, I don't want to rock the boat anymore with him. I'd rather we all be on friendly terms for Madison's sake. We can address this more after she and Luke are married."

"Good idea," Michelle agreed, relief washing over her. She always felt like the referee between her husband and her son these days. It was sad because those guys had been so close when Caleb was younger. Adolescence was certainly challenging at times.

"At least we know he hasn't had any major brushes with the law," Steve added. "Not that drunk driving couldn't end up being serious. But maybe he learned his lesson. Both of those charges were from a while back. Maybe he's a decent guy now."

"Maybe," she replied, taking Steve's hand in her own and breathing a silent prayer for their son.

CHAPTER NINETEEN

"I've decided to take a karate class this summer," Caleb announced the next morning over breakfast.

"Really?" Michelle asked. "When?"

"Tuesday nights starting in a couple of weeks."

"After the wedding, right?" she asked.

Caleb got a disgruntled look on his face. "Is that all this family can think about? No, it's the Tuesday before the wedding," he answered defensively. "But it's just for one hour that week. Think you can spare me?"

Michelle was taken aback by the tone of his voice. This wasn't like Caleb. Maybe he was feeling like a third wheel with all the attention going to Madison these days. She decided to cut him some slack. "Sorry, bud. I'm sure it seems like that's all we talk about lately. I'm sure it won't be a problem for you to take the class that week."

His voice softened. "Thanks, Mom. Sorry I snapped."

Madison sat on a bench by the shoreline, her Bible in hand as she gazed out over the turbulent waves and the gray horizon. She'd thought a lot about what Taylor had said about being completely open and transparent with God.

As she began to pray, memories washed over her, one after the other. Walking on this same beach with Miles, how he'd made her feel so special and beautiful, and then how she'd given her whole self to him, losing not only her virginity but also her integrity and self-worth.

Tears pooled in her eyes, as she once again became that high school girl. When Luke, her crush since middle school, had left for college, she'd felt so bereft, like a ship without a sail. Flipping through fashion magazines and studying the popular girls at school, she'd found herself lacking. Not thin enough, not pretty enough, not stylish enough.

After spending time and effort running and dieting, revamping her wardrobe, and adding layers to her makeup, she found herself the object of attention by the new guy at school. Miles was so cute, and even the popular girls were vying to catch his eye. But for some reason, he'd chosen Maddie.

She smiled through her tears as she remembered him asking her out and then the way he draped his arm over her shoulder and would even kiss her in the hallway between classes—right in front of those envious cheerleaders! He made her feel so attractive and even sexy.

Soon their kisses had progressed to new levels of intimacy, and Madison could remember how her body had responded with cravings that made it difficult to say no. She'd held her ground for a while, but then one day…She shuddered as she remembered that afternoon, alone with him at her house. Her parents had forbidden them to be there without either her mother or father home. But it seemed silly to Madison, and she defied their rule, only to her eventual regret.

Miles said he loved her. And Madison believed she loved him, too.

Then, it seemed like things began to cool with him. When her conscience got the better of her, and she reigned in their physical relationship, he reigned in his affection and attention. Soon he was working the cheerleader circuit behind her back.

Madison's heart ached, just replaying the memories of his rejection and the shame she'd felt in the aftermath. There was no excuse for her. She'd known better from the start.

Gazing out over the water, she shook her head. If only she'd waited! The following summer, when Luke returned home from college, they'd reconnected. And on the short-term mission trip to the orphanage, he'd confessed his feelings for her.

At first, she pushed him away. She was damaged goods and didn't deserve a godly guy like him. But Luke had persisted and had given her the gift of grace.

Madison reached up and fingered the necklace she'd worn ever since—a gift he'd given her to express how much both he and God loved her. Feeling the tiny ladder and cross, she remembered what he'd said that day. First, he'd told her how much he loved her, not just romantically, but as a person and a friend. Then he said, "I know you think you've really blown it. But who on this earth hasn't." He reminded her of God's unconditional love and Jesus' gift of the cross.

Then he'd said something she would never forget. "If there was any way I could help you climb a ladder beside the cross and look into His eyes, I know you'd see a love you're not letting yourself receive…a love that never ends."

She'd told him everything. All about how she'd given herself to Miles and didn't deserve Luke's love. He turned the fault partly on himself, telling her that if he'd only been honest with himself and Madison before he went off to school, none of it would have happened. And then he reassured her that what they had would be completely different; it would be like Madison's first time all over again.

"Oh, God," she prayed, tears streaming down her face. "I've really blown it in the past. The truth is I'm not worthy of Your love or Luke's." She felt her heart sink as she allowed the full weight of her sins to encompass her.

Finally, she said the words she'd feared for such a long time. "I'm a wretched sinner, Lord." Like a sudden storm, the winds of regret let loose completely. Her chest began to heave as she poured out her grief along with her tears.

After the storm in her heart had subsided, Madison closed her eyes and imagined all the dark scars of sin within her. She asked God to scrub them all away with His love and mercy.

And then it happened.

A peace washed over her. A peace she'd never experienced before. The peace of total surrender. Miraculously, a shaft of sunlight pierced through the heavy clouds shadowing the ocean, lighting up the horizon with sparkling radiance.

Almost as if she could hear His voice audibly, the Holy Spirit spoke to her heart, "I have loved you with an everlasting love. Your sins are washed away, and you are clothed in My white robe of righteousness."

Maddie sat very still, soaking in the love of her heavenly Father and the forgiveness she'd denied herself for so very long. And then she recognized a new feeling—complete freedom from the past.

That Sunday at church, Madison sat beside Luke in the second pew from the front. She felt so very close to God, and to this man who would soon be her husband. Next week at this time, they'd be Mr. and Mrs. Luke Johnson. Her heart soared at the thought.

As they listened to the message Luke's father delivered from the pulpit, they leaned their heads together, sharing the same Bible that rested partly on his lap and partly on hers. At one point, when Ben mentioned the blessing of raising a houseful of kids, Luke nudged her with his elbow. When she looked at him, he smiled and winked. Then he pointed to himself and her. "That'll be you and me someday," he whispered.

Caleb, who sat on the other side of Madison between her and her parents glanced over at them and cleared his throat. Madison flashed him a smile as he rolled his eyes at her.

Steve leaned slightly forward and looked down the pew at them, giving them a "what's up?" expression.

Madison feigned innocence, raising her eyebrows and tipping her head toward Caleb, which just roused her brother even more. He looked at his father and shook his head in mock disdain.

Try as she might, Madison had a hard time focusing on the message for the remainder of the service. She kept imagining what it would be like ten years from now, as she and Luke raised however many kids they ended up having.

She knew her future pregnancies would be higher risk because of a condition she'd been diagnosed with as a young child, a bleeding disorder called von Willebrand disease. But her hematologist had assured her that with the proper prenatal treatment and monitoring, and extra precautions during delivery, she should be able to have children.

Luke wanted a slew of kids, and Madison was getting used to the idea. As with most new phases of life, she had her anxieties and apprehensions. Would she be a good mom? The role seemed a bit daunting to her.

One step at a time, she reminded herself mentally. Taylor was helping her look at life differently now, not borrowing trouble from tomorrow, and trusting that God would provide for her every need that very day. She'd helped Maddie see that she was missing out by living too much in the regrets of the past and the worries of the future, rather than soaking in the blessings of the present.

As Ben wrapped up his sermon and the worship team came back to the front, the congregation stood to their feet for the final song. Luke clasped Madison's hand in his as they lifted their voices to God, praising Him for His faithfulness and love. Leading her by the hand, Luke guided Madison to the front, where they were meeting his folks to go out to lunch.

Soon his family would also be hers, Madison thought with a smile. Ben and Kelly were already like an uncle and aunt to her. They'd been close friends with her parents since before she was born. *God must be smiling to see all this,* Maddie thought. *He sure is in the details of life,* she observed silently as Kelly moved in and gave her a big hug.

"Can I borrow the car?" Caleb asked his mom. "My karate class is starting in less than half an hour."

Michelle handed him the keys. "Would you mind filling up the tank? I've got some errands to run for the wedding tomorrow morning."

"Sure. No problem," he replied, heading out the door.

A few of the other students in the class were already on the mat when Caleb walked in. Two looked like they were just a little older than Luke. The third was closer to Caleb's age.

Over the next few minutes, five other students appeared and found places to sit on the mat. The class was supposed to start at seven, but there was no sign of Adam. Caleb made small talk with the other young guy, discovering that he was also a student at the high school. They compared notes about overlaps in teachers and classes. The guy seemed decent enough, although his language cued Caleb that he probably wasn't a Christian.

Finally, at five after seven, Adam strode into the room, his presence silencing the small talk among the students.

"My name is Adam Wilson," he began. "I'll be your instructor over the next six weeks." Explaining the format and routine of the class, he eventually had them do a few simple stretches and then taught them the first night's poses and moves.

Caleb noticed that Adam didn't smile much. He kept his instructions short and to the point, demonstrating as he went along and then watching the students for their form as they attempted to copy what he had shown them.

He spent a little time talking about the importance of focus and mental exercise throughout any martial arts undertaking. "You can know all the moves in the world and be completely defeated if you don't discipline your mind and keep a razor sharp focus," he explained. "Karate is not based on brute strength or weight. It is a science of learning to anticipate your opponent's moves and artfully respond to use his own force against him."

At the end of the hour, he taught them the concluding bow and then directed them to practice what they had learned throughout the week ahead. After making sure there were no questions, he dismissed them and began walking out of the room.

Caleb caught up to him, not quite sure what he was going to say, but hoping for at least a moment or two of conversation. "Good class," he said.

Adam nodded. "Thanks." No smile, just a very brisk response as he continued walking.

"See you next week," Caleb added, feeling lame.

"Right," Adam called over his shoulder.

Caleb watched him leave the studio and walk out to his car, pulling immediately out of the parking lot and driving away.

The guy Caleb had been talking to before class patted him on the back. "See you around."

Caleb turned and lifted his chin in acknowledgment. "See ya."

As he climbed into the car and drove home, he was so preoccupied with thoughts about Adam that he completely forgot to gas up the car.

Walking into the kitchen from the garage, he was greeted by his mother. "How'd it go?" she asked, looking apprehensive.

"Fine."

"Did you gas it up?" she asked, holding out her hand for the keys.

"Sorry, I forgot," he replied. He could see her irritation mixed with exhaustion, as she gave him one of her looks and then gazed back down at the lists of last minute wedding details.

Just then Madison walked in. She looked at her mother and then turned to Caleb. "What's up?"

"I forgot to gas up Mom's car," he replied, grabbing a cookie from the counter. "Give me back the keys, and I'll go do it right now," he mumbled, his mouth full.

Michelle held them out to him. "Come right home afterward," she said. "I may run over to the ATM."

He nodded.

"And Caleb?"

"Yeah?"

"I want to hear more about your class," she said, her tone communicating her curiosity.

But by the time he returned, she was in a conversation with Madison about the boutonnières. Caleb took the opportunity to slip upstairs and avoid talking with his mom. There really wasn't anything to say, anyway. For once, he was glad everyone was focused on the wedding. Even his dad seemed to have backed off.

CHAPTER TWENTY

The last four days had been a whirlwind of last minute details for both Madison and her mother. Tomorrow was the big day! She'd soon be married to the man of her dreams and her very best friend.

Madison checked herself in the full-length mirror. Her floral sundress accented her blue eyes and fit like a dream. Heart swelling with joy, she felt like she could cry. It was really going to happen! Tonight was the rehearsal dinner, and tomorrow the wedding.

Opening her door, she could hear laughter downstairs as her Uncle Tim and his wife, Traci, chatted with her parents. Traveling up from Seal Beach for their niece's wedding, they'd arrived late last night, and surprised them all with a visibly pregnant Traci.

"Why didn't you tell us?" Michelle asked as she embraced her sister-in-law.

"We wanted to wait until the end of the first trimester, and then we got the invitation for the wedding, so we decided to just wait and surprise you in person," she explained, looking over at Tim with a conspiratorial smile.

"Does Mom know?" Michelle asked her brother.

"Nope. You're the first," he replied.

"Other than my parents and sister," Traci added.

"I can't believe I finally get to be an auntie!" Michelle exclaimed, giving her brother a playful shove. "You kept me waiting long enough," she added with a grin.

"Don't tell Mom," he replied with a wink. "Let's all just pretend like nothing's different and see if she notices."

Everyone laughed. "Right," Michelle said. "Like she wouldn't notice!"

Madison smiled thinking of a new baby cousin. She was due in early December, and Uncle Tim promised to try to come up for the holidays when Maddie and Luke would be home from the mission field on their two-week holiday vacation.

Smiling to herself, she tried to imagine her uncle as a dad. He'd always been so carefree—more like a kid than an adult. She knew Traci would be a great mom, but she figured Tim would probably be one of those playful parents who relied on his partner to be the disciplinarian.

She did have to give him credit, though. He was a lot of fun! And Traci and Uncle Tim were perfect for each other—with his outgoing, rambunctious nature drawing her out of her shyness, while her calm, thoughtfulness civilized his wild side.

They were much older than Madison and Luke when they got married. Maddie had a feeling that was a good thing, especially for Tim. He definitely wasn't ready to settle down at twenty-two.

Now, Uncle Tim was almost forty, and Traci was thirty-five. They'd been married for two years. *I'm glad they're starting a family before it's too late*, Madison thought to herself. If she and Luke had kids in the next few years, their kids would be more like cousins to Tim and Traci's than she and Caleb would ever be.

Kids. The idea was exciting but scary. Well, she didn't have to think about that now.

Knocking on Caleb's door before heading downstairs, Madison called out, "Time to go, Cale."

"Be right down," he replied without opening the door.

The church was so quiet compared to the usual Sunday hustle and bustle. Kelly and Ben were sitting in the front pew discussing something when Madison and her family walked in.

Turning around, Ben smiled and stood up to greet them with Kelly on his heels. As they all exchanged hugs and hellos, Madison glanced over the sanctuary. As if reading her mind, Kelly said, "Luke will be right here. He left something at home."

Madison smiled. Luke had been a little distracted lately. The last time he was over at her house, he forgot his keys, came back inside, and then after kissing her goodbye one more time, walked out without them again. "Guess I'm just having a hard time saying goodbye," he'd commented with a grin the second time back to retrieve them.

Starting tomorrow, they wouldn't have to say goodbye at night again. It was hard to fathom. Instead, they'd be just saying 'goodnight' and falling asleep in each other's arms.

"Hey, there," Luke's voice interrupted her thoughts as he came up from behind and wrapped his arms around her waist.

Turning her head, she smiled and said hello. Then he released her and greeted everyone before Kelly took over as the wedding director.

Step by step, she walked them through the entire ceremony. Madison tried to concentrate on what she said, but she kept wondering if she'd remember everything and do it all just right tomorrow.

Ben must have noticed because he leaned over and said softly, "Don't worry, we'll coach you through it all as it happens. You just show up in that gown of yours and leave the rest to us."

Relief washed over her, and she began to relax and even kid around a little with Luke.

Soon the rehearsal was wrapped up, and they all headed over to the Cliffhanger Restaurant to meet up with Madison's grandma Sheila, step-grandfather Rick, and great grandma Joan.

As they filed into the restaurant, Sheila rose from her seat on a nearby bench, followed by Rick. They began greeting everyone and explaining that Joan felt a bit under the weather and wanted to rest up for the big day tomorrow. Madison and her mom stood side by side watching Sheila as she came to Tim and Traci. Momentarily, she didn't notice. Then, squealing, she exclaimed, "You're having a baby!"

"Nah," Tim said. "Traci's just putting on a few pounds," he teased.

Soundly clapping him on the back of the head, Traci grinned and hugged Sheila. "We're due in December. It's a girl."

Madison and her mom exchanged smiles as they shared a moment of joy. By the way Michelle looked at her, Madison could tell her mother was probably imagining a future announcement of the same kind from her and Luke.

After the excitement, the hostess called their name for their table, and they began what would be Madison's last family meal as a single girl.

165

CHAPTER TWENTY-ONE

Madison awoke bright and early the next morning. She lay in bed looking around the room and thinking about all the years she'd woken up here. So many memories of times playing with friends, doing homework, and just retreating from life for some alone time.

Then she flashed on a memory of her and Miles lying on the floor in each other's arms giving in to their flesh. Shuddering at the thought, she quickly dismissed it. *I won't let Miles spoil this day*, she thought determinedly.

Rising to her feet and parting the curtains, she could see that the sun was working to peer through the morning fog. She shot up a silent prayer for a sunny day, and then stretched for a moment and started getting dressed. There was much to do, even this morning. Although the wedding wasn't until late in the afternoon, she had appointments for hair, nails, and makeup—all before noon—followed by lunch and then some formal photography before the ceremony.

She and Luke had decided not to see each other until she came down the aisle. But the photographer would be taking a myriad of other shots on the church grounds before that. Some photos of Madison with the ocean in the background, group shots of her with her bridesmaids, as well as Luke with his groomsmen, and some portraits of Maddie with her mother, grandmother, and great-grandmother, as well as a few of just their immediate family—Mom, Dad, and brother Caleb.

After she was dressed in her casual garb for the morning appointments, she took one more lingering look at her gown hanging on the closet door. Carefully fingering the soft fabric, she felt almost like a princess about to get ready for the big ball. Smiling, she thought of all the times she'd played dress up, donning sparkling costumes, tiaras, and little girl high heels.

Today would be the real deal.

Before she went downstairs, she looked in the mirror. "Here goes," she told herself with a smile. Then saying a silent prayer of thanksgiving, she walked out of her childhood bedroom and into her new life.

With a head full of curlers and surrounded by her bridesmaids, Madison sat still while Tara, a friend of Lucy's who'd become a cosmetician, applied Maddie's makeup. "I'm going to add a little gray here to give you a wide-eyed look," she said. A moment later, she handed Madison the mirror. "What do you think?"

"I like it," Maddie replied.

The photographer, who was taking candid wedding prep shots, leaned over Madison's shoulder and took a picture of her looking into the mirror. "Nice," she murmured to herself as she backed out of the way again.

Soon it was on to hair. Tara helped the bridesmaids first and then turned her attention to Madison. Carefully unwinding the curlers, she began teasing and spraying as she guided the curled tendrils into place and set the tiara at the crown of Madison's head. All that remained would be to secure the veil after her gown was on.

When Tara was finished, Madison stood back and gazed at her image in the mirror. *Wow. I do look like a princess*, she thought.

Her mother came over and stood beside her, also looking into the reflection. Neither of them noticed the photographer snapping away, as they turned and looked at each other, both of them with tears in their eyes.

"Don't get me started, Mom," Madison chided. "My makeup will be ruined."

Her mother smiled. "I love you, sweetheart. This is going to be the beginning of a great future for you and Luke."

After a light lunch, it was time for Madison to slip into her gown. With her mother holding it open on one side, and Lucy on the other, Maddie carefully stepped into the sea of white.

"This dress is so amazing," Lucy said. "I love it more every time I see it."

Madison smiled. "Me, too!"

After her mother had zipped it up, Tara stepped forward with the veil and anchored it in place behind the tiara, gently spreading it out across Maddie's shoulders and back.

"Don't move," Michelle said, as Madison soaked in the image in the mirror. "I want your father to see you." She disappeared for a moment and then returned with Steve in tow.

Madison slowly turned around, hoping the veils would stay perfectly in place. "What do you think, Daddy?" she asked.

Steve stood staring at her, his eyes pooling with tears. Finally, he managed to say, "I think my little girl is all grown up." He wrapped his arms around her momentarily, and the photographer caught it in a quick shot.

"I'll always be your little girl, Dad," she said, wiping a tear from his cheek.

His eyes full of emotion, Steve replied, "Yes, you always will."

The sun was shining, and a cool breeze wafted off the ocean, as Madison, her bridesmaids, and her family slipped into the room next to the church foyer, where they would await the start of the ceremony.

True to his word and his practice, Pastor Ben came in and gathered Madison and her parents into a corner of the room where he prayed with them and their transition from being Madison's covering and her spiritual leaders to her close alliances and friends. Then he asked Steve to also pray for Madison's role as a new wife and partner to her husband, Luke.

As they hugged afterward, Kelly walked up. "It's time," she said.

Ben smiled, gave Steve a pat on the arm, and quipped, "Stiff upper lip, now Dad," before disappearing through the side door.

Kelly lined up the bridal party out in the foyer, with Madison's great grandmother Joan and her grandparents Sheila and Rick at the front of the line. Caleb offered his arm to Grams, and Joan locked hers with his. She turned and smiled at Sheila before being escorted down the aisle to her seat up front.

Next, Grandma Sheila was escorted in by her husband, Rick.

Lucy assumed her mother's usual role of pacing the procession, so that Logancould escort Kelly up to her seat as the mother of the groom.

Caleb was back to walk his own mother down the aisle next before taking his place in front with Luke, Logan, and the other groomsmen.

One by one, the bridesmaids walked gracefully in, their bouquets clasped firmly in front of them. Then Lucy, maid of honor, turned and winked at Madison before leaving her alone with her father.

"Are you ready, princess?" Steve whispered into Maddie's ear as the music switched to the traditional bridal chorus.

She turned and looked into his eyes and saw a combination of pride and joy mixed with a tinge of sadness. "I love you, Daddy," she replied. "Let's go."

As they entered the sanctuary, seeing all the guests on their feet facing her in eager anticipation, she breathed deeply and smiled. She'd planned to look to each side as she entered as a silent greeting to these loved ones, but she found herself keeping her focus on Ben and the altar until she got close enough to see Luke off to the side. Peace and deep happiness settled over her as she locked her gaze on him.

Luke was so handsome. With his head tipped slightly to the side and a loving smile on his face, he looked as eager to marry her as she was to be his bride.

As they approached the altar, Ben opened the ceremony by greeting everyone and then asking, "Who gives this bride in marriage?"

Steve replied, "Her mother and I do."

As Luke moved forward, Madison's father gently moved her arm off of his and onto Luke's. Steve kissed her on the cheek and then took his seat beside Michelle.

After opening in prayer, Ben started talking about his son Luke and how he had grown into a fine young man who loved the Lord and wanted to dedicate his life to serving Him. He spoke of Luke's passions in life and led into his relationship with Madison, one that had begun when they were both young teens and had blossomed into a lifelong commitment.

When her future father-in-law switched his focus to talking about Maddie, she was so touched by his love and praises for her. Speaking so highly of his son's bride, Ben painted a picture of a young woman who was the very best suited for his number one son. What a joy to think that this godly man, her father's good friend and their family pastor would now be second in line to Madison's own dad.

The marriage of two families along with hers and Luke's hearts.

Soon they were exchanging vows and rings. As Luke slipped her wedding ring onto her finger, Madison's eyes blurred with tears.

"I love you," he whispered.

"I love you, too," she replied so softly that the air carried her words away.

Then Ben explained to the guests that Luke and Madison would be taking communion together as husband and wife. He ushered them over to the table with the elements and the three of them bowed heads together as Ben prayed, and then Luke followed suit. Next, Luke served his bride communion, and they partook together.

Leading them back to the center, Ben spoke about the sanctity of marriage, sharing a few Bible passages, and then exhorting the guests to stand in unity with Madison and Luke and help them uphold the vows they had exchanged.

"There will be tough times," he promised the newlyweds. "But never times when God will not meet you and carry you through together as a couple. And we," he gestured to the congregation, "will all be there to support and encourage you, too."

He closed the ceremony with a prayer and benediction, and then Ben said, "And now, by the power vested in me by the state of Oregon, I pronounce you husband and wife." Leaning toward his son, he added, "You may kiss your bride."

Applause broke out in the sanctuary as Luke leaned down and kissed her, gently at first and then with deep feeling. Madison's heart reeled. She was married! Her dream had come true!

Ben turned them toward the guests and said, "I present to you Mr. and Mrs. Luke Johnson."

The music began playing, and Madison took Luke's arm as they descended the stairs at the altar, stopping to hug and kiss Kelly, Michelle, and Madison's grandmothers. Then, before they turned to walk out, Madison turned to her father and gave him a big hug. "Still your little girl," she whispered into his ear before linking arms with her husband and leading the recessional out of the church.

The reception was a blur of greeting their friends and family, trying to eat some of the delicious dinner, and then the dances that followed. Madison and Luke were inseparable as they mingled with the guests. It wasn't until the mother-son dance that they left each other's side.

Watching Luke on the dance floor with his mom was such a touching moment for Madison. She'd always known Luke to treat his mother with utmost respect. And she could see his tender affection for her as they swayed together to the music and spoke quietly to each other, occasionally laughing softly in some secret memory.

Then it was Madison's turn. Steve was at her side immediately, leading her into the center of the wooden floor before taking her in his strong arms. As they danced, Madison caught her mother's eye on the sidelines. She looked so happy and a bit nostalgic. Maddie thought about the times she'd danced as a little girl, standing on her father's feet. They exchanged smiles as he pushed her off into a twirl, eliciting cheers from the onlookers. As the song ended, he pulled her in close one last time. "Luke is a very blessed man," Steve said to her.

"Thanks, Daddy," she replied, kissing him on the cheek once again.

"And now, for the bride and groom's first dance," the MC announced.

Luke met her and her dad on the floor and took her hand. The tinkling of silverware on glasses signaled the guests' call for a kiss. Luke leaned over and kissed her, lingering for a moment as the song began playing. Then he whisked her into his arms, and she felt like Cinderella at the ball as they danced in perfect harmony. As the song ended, Luke lowered her into a dip before giving her a hug.

A roar of applause and more tinkling of glasses evoked another kiss. Each one sent Maddie's heart racing with joy and anticipation.

Finally, it was time to cut the cake. They'd agreed not to smash it into each other's faces, but that didn't keep Luke from licking the extra frosting off of Madison's fingers. She loved the feeling of intimacy that was building over the evening. And, although she was a little nervous, she could hardly wait for the reception to end so they could begin their first night together as husband and wife.

By nine o'clock, they were both ready to leave. The bouquet had been tossed, with Lucy as the lucky recipient, and the garter had been shot through the air and caught by one of Luke's college friends. As the guests continued to enjoy the live band and cake and coffee, Luke put his hand on Madison's back and asked, "Are you ready?"

She nodded.

While her husband went to flag the MC about their departure, Madison walked over to her family's table to say goodnight. Great Grandma Joan looked tired, and Sheila and Rick were preparing to take her home. Michelle had slipped off her shoes and was leaning into Steve as his arm draped over her shoulder.

"I'm glad we get to be here for your send off," Sheila said. Then she leaned over to her mother and added, "We'll leave right after they do."

"No rush, honey," Joan replied. But her eyes looked heavy. "It was such a beautiful ceremony, sweetheart," she said to Madison. "I wish my Phil had lived to see it."

Madison felt sad for Grams. She tried to be such a trooper. But it was clear that she'd be happy to be finally home in heaven with her beloved husband.

"If it's at all possible, Grams, I'm sure he was watching."

Her great grandmother smiled. "I hope so, dear."

Luke walked up that moment, and the MC spoke into the microphone announcing the couple's departure. "If you'd all just gather over by that exit," he said, gesturing to the door, "we'll give them a bubbly send off."

The guests grabbed the tiny bottles of bubble solution and clustered around the double doors. Luke clasped Madison's hand in his and led the way through the tunnel of bubbles that filled the air. As they reached the door, he turned and smiled, waving to the guests before they headed out to the waiting limousine that Tim had rented for them as a wedding gift.

"No way are you driving off in a plain old car," he'd quipped. "My niece will leave the ball in class."

Luke helped her climb into the limo, lifting the train of her dress and helping her settle into her seat. As soon as he was in, he pulled off his necktie. "That's better," he said with a grin.

As the chauffeur pulled away from the curb, their lips met once again, this time both feeling a new freedom to give in to their passion.

CHAPTER TWENTY-TWO

Before Madison could step into their hotel room, Luke stopped her. "Where do you think you're going?" he asked with a sly grin. Sweeping her off her feet, her husband carried her over the threshold. "I've been looking forward to doing that for a long time," he said, planting a kiss on her lips before lowering her to the ground.

Madison laughed. "I would have let you carry me over the threshold after each date if I knew it meant that much to you," she teased. As Luke rolled their overnight bags inside, she turned to look over the room.

Pink and red rose petals created a path to the big king-sized bed and covered its surface in a big heart shape. On the table in the corner was a large basket filled with goodies. Sparkling cider with two stemware glasses labeled bride and groom, chocolates, and a variety of exotic cheeses and crackers were nestled into the iridescent cellophane lining and crinkle cut red and pink paper. Red confetti hearts were sprinkled over the table, surrounding the basket. And heart-shaped Mylar helium balloons that said "Just Married" were tied to the chairs.

"Wow," Madison said. "Did you know about this?"

Luke smiled. "Lucy mentioned something about needing to drop off a few things for you in our room when she came home at lunch time. But I didn't know this was what she had in mind when she said a few things," he replied. "Shall we break open this bottle while it's still chilled? Or I can put it in the little fridge over there," he said, pointing to an under-the-counter unit.

"I think we should indulge," Madison replied. "The cheese and crackers actually look pretty tempting, too. I didn't eat much dinner."

He nodded. "Me neither." Pulling out one of the chairs, he said, "Mrs. Johnson?"

"I'm liking the sound of that," Madison said, kissing him before she sat down.

Luke opened the sparkling cider and poured a glass, handing it to her before he poured his own. "A toast to my beautiful bride."

They gently clinked glasses then interlocked their arms before drinking. "Now for the food!" Madison announced, pulling out a box of crackers and opening the cheese. "How do you suppose they kept everything cool from lunch time until now?"

"So, I'm thinking that might have been why Logan took so long dropping off my car here for us to use in the morning. You knew he left during the reception for a while, right?"

Madison shook her head. "No. I had no clue."

"I'm guessing my car will have some things tied to the rear bumper and some writing on the back window," Luke said. "Logan and Caleb were gone for over an hour."

"Wow. I never missed them. Must be because I only had eyes for you," she teased demurely.

Luke smiled and leaned over, kissing her gently. "Okay, let's eat!"

They dug into the cheese and crackers, feeding each other along the way. Madison could feel her stomach stretching with the food, and she was getting eager to get out of her long gown. "I've had enough," she remarked. "How about you?"

"Me, too. I'll just put the rest of the cold stuff in the fridge."

Madison began heading for the bathroom to change, reaching up in back to try to unzip her gown as she neared the door. Although she could touch the zipper pull, she couldn't get a hold of it. "Can you help me?" she asked over her shoulder.

"I'd be happy to," he replied.

Madison could feel Luke's hands shake a little as he started opening the zipper. Rather than reaching back to take over, she just stood there and let him keep unzipping. Their playful mood changed quickly, and Madison felt a surge of emotion as he reached the small of her back. Turning around, she faced him, and as they kissed, she let the dress fall to the floor. Their lips never parted as Luke drew her close, his breathing changing along with hers as his hands nervously unhooked her bra and gently began to explore her body.

Not once did she think of Miles.

After a night of tender lovemaking, Madison felt she was finally home in the arms of the man God had created just for her.

The next morning, Madison awoke with her head on Luke's chest and his arms cradling her. His rhythmic breathing told her he was still asleep. She tried to lie still, soaking in the memories of the past twenty-four hours. Tears filled her eyes as she thought of God's grace and mercy in her life. He'd faithfully taken her through the heartaches of adolescence and into a marriage with the man of her dreams. Now, here they were, under the covers together completely naked and yet without any shame. She would have stayed right there forever if she could.

Nestling in even closer, she felt Luke start to stir.

"Mmmmm…I like waking up to you," he said, kissing the top of her head.

She looked up and smiled. "Good thing 'cause you're stuck with me now!" she replied.

He pulled her close. "I think I can get used to that," he said.

Soon they were lost in each other's arms again, learning everything they could about each other and developing new levels of intimacy as they submitted to their love and the passion it evoked. An hour later, resting nestled together once again, Luke noticed Madison's tears welling up. "Are you okay?" he asked softly, his face full of concern.

She nodded and smiled. "I just never imagined I could be this happy."

He kissed her and held her close. "Me, neither."

They both drifted off to sleep for a while and awoke hungry. Luke ordered room service, and soon they were feasting on eggs, sausage, and waffles with blueberries. Glancing over at the clock, he said, "We'd better call downstairs for a late checkout." The front desk was very accommodating, and they were given an extra hour and a half to finish eating and pack.

By two o'clock they were on the road headed north with passers-by honking and waving in response to their decorated car. Logan and Caleb had painted "Just Married" on the rear window and the side windows in the back seat. The car had cans strung to the tail bumper, which Luke removed before they headed out of town. But he left the white streamers and balloons that would follow them all the way up the coastline into the Olympic peninsula.

They had reservations at three bed and breakfasts—all with specially designed romantic rooms for honeymooners. With only a couple of weeks before their departure to the mission field, they were determined to soak in the seven days they had alone, just the two of them, before returning home to open gifts, pack, and say their goodbyes.

All three stops proved delightful. Their first room was in a renovated Victorian mansion overlooking a meadow surrounded by beautiful pine trees. It had a claw-footed tub, which they managed to squeeze into together for their first bubble bath as a couple. Afterward, they nestled in the white terrycloth robes provided by the inn, as they kept warm by the fireplace across from the foot of the big four-poster bed.

Dropping their robes and slipping under the covers, Madison felt like she was floating on a cloud. "I'm liking this featherbed," she murmured as Luke propped himself up on his side to look at her.

"We just might have to get one of these when we get our own home," he replied with a nod.

Their second stop was a barn that had been converted into an inn. Their room was upstairs in what had once been the loft. It looked out over fields of crops and rolling hills. With beautifully crafted natural wood walls, floors, and ceilings, and country décor, their room was both spacious and inviting. Illuminated by a wall of soaring multi-paned windows, they could enjoy breezes from the nearby coastal area during the afternoon and then snuggle by the potbellied stove at night. Not wanting to be apart for a moment, they enjoyed the oversized double shower and scrubbing each other's backs.

During the following day, they took a hayride out to pick berries and then had a relaxing few hours in town strolling through antique shops and enjoying lunch at a barbecue restaurant.

The final destination of their trip was a majestic glass and cedar home on a cliff overlooking the sea. They spent their last few nights there. Nights they would remember fondly when they were landlocked in China, and the sound of the ocean was far away. It seemed as though they couldn't get enough of each other the entire week. Not only were they becoming one flesh in their most intimate moments, but they were becoming one heart and soul as well. Madison found herself keenly aware of Luke's needs and feelings, not just physically, but emotionally, too. And she noticed how he was cueing in on her.

"I never realized this is what God meant when He said the two shall become one," she remarked to Luke one night as they were resting in each other's arms. "Every part of me feels connected to you in ways I've never felt with anyone before."

He nodded. "It's amazing, isn't it? How in one week, we've changed so much. I'll never be the same."

"Me neither," she replied, as a feeling of complete peace washed over her.

CHAPTER TWENTY-THREE

"Are you ready, babe?" Luke asked as they rolled their suitcases out to the car.

"For?"

"For our happily ever after?" he replied with a wink.

"Yep," she answered. "I'm ready to go wherever you do."

"Okay, then. First stop, Sandy Cove. Next, the great adventure—China."

She laughed. Nothing he could say or do at this point would seem daunting to her as long as she was at his side.

It was a six-hour drive back to Sandy Cove. Luke played some soft contemporary Christian worship music as they traveled south, and Madison found herself dozing off once, forcing herself back awake to keep him company and help him stay alert.

They stopped for a late lunch at two-thirty and rolled into town just in time for dinner, arriving at Maddie's parents' house at half past six. She and Luke would be staying there for the final week before their trip to China. A twinge of anxiety bit Madison as she thought about them staying in her bedroom. Would memories of Miles invade their privacy? She shuddered at the thought.

As they pulled into the driveway, Michelle and Steve came out to greet them. "Welcome home, sweetheart," her dad said as he took Madison into his embrace.

Home. It would never be the same. She felt like a lifetime had passed since she'd slept here just one week before. Now home was in Luke's arms. But she just smiled up at her father and nodded. "Thanks, Dad. And thanks for everything. The wedding, the reception, everything," she added, planting a kiss on his cheek.

"Anything for my girl," he replied, giving her a squeeze before he turned to embrace Luke. "You, too, son. Welcome home."

Just then, Luke's parents drove up with a car full of family. "Sorry we're a little late," Kelly said as she climbed out of the passenger seat. "My potatoes were taking longer than I expected." In her hands she held a basket with a covered baking dish inside.

"No problem," Michelle replied, walking to her friend to help. "The kids just got here, so your timing is perfect."

"Hey, guys!" Lucy called out as she hurried over to greet Luke and Maddie. "Did you like the special hotel décor?" she asked with a sly smile.

"Loved it!" Maddie exclaimed. "I can't believe you managed all of that during your lunch time. You were hardly gone an hour!"

"Where there's a will, there's a way," she said before asking, "Did my brother take good care of you?"

Madison looked over at Luke and they made eye contact and smiled at each other. "Yep," she replied.

"Well, let's all go inside," Michelle said. Turning to Steve and Ben who were talking off to the side, she added, "Honey, would you help me get the roast out of the oven?"

"Duty calls," Steve told his friend as he followed Michelle into the house.

"Where's Caleb?" Luke asked once they were all seated for dinner.

"He had his karate class tonight," Steve said. "I tried to get him to skip it, but he was pretty adamant about going."

Madison flashed to her brother and his current obsession with knowing his biological father. A dark cloud of worry threatened to settle over her until Steve asked Luke to lead them in a blessing. As her husband began to pray, he reached over and took her hand, and Madison's anxieties seemed to dissolve.

When the karate class was ended, Caleb walked up to Adam. He knew he should be getting home to see Madison and Luke, but he wanted to try to at least talk to Adam one-on-one before leaving. "Do you have a minute?" he asked as he approached the instructor.

"Not really. I've got a private lesson about to start," Adam replied. "What did you need?"

Private lesson! Great idea, Caleb thought to himself. "Actually, I was wondering if I could maybe set up a private lesson with you."

"Sure. Talk to them at the front counter. They'll give you my schedule." Adam turned and started walking away. Then he paused and looked back over his shoulder. "If you want to wait until after this guy's lesson, I can give you a few pointers to work on."

Caleb hesitated. He really should be getting home. "Sure," he replied. "I'll just hang back in the bleachers and watch."

A few minutes later, the girl up front came back and said, "Adam, your private lesson just canceled."

Caleb heard him curse under his breath.

"This is the second time that guy's bailed on me," Adam told her. "Next time he asks to schedule a lesson, have him come and talk to me in person."

"Will do," she promised, heading back to her spot at the front counter.

"So, do you want to take his place?" Adam asked Caleb.

"Okay, sure," Caleb replied.

"Go settle up with Amy. She'll collect the fee and then we'll get started."

"Oh, man," Caleb said as he opened his wallet. "I'm out of cash. Can I bring it next time?"

Adam hesitated. "Let's wait until you've got the money. I've been stiffed too many times lately."

Probably for the best, Caleb thought, already feeling guilty about not being home for dinner. "Okay. I'll bring the money next time," he replied. Adam was already walking out the door. He just lifted his hand without turning around.

Madison and Luke were just getting settled into the living room to open their gifts in front of their families when Caleb walked in. "Hi everybody," he said with a wave and a smile. "Hold off for a sec, and I'll go change out of my ghee."

Logan popped up off the floor and followed him. "So, how'd it go?" he asked once they were out of earshot.

"I almost took a private lesson from him after class," Caleb said. "But he wanted me to pay up front, and I didn't have any money with me."

"Seems crazy to pay him for a lesson just so you can talk to him," Logan remarked. "Maybe you could just hang out for a while after class and get to know him that way."

"He's not going to hang around and socialize, Logan. He pretty much leaves right away unless he has another class or private lesson."

"Caleb? Are you guys coming?" his sister's voice came from downstairs.

Caleb leaned out the door as he grabbed a tee shirt from on top of his dresser. "On our way," he called back down.

After the newlyweds had finished opening all their wedding gifts, Ben and Kelly rounded up their kids and headed home. Caleb flipped on the television and started watching a game with his dad and Luke, as Madison and her mom cleaned up the last of the wrapping paper and took the dessert plates to the kitchen.

"Everything's all set for you two in your bedroom," Michelle said. "I put clean sheets on the bed, along with an extra pillow. There are clean towels stacked on the bathroom counter, too."

"Thanks, Mom," Maddie replied. She felt like a guest in her own house. It seemed so surreal to have her mother prepping the room for their weeklong stay. Plunking herself down beside Luke on the couch, she began to feel the weight of exhaustion from the busy week they'd just had. Resting her hand on his knee, she said softly, "I think I'll go get ready for bed."

Luke turned from the game and looked at her. "I'll be up in a minute."

"What was that?!" Caleb exclaimed at the home plate umpire in disgust. "That guy needs glasses," he muttered.

Luke's head pivoted back to the television. "He's out?"

"Yeah, thanks to the blind ump," Caleb replied.

Madison shook her head. She'd never understand how these guys could get so emotional about a game on television. They didn't even know any of the players. At least when she went to Caleb's games, they knew most of the kids on his team. She sighed and said, "Well, I'll leave you guys to your blind ump. See you in the morning."

As she stood, Luke grabbed her hand and pulled her back for a kiss. "Be right up."

Walking into her bedroom, Madison was surprised how orderly and immaculate it looked. When she'd left here the morning of her wedding day, it had been strewn with clutter from one end to the other. Now everything was in its place, and the bed was made and turned down with two pillows propped against the headboard side-by-side.

She tried to picture Luke climbing into her bed. And waking up in the morning with him here beside her. *This is really weird*, she thought. Even though she'd had Miles up here when her parents weren't home, they'd never gotten into her bed. Their passion had been spent on the floor instead.

And Luke had never even sat down in here, always opting to stand at the door to flee all appearances of impropriety.

Unzipping her suitcase, she looked through the lingerie she'd taken on their honeymoon. What had seemed fun and pretty in their B & B's, suddenly seemed too sexy for her bedroom in her parents' house.

Turning to the closet, she rifled through her nightgowns hanging in there and chose a football jersey style sleep shirt to wear instead. As she slipped out of her clothes and into it, she heard a soft knocking on the door. "Can I come in?" Luke asked.

She walked over and opened it. "Sure, make yourself at home," she replied, hoping she sounded relaxed and casual in spite of her sudden nervousness.

He closed the door behind himself and leaned against it. "You look cute," he said, smiling.

"I just felt a little, I don't know, kind of, funny," she stammered, "you know, wearing those here," she added gesturing to the open suitcase with the lingerie peeking out.

Luke laughed. "I get it," he replied, coming over and taking her in his arms. "We'll just have to be very quiet," he added in a whisper.

Madison willed herself to relax into his embrace. "I'm actually kind of tired tonight," she said.

He pulled back a little and studied her for a moment. "But we're okay, right?"

"Of course," she replied, reaching up and cupping his face in her hands as she kissed him.

That night, as they slept in each other's arms, she dreamed they were making love, but when she looked into his face, he turned into Miles.

CHAPTER TWENTY-FOUR

The week slipped by quickly. Madison was caught in a whirlwind of emotions. She was relieved to be leaving behind her memories of Miles but was sad to be going so far from her family. It would be several months before they came home, and she knew they were very blessed even to have that opportunity to look forward to.

As she finished her final packing and awaited Luke's return from his house, where he, too, was packing up his things for their trip, Madison prayed for strength— strength to say goodbye, to travel to a distant country, and to serve God alongside her new husband.

Her mom peeked her head into the bedroom. "Are you about ready, honey?" she asked. "Luke just pulled up out front with his parents, and we'll need to leave for the airport in about thirty minutes."

One last look around her room, and Madison was on her way. After saying their goodbyes to Caleb and Luke's family with some tearful hugs, Madison and Luke were off to Portland with her parents to catch the flight that would take them to Beijing.

Steve insisted on parking the car rather than dropping them at the curb. The lines for checking their luggage were surprisingly short, and soon Madison found herself in her mom and dad's embraces as she prepared to leave them for three months. Her mother was first, reminding her to email and call "at least a few times a week!" When her dad wrapped his arms around her, she suddenly felt the impact of their upcoming separation.

"I love you, sweetheart," he said softly, just like he had during the wedding. And again, she could see tears in his eyes.

When they finally parted, Madison looked at both of them and said, "You guys take care of each other while I'm gone. And keep Caleb in line," she added with a smile, denying herself the emotions that were surging inside.

Steve looked Luke in the eye and said, "And you take care of our little girl. We're counting on it."

"Yes, sir," Maddie's husband replied seriously and then gave them each a final hug. Turning to Madison, he said, "We'd better go."

Less than an hour later, they were on their plane headed to a whole new life together.

Madison was roused from sleep by a hand on her shoulder. "Would you like a hot towel and some orange juice," the flight attendant asked, extending a plastic wrapped towel held by tongs.

Luke stirred beside her and opened his eyes, too, joining Madison in reaching for the offerings.

After wiping her face and hands with the hot towel, Madison brought her seat to the upright position and drank her cold juice. Feeling refreshed, she leaned over and kissed Luke and then said, "I think I'll walk around and stretch my legs a bit."

"Me, too," he agreed.

As they roamed through the wide-body cabin, Madison noticed how easily Luke could strike up conversations with other passengers. Returning to their seats, she remarked, "I'm surprised how many people onboard know English so well."

He nodded. "Yeah. It's the global economy, I think. But don't get your hopes up about the workers at the orphanage. From what I've been told, many don't speak English. Hopefully, we'll pick up some Chinese pretty quickly," he added. Seeing the breakfast cart coming their way, he took her hand, and they prayed together, thanking the Lord for their safe travels so far and for the food that they were about to eat.

After breakfast, they settled into some reading. Luke had his Bible open on his lap, and Madison dug into a book she'd been reading about Billy Graham's wife Ruth and her parents' medical missionary work in China in the early 1900's. She was fascinated by the colorful life of this famous evangelist's wife. *I wonder what kind of life our kids will have,* she thought to herself, knowing full well that her future with Luke would be anything but boring.

By the time they'd eaten lunch, she was eager to land and get off the plane. Only a couple more hours, and they'd be at their destination. She pulled out her iPod and offered one earpiece to Luke. He smiled and placed it in his ear as she nestled into his shoulder. Allowing her mind to drift back in time, she remembered the very first time they'd listened to music together this way. She'd only been eleven at the time and had a wild crush on thirteen-year-old Luke. *Wow, who'd have thought we'd make it this far,* she silentlymused as she soaked in the familiar Christian pop tune.

The last hour of the flight was a little rough as they hit turbulence from a storm. Madison was white-knuckling her armrest while Luke seemed completely nonplussed. "Just look at the flight attendants," he said. "If something were wrong, they'd look worried."

She glanced over and noticed that two of them were chatting normally, even laughing at stories they were exchanging. Although they'd been warned to keep their seat belts fastened, there were no other big announcements about the bumpy ride.

Just relax, Madison coached herself in her head. But she was very relieved after the storm was behind them. Soon they were on the ground and collecting their carry-on gear to prepare for exiting.

The Beijing airport was breathtaking in its scope and design. Walkways with gleaming white floors and expansive arched skylight grid ceilings brought beauty and light into the terminals. Strategically placed soaring sculptures, domes, and ornate pagodas made the place feel almost like a museum of modern art and Chinese architecture.

"This place is amazing," Madison said.

"I was just thinking the same thing," Luke replied, draping an arm over her shoulder, as they looked skyward at the intricate web of windows overhead.

After retrieving their luggage, they found their way to the rendezvous point where a driver from the orphanage would be picking them up. Through a sea of people, Luke pointed to a man holding a sign that said Children's Garden. "That's it!" he exclaimed, leading Madison over to meet the driver.

They introduced themselves and were relieved that the man spoke broken English, enough to confirm that he was indeed their transportation to the orphanage as he gestured for them to follow him. He'd brought a rolling cart for their luggage, and he soon had all the bags securely on wheels, which he skillfully maneuvered through the crowds to the exit.

Luke helped the man transfer their suitcases to the back of the van. Then he gave Madison a hand climbing into the back seat before slipping into the front passenger position himself. In his usual friendly manner, Luke made conversation with their driver to the best of his ability as they traveled out of the airport parking structure and through the city.

Finally out in the country, Madison felt herself relax and begin to enjoy the scenery. They drove for about an hour before arriving at the orphanage complex hedged about by a tall, stone wall with an iron gate across the driveway. Signs in Chinese and English noted that they were entering the Children's Garden. As the gate swung slowly open, their driver eased into the complex, carefully watching for any young residents who might have wandered from their playground or residence.

Luke turned around in his seat and looked at her. "We're home," he said with a wink. Although Madison returned his smile, she suddenly felt very far from home indeed.

CHAPTER TWENTY-FIVE

After meeting Erick, the senior director of the orphanage, the night before, they'd unpacked their suitcases, had an early dinner, and retired for the evening. Now it was early morning, and Madison opened her eyes to see her husband on his knees beside their bed. Hands clasped and resting on the mattress, his head was bowed low, and she knew he was seeking out their Father.

She quietly slipped out of bed and knelt beside him. He glanced over and smiled, wrapping an arm around her shoulder and pulling her in close. "And thank you, Lord, for my beautiful bride and her willingness to undertake this ministry venture with me. In Jesus' name. Amen."

"Amen," she echoed.

Soon they were being escorted through the grounds and oriented to their new positions. Erick explained the difference between Children's Garden, which was a privately run orphanage functioning under the umbrella of foster care versus the government run facilities. "We have the freedom to walk out and talk about our faith here," he said. Then he explained that Luke would be coordinating the caregiving staff and managing the business side of the facility, while Madison would put to use her nursing skills in the infirmary. After detailed job descriptions and a thorough tour, Erick asked, "Any questions?"

Luke looked at Madison. "What do you think? Any questions?"

"I'm sure I'll have plenty as we get going. But I think I pretty much know where to start," she replied. "I'd like to take a few hours this afternoon to review the vaccination schedules of the kids as well as any ongoing medical conditions in their charts. And I'll want to meet with the doctor when he comes through in the morning. It seems like the nurse's assistants have things under control in the infirmary," she added with a smile. "But I'm a little concerned about that one infant in the far crib. Her breathing is pretty labored."

"She has a heart condition," Erick said. "We're not hopeful about her chances. The doctor says she needs open heart surgery, but there are no funds for that here."

Luke inserted himself into the conversation once again. "How expensive are we talking here?"

"Likely several thousand U.S. dollars," he replied.

"How old is she?" Maddie asked.

"She's nine months old."

"Really? She looks more like three," Madison observed.

"It's the heart condition. She hasn't been able to grow and thrive normally. We're certain that's why she was abandoned by her parents," he explained.

Luke put his hand on Madison's shoulder. "I'll contact my dad about putting out a plea through the church for funds."

"Good idea, honey."

After a moment's silence, Erick said, "Well, if you don't have any more questions for now, I'll take Luke back to the office to go over the paperwork he'll need to start with, and you can head over to the infirmary."

"Sounds good," Maddie replied.

Luke bent down and gave her a quick kiss. "See you at lunch," he said.

By the end of the day, both Madison and Luke were exhausted. They'd both spent the day getting into their new roles and then allowed themselves the chance to play with the healthy kids when they congregated in the recreation room before dinner.

Getting ready to retreat to their room for the night, Madison felt an urge to go back to the infirmary to check one more time on little baby Lily. Her tiny body slept in a ball in the center of the crib, her breathing uneven. Not wanting to awaken her, Madison stood and leaned quietly over the rail, praying silently for this precious little one.

Luke, standing beside her, placed his hand on her shoulder and whispered into her ear, "She seems to be sleeping okay."

Madison nodded, watching Lily for another minute and then turning and taking Luke's hand as they slipped out of the infirmary. Once they were in their quarters, she sank down onto the bed and sighed. "I don't think Lily has much time if she doesn't get that surgery. I've seen this before in my pediatric rotation at the hospital. Her breathing's just going to get more and more labored until her heart finally gives up."

Luke sat down beside her and pulled her close. "Let's hope Dad can drum up the funds. I'll write letters to other churches and organizations as well," he promised.

As Maddie tried to fall asleep that night, she kept seeing little Lily in her mind. Eventually, she drifted off into a restless series of dreams about the baby disappearing from her crib or dying. By morning, Madison was even more concerned.

Shortly after dawn, she slipped out of bed, got dressed, and left their apartment, closing the door as quietly as possible to avoid waking Luke. The infirmary was quiet and dark. Tiptoeing over to Lily's crib, she peered down to see a still form.

All of her nurse's training kicked in immediately. Lifting the tiny baby into her arms, she could see the blue lips that indicated oxygen deprivation. After finding no heartbeat, she immediately began CPR, desperately pleading with God as she worked on little Lily.

Her efforts were rewarded with a sudden gasp of air as the baby's lungs kicked in to do their job. Madison breathed a prayer of praise as she lifted her tiny charge into her arms and held her close to her heart. Although Lily's breathing was still irregular, her lips began to turn light pink as her body began to move.

"You cannot be left alone," Madison whispered into Lily's ear. Suspecting that she was breaking regulations, but unwilling to take the chance of losing this little patient, Maddie carried Lily back to their apartment. Soon the orphanage would spring to life, and then she'd figure out what to do.

As she opened the door to the apartment, Luke stirred. "Honey? Is that you?" he asked softly.

"Yeah," she replied in a whisper.

Luke pushed himself up on his elbow and glanced over at her. "Where have you been? And what is that?"

She sat down beside him and lowered Lily so he could see her face from inside the blanket. "I was at the infirmary checking on Lily. She stopped breathing, Luke. We can't leave her alone. Not at all."

Sitting up and rubbing his eyes with the heels of his hands, he swung his legs over the side of the bed and sat next to her. Peering down at Lily's face and then up at Madison's, he said, "We'd better talk to Erick. I'm sure there's specific protocol on this."

Nodding in agreement, Madison said, "For now, I'm going to make a sling out of the scarf Grandma gave me and use it to carry her. That way I'll have my hands free, but I can continuously monitor her breathing."

"Okay. Here, let me hold her while you get that ready." He reached out and took the tiny babe in his arms, cradling her to his bare chest. "She's really adorable," he murmured.

"Yeah," Madison replied. "I love her eyes. It seems like she's looking right into your soul."

After digging through their luggage, she found the scarf and tied it around the back of her neck, spreading the fabric in front to create a baby sling. With Luke's help, she was able to nestle Lily into the pouch. "There. That's perfect," she said, feeling thankful she'd gotten the idea.

Hopefully, she'd be allowed to carry the baby and still do her regular nursing tasks. Since there were not many children in the infirmary right now, she thought she could probably manage. The problem would be helping those who might be contagious. At that point, she'd have to put her down again or hand her over to one of the assistants.

As they walked into the dining hall for breakfast, they spotted Erick sitting near the windows with another staff member. Luke took Madison's hand and led her through the maze of tables over to Erick's.

"Good morning," the senior director said as they approached. "What have we here?" he asked as he gestured to the sling.

"It's Lily," Luke began.

"She stopped breathing early this morning," Madison added quickly. "I went to check on her, and she was already beginning to show signs of cyanosis. I performed CPR, and she revived immediately. But I don't think it's safe to leave her alone right now."

"I see," he replied. "Okay, well let's consult with Dr. Su when he arrives."

"So, it's okay to wear her in the sling for now?" she asked.

He looked up at her and smiled. "Sure. But remember you have other patients to contend with this morning. There are three girls and a boy with suspicious rashes and fevers. You'll need to look in on them."

"Okay, no problem. I'll have one of the assistants hold her while I do that," she said.

Dr. Su arrived late that morning. Erick introduced him to Madison and updated the doctor on Lily and the other children in the infirmary. "We'll need to check them for measles," Dr. Su replied in response to the description of the rashes and fevers.

"And what is going on with this little one," he asked, peering into the sling Madison was wearing.

She carefully lifted Lily out and handed her to the doctor, giving a complete description of the morning's events. "I'm glad I got there in time," she added. "She had all the signs of cyanosis. But thankfully she responded right away to CPR."

"I'm glad you followed your instincts and checked on her," he replied, placing the infant on an examination table near her crib. After listening to her heartbeat, he handed another stethoscope to Madison. "Have a listen."

She warmed the diaphragm in her hands before placing it on Lily's chest. She could hear the tiny heart struggling with arrhythmia and sounds of congestion in the lungs indicated imminent heart failure.

"I'm afraid this little one doesn't have much time to wait for a surgery," the doctor said as he shook his head wistfully.

Madison wanted to scream. Her frustration at the doctor's apparent resignation over the infant's chances rose up to clash with her practical recognition of the daunting task of finding funds for such an expensive procedure. The orphanage just didn't have that kind of financial wherewithal. And the country did not offer free medical care to abandoned infants.

Lily might have a couple of months, tops. But more likely, she needed surgery within the next few weeks. She could even be gone by tomorrow if she wasn't monitored closely enough.

"Let's have Lian watch Lily while we check on the sick children," Dr. Su suggested, gesturing to one of the assistants who was bringing fresh bedding in from the laundry room.

As she approached, Madison carefully handed the baby over to her and was dismayed to see Lian immediately place the infant back in her crib. "I have beds to change," she explained curtly. "I'll watch her."

Madison turned to the doctor, hoping for his intervention, but he simply nodded, picked up his clipboard and led the way into the room for contagious diseases. Three young children, no older than preschool age, were in beds along the wall. Another assistant, whom Dr. Su introduced as Suyin, was bent over one bed wiping a brow with a damp cloth. She backed away immediately upon seeing the doctor, leaving him ready access to the child.

He spoke to her in Chinese and then explained to Madison, "I asked about the timing of the onset of the rash. When I was here last time, they only had fevers. We'll run nasal swabs on these children to determine whether they are suffering from rubella or roseola. If it's rubella, we could easily have an outbreak throughout the orphanage." He looked concerned. "You aren't pregnant, are you?" he asked.

Madison shook her head.

"Okay, good. We wouldn't want you around any of these kids if you were. Until we get the results of the swabs, that is."

"I'll take care of those right away," she replied. "The supplies are in the closet over there, right?" she asked, pointing to a door at the end of the room.

"Yes." Dr. Su handed her a key on a small chain. "We keep it locked at all times."

Starting in the direction of the closet, Madison paused and turned back to the doctor. "Shouldn't I be immune to rubella since I was immunized as a child?" she asked.

"Although it's likely, I'm afraid there's no guarantee that you'd be completely immune. Unfortunately, the best immunity is built when your body is fighting off the actual disease itself."

Madison nodded. "Right." After retrieving the swab kits, she went right to work. As she took her samples, she could see Dr. Su speak to Suyin in their native language, pointing to charts as he filled her in on his treatment plan for the three young children.

Turning to Madison, he said, "I've given her all the instructions for their care. If you'll just check on them every few hours and keep any other sick children out of this room for now, we can utilize the vacant dorm wing as a backup infirmary. Hopefully, no one else will get sick before we get the results on these swabs," he added, taking the samples from her and slipping them into his medical coat.

Before they headed into the office to go over the charts of the various residents with ongoing medical conditions, Madison peeked back in on Lily. The baby was sleeping quietly with Lian sitting in a chair nearby.

"She'll keep an eye on her," Dr. Su said reassuringly. Opening the door to the adjacent office and gesturing for Madison to enter, he offered her a seat across from his desk and then pulled out a portable file box. "This contains the charts on all the children who we need to monitor for health conditions," he explained. Pulling out one file at a time, Madison looked at each child's photo on the inside flap and then went over the particular medical need or needs of that individual. Most related to allergies, asthma, or congenital issues like vision or hearing loss, cleft palate, clubbed foot, or spinal issues.

"Many of these little ones were abandoned because of health concerns," he explained. "The combination of medical costs and raising children in general, along with the cultural issues of limited family size, prompt parents to release these kids to an orphanage.Then they can try for other offspring, who will be able to care for them in their old age and continue the family name."

Madison's heart ached as she looked at the faces of these innocent children, cast aside by their parents because of their imperfections. As if reading her pain, Dr. Su added, "Many of these children find homes, Madison. Not most. But many. You'll see that Americans often adopt a special needs child, especially those whose medical conditions can be corrected or easily managed."

She nodded. "Erick has explained some of the adoption processes to us. I hope we'll see some of these kids find good homes," she added as she handed the stack of folders back to the doctor.

"You will," he reassured her. "You will."

CHAPTER TWENTY-SIX

Caleb's private lesson was about over, and he was determined to talk to Adam this time. "I need to ask you something," he said after they wrapped up their session with a bow.

"Yeah?"

"Do you remember someone named Amber Gamble?" he asked.

Adam stopped in his tracks. "Why?"

"Because she knows you," Caleb replied evasively.

"I knew her a long time ago. But I thought she moved away. Out of state or something."

"She did. She lives in Arizona," Caleb said.

"So how do you know her?"

"She's my mom. Well actually, my biological mom. I'm adopted," he explained.

Adam nodded. "I see."

"Anyway, my parents kept in touch with her, so I've known her all my life."

"That's cool. But I don't see what this has to do with me. Amber would have no way of knowing I teach karate, so how did you know that we knew each other?"

Caleb's heart was racing, but he forced himself to blurt it out. "She told me you're my father—my biological father, that is."

Adam cocked his head and frowned as he studied Caleb's face. "You're kidding, right?"

He shook his head. "No. Serious."

"Well, Amber's crazy then. I'm not your father," he said curtly as he spun around and began walking out of the studio, with Caleb on his heels.

"Just hear me out," Caleb begged.

Turning to face him again, Adam's hardened expression almost stopped Caleb from pressing on. But he'd waited awhile for this opportunity, and he wasn't going to let it pass. "I'm not asking anything of you," he said, "other than just to know you. Amber told me you're the one."

Adam rolled his eyes and then punched his finger against Caleb's chest. "You listen to me, kid. Amber's screwed up. I'm not your dad. Got it?" he asked leaning so close to Caleb's face that his breath was hot on Caleb's cheeks. "Amber was easy with lots of guys, if you get my drift. Sorry to break your bubble about your mother, but she was just a fling for me. Nothing more."

"But she said she told you she was pregnant," Caleb said, as he attempted to defend Amber's reputation. "She said you knew, and you just walked away."

"Right. Whatever. Amber was looking for someone to take care of her. And she used that line with me to try to rope me in. But I knew better. And you, my friend, need to know that I'm not, I repeat *not* your father. Got it?" he asked as he stared Caleb down.

Caleb stared back at him, fighting off anger as well as tears. "Maybe I should be glad about that," he replied before turning and walking out the door.

After he got into the car, Caleb started driving. Nearly blinded by his emotions, he headed out of town, hopping onto the highway and gunning the engine. He drove for fifteen minutes, racing the other cars and weaving in and out. Finally, another driver, feeling anger at being cut off, swung into Caleb's lane and forced him off the shoulder and into the wall.

The sound of metal and cinderblock rang in Caleb's ear as the car skidded and scraped along the solid barrier. By the time it came to a stop, he was shaking inside and out from panic and rage. Determined to catch up with the other driver, he sped back out into the lane and darted between cars as he continued to accelerate. Finally spotting the culprit ahead, he put his foot to the floor, never looking in his review mirror to see the flashing lights on his tail.

A voice from a bullhorn ordered him to the shoulder again. He hesitated for a moment, eyeing the target in front of him before slamming his hand on the steering wheel, cursing, and pulling over to stop.

Staring out the windshield as he waited for the officer to approach, he thought about all the injustices he'd just witnessed that evening—a denial of his father's paternity, even when Caleb insisted he wanted nothing from the man but to know him; the other driver pushing him off the road and into the wall; and now a cop about to punish him for going after the culprit.

By the time the officer was tapping on the passenger window, Caleb was seething. But he was smart enough to know that lashing out at a cop would only add insult to injury. Taking a deep breath, he powered down the window and leaned across the front seat, handing his driver's license and the vehicle's registration to the policeman.

"Do you know how fast you were driving, young man?" the officer asked.

"No. I was trying to catch up with the guy who ran me off the road and then took off," Caleb replied.

The officer stood up and surveyed the side of the car. Then leaning back down at the window, he said, "Can you give me a description of the vehicle?"

Caleb rattled off the model and color. "I almost caught up with him before you pulled me over."

"And what were you planning to do then?"

Caleb paused. "Uh, get his license plate I guess."

The officer nodded. "Well, I clocked you at eighty-five miles per hour on that little chase of yours. That, along with the fact that you were weaving between cars, placed other drivers and yourself at risk. I'm sorry about the damage to your vehicle, but that's no justification for your reckless driving."

As he took out his citation pad and began writing, Caleb felt his anger surge again. I can't believe this. The guy's going to write me a ticket even though I had every reason to go after that jerk.

Half an hour later, Caleb drove into their driveway at home. His father met him on his way in. "Where have you been? Your lesson ended an hour ago?"

Before he could answer, Steve added, "And what happened to the car?" Now he sounded like he was about to blow a gasket.

"A guy edged me off the highway and into a wall," Caleb muttered.

"What were you doing on the highway?"

"I needed some time to think."

"About what?" Steve asked.

Caleb just shook his head and started toward the house.

"Hey, I asked you a question," his father said.

"Yeah, you've always got your questions, don't you?" Caleb replied as he continued to walk toward the house, turning back for a moment to add, "Oh, and I got a ticket." Tossing the citation over his shoulder, he stormed inside.

Steve called after him but to no avail. Stooping down, he picked up the ticket and read the violation. "Eighty-five miles per hour? That kid just lost his driving privileges."

"What's going on with Caleb?" Michelle asked as Steve stormed into the house after their son.

"He wrecked the car."

She stood up, feeling her heart race. "What happened? Is he okay?"

"Some guy nudged him into the wall on the side of the highway."

"The highway?" Now she looked as confused as Steve felt.

"Yeah. He said he needed some time to think, so he went for a drive. That's when the guy ran him off the road."

"Oh my gosh! Poor Caleb! We should go up and talk to him."

Steve looked incredulously. "Poor Caleb? Get this— he was driving eighty-five miles an hour." Handing his wife the citation he added, "There's more to this story, like maybe a reason the other guy was pushing him like that."

"There's no excuse for someone running someone else off the road," she countered as she headed for the stairs.

Steve moved to block her path. "Michelle, wait. Think about it for a minute. I agree with you that there's no excuse for what happened. But Caleb was clearly in the wrong here, too." He held her eye. "Let me go talk to him."

She looked at him hesitantly. "Okay, but give him a chance to explain, alright? Sometimes you forget you're not in a courtroom here."

Steve felt himself bristle a little. *Don't react,* he heard in his spirit. Taking a deep breath, he said as calmly as he could, "I'll try to remember that."

CHAPTER TWENTY-SEVEN

As Caleb sat on his bed with music blasting into his ears from his iPod's headset, he thought about the two men he'd set off that night—Adam, who was supposedly his biological father, and Steve who had raised him as his adoptive son.

Both of them didn't seem to care a bit about him tonight. Adam didn't even want to admit he was related to Caleb, and he said some pretty ugly things about Amber in the process. And after Caleb's dad saw the car, he about bit his head off.

He thought about the citation, knowing it would be an automatic grounding and probably the loss of his karate lessons for the rest of the summer.

Suddenly Steve poked his head into the room, and Caleb pulled out his earpieces.

"I've been knocking out here," Steve said. "You must have had that music up pretty loud."

Caleb shrugged. "I guess."

"Mind if I come in?"

"Be my guest," Caleb replied, turning his attention back to his phone to pause the music.

Steve walked over and sat on the chair at Caleb's desk next to his bed. "Want to tell me what happened? I mean the whole story?"

"I already did. Some jerk swerved over and pushed me out of my lane and against the wall. I tried to catch him but got a ticket instead. So he's free, and I'm busted."

"Let's start with the ticket. Eighty-five miles an hour? What were you thinking?"

"I was thinking I'd catch up to the guy and get his license plate so we could turn him in. But the cop made sure that will never happen," he replied. "So now you can just ground me and tell me that I'm going to pay for the repairs, and everything will be perfect."

His dad stared at him and didn't say a word. Caleb could feel the thick cloud of disappointment. He knew that any second, he'd be toast.

Instead, his father walked over and sat by him on the bed. He put his hand on Caleb's knee and said, "I'm trying to understand all this, bud. Help me out here." He sounded like he really meant it. "What started all this tonight?"

Caleb hesitated. He could feel his anger and even tears threatening to spill. Without making eye contact, he muttered, "Nothing much except my real father is a total jerk and doesn't want anything to do with me." Then he turned and looked at Steve. "That's all. No big deal."

The look on Steve's face hurt almost as much as Adam's rejection. *Bet that real father line went over well with him. Now I'm just as much a jerk as Adam.*

Steve shook his head with a puzzled expression. "What are you talking about? Did you go to see Adam?"

"He's my karate teacher, Dad. That's why I've been taking the lessons, so I could get to know him and tell him who I am."

Steve dropped his head into his hands and rubbed his forehead then raked his fingers through his hair before looking up again. "Start from the beginning, okay?"

Caleb was in no mood to go over everything, but he knew his dad would press him until he did. "There's not that much to tell. I found Adam because Amber told me where he used to live, and he's still there. I talked to some lady who lives there, and she told me he was at the martial arts studio. The next time I drove by there, I saw him leave and followed him to the studio. Then I went inside and signed up for his class. And now I'm taking private lessons from him. Or at least I was," he muttered under his breath.

His dad looked surprised and upset. "Don't you think it would have been a good idea to discuss all this with us first?" he asked.

Caleb rolled his eyes. He hated the way he felt and the way he was talking to his dad, but he couldn't seem to stop himself. "You wanna know why I didn't discuss it with you first? What? So you could tell me how stupid it was to want to spend time with him and get to know him?" He looked away and then added, "I get it, Dad. I figured you wouldn't want me to know him. Fine. That's why I didn't tell you. But you don't have to worry. Adam doesn't want to have anything to do with me. So you can just relax and be happy."

He could see his dad stiffen. "I'm not happy, Caleb. Not about Adam and whatever happened between you two. And not about this citation or the car."

Turning his back on Steve, Caleb replied, "Fine. Whatever. That makes two of us."

After a few moments of silence, his father said, "We need to talk about this again when you've calmed down, young man. In the meantime, I think we both need to spend some time in prayer."

"Right," Caleb replied sarcastically. "That'll fix it."

"Knock off the attitude, Caleb. And don't plan on using the car for a while," Steve added. "You'll need to start contributing to the insurance cost around here, too. They're not going to let you off the hook with traffic school twice in one year."

"Fine. Whatever."

Over the course of the next few weeks, Caleb resisted going to church and avoided spending time with his family and friends, as he pulled away from all the people who loved him most, believing that they did not understand him. *Who cares? I don't need any of them—not Adam, not Mom and Dad, not Madison, not Logan. None of them. They don't get me and they never will. And God? Well, apparently He's not going to answer my prayers anyway, so why should I bother?*

The more he thought about it, the more determined he became never to let anyone ever hurt him again. He'd graduate soon, and he could take off on his own.

CHAPTER TWENTY-EIGHT

Madison sat in the shade watching the children play on the playground as she ate her lunch. The rubella outbreak had exhausted her over the past three weeks as the infirmary experienced an ever-growing population of children. While caring for their needs, she'd also tried to keep a vigilant eye on Lily, who was losing ground as they awaited funds from back home for her surgery.

Oh Lord, please help. I don't think she'll make it much longer,Madison prayed silently, her heart heavy with concern. She'd had to rely on Suyin and Lian to keep watch over Lily. If it weren't for the rubella cases, Madison would have been at her side much of the time. At least she hadn't gotten sick herself. That was something to be thankful for.

Each day seemed to go by in a blur. Luke was up before dawn, organizing the short-term mission team that arrived the week before. They'd come loaded with supplies for the school, the dormitory, and the infirmary, along with eager hearts and hands to serve. It was an interesting conglomeration of ages ranging from the early twenties to a couple in their seventies. All fifteen needed assignments each day, and it was Luke's responsibility to coordinate those tasks.

Maddie usually arose early with Luke. After a quick breakfast together, she'd head over to the infirmary, and he'd be off to meet with the team. Often they didn't see each other again until dinner.

Although Madison was busy and felt confident in her role as a nurse, loneliness followed her around like a lost sheep. The caregivers and kids spoke in Chinese to each other, leaving her separated by the invisible boundary of language. She was beginning to pick up some words and could carry on the most basic conversations, but trying to follow native speakers as they conversed with natural flow and pace, left her an outsider looking in and guessing what they were saying. Even the music and loud televisions in some of the common rooms reminded her throughout each day that she was far from home.

Sharing dinner with her husband and members of the mission team gave her a welcome opportunity to interact with others. The zeal of the team members also helped Madison remember the blessing of their call to serve here at the Children's Garden. When a child in the infirmary smiled at her or hugged her close, she felt the joy of the Lord surge within. And cradling Lily in her arms evoked deep feelings of love and compassion that had driven Madison into nursing in the first place. Now she was using her hard-earned skills and knowledge to make a real difference in the lives of these sweet children.

Still, she longed for home and the sound of the surf and the familiar chatter of family around the dinner table.

Smiling as she watched one young man from the team twirling a child in the air, she thought about tonight. Luke had promised they could call home. And she could hardly wait. "Oh please let there be good news about the fundraising for Lily," she whispered softly in prayer.

It was ten o'clock that night before Luke and Madison were in their quarters and ready to phone home.

"How are all the kids doing tonight?" Luke asked, referring to the rubella patients.

"Most of them should be able to go back to the dorms in the next few days," she replied, "barring any complications, that is."

"And Lily?"

Madison sighed. "She's getting weaker every day, Luke. I'm really concerned that we may lose her."

"Well, hopefully, we'll get good news from Dad," he said.

"So what time is it there?" Maddie asked. "Six o'clock in the morning?"

"Seven. So we should be able to catch everyone up but still home." He reached over and squeezed her hand. "Wanna go first?"

"No. You first. Then maybe I'll have good news to share with Mom and Dad about Lily."

"Okay, you're the boss!" he teased, pulling out his cell phone and punching in his parents' number. As it began ringing, he draped his arm over her shoulder and pulled her close.

He could hear his father's voice as if it was in the next room. "Luke! Honey, Luke's on the phone."

A moment later, his mom's voice joined in. "Luke! How are you? Tell us everything that's going on out there."

Luke laughed. "Okay, okay, Mom. But first how are all of you?" He could hear voices of siblings in the background asking if they could talk, too.

"We're all fine," Kelly replied. "Although your dad's been pushing himself too much as usual," she added, a hint of concern in her tone.

"Don't worry about me, son," his father quickly added. "So how are the newlyweds? And how's the orphanage doing?"

"Maddie and I are doing well. I'll let her say hi in a minute," he said. "Children's Garden is pretty busy right now. We have a fifteen-person team here from Arkansas, and the kids I emailed you about with the rubella outbreak are still recovering in the infirmary, so that's keeping Madison's spending a lot of time with them."

"And don't forget about Lily," his wife urged, gripping his leg.

"Here, I'm giving the phone to Madison. She wants to ask you about Lily's fundraising." He handed the phone to his wife. "You're on, babe," he said with a smile.

"Hi Mom, Dad," she said. Luke loved hearing her call his parents that. How sweet to have a wife who loved his folks, too.

"So, I've been eager to hear how the fundraising is coming for Lily's surgery. She's getting weaker, and I'm afraid we could lose her."

Luke watched her face as she listened to his parents' reply.

"Uh huh. Okay. Yeah, I know what you mean." There was a pause, and then Luke saw her expression light up. "Wow! That's so great! Okay, I'll tell Dr. Su to start making the arrangements." She looked over at him and said, "They've got most of the money. And Grandma Sheila and Rick offered to pay the difference."

"That's wonderful!" Luke said, her joy infecting him as well.

Madison turned back to the phone. "Okay, so I'll put Luke back on. But please tell everyone how much I appreciate this. I've gotten pretty attached to her, as you might have noticed," she added before saying goodbye and handing him the phone.

Luke knew his wife was eager to call her parents, so he kept the rest of the conversation as short as possible. He asked his father a few questions regarding the transfer of funds for Lily's surgery and then added, "Don't overdo it, Dad. Mom sounds a little worried about you."

"I'm fine. Really," Ben replied.

But Luke noticed a slight drop in his father's voice. He made a mental note to pick up his prayers for the man who'd been his hero all of Luke's life.

"My turn?" Madison asked, excited and eager to call her folks.

Luke leaned over and kissed her. "Your turn, babe."

Her hand shook a little as she punched in the number. This was the first time she'd be talking to her parents since she called them to let them know she'd arrived at the orphanage safely three weeks ago. Never in her entire life had so much time passed between hearing their voices.

"Madison, is that you?" her father asked.

"It's me, Dad!" she replied, grinning ear to ear.

"Let me get your mother on the other line," he said, calling out, "Michelle, it's Maddie. Pick up the phone up there."

"Maddie!" Michelle exclaimed. "How are you? Is everything okay?"

"Hi, Mom. Yeah, we are fine," she replied. "But I miss you guys so much."

"We miss you, too, honey," her father said.

"Tell us about the baby. Lily, I mean," Michelle added. "Ben announced at church that we've reached the goal for her fundraising."

"Yeah, we just talked to him," Madison said. "You knew about Grandma and Rick, right?"

"What about them?" Michelle asked.

"They donated the balance to meet the goal."

"They did?"

"Yeah. I'm surprised you didn't know," Madison said, glancing over at Luke and mouthing, 'Mom didn't know.'

Madison's father jumped back into the conversation. "I'm not at all surprised, Michelle. You know how Rick is. He keeps his generosity under wraps."

"True," Michelle replied. "But I would have thought Mom would have said something to me. At any rate, that's great news, Maddie. So, will Lily get her surgery soon? And how's she doing? We loved the little picture you sent us in the mail. She's adorable."

Madison's heart swelled hearing her mom talk about Lily. It was encouraging to know that her parents were also invested in this little life that had become so important to Madison. "Luke and his dad discussed the transfer of funds, so I'll be talking to the doctor tomorrow about setting up the surgery. It's not coming a moment too soon, though, Mom. She's really getting weak. Please just pray that she makes it to the surgery and survives the operation."

"We will, sweetheart," her mother promised.

"I'll have the men's breakfast group pray, too, honey," Steve added. "And how about you? Are you enjoying your work there?"

"I am, Dad. It's great working with the kids. And Dr. Su is wonderful," she said, hoping she sounded upbeat.

"Why do I feel like there's a 'but' in your voice?" he asked.

Madison paused. She didn't want to talk about her struggles with loneliness when Luke was sitting right beside her. What was it about her dad that he could read beneath the surface? Maybe it came with years of being an attorney.

"No 'buts' Dad. I'm fine. Really. It's just an adjustment period right now. And I'm trying to learn the language, so that's an added challenge." There, that was the honest truth without going into details about her loneliness and homesickness, which she knew would place an added concern on Luke's shoulders that he didn't need right now.

"How's Caleb doing?" she asked, changing the subject.

"He's had a rough few weeks," Steve replied.

"It's nothing for you to worry about, though," Michelle interjected.

"Is he around? I'd like to talk to him. He emailed me about the whole Adam thing. I've just been so busy, and I wanted to give him a thoughtful reply."

"He had an early shift at the Coffee Stop this morning," her father said. "He'll be bummed that he missed your call."

"Well, tell him I'm praying for him. and I'll email as soon as I can," she promised, feeling a lump in her throat as she prepared to say goodbye. "We'll call again in a couple of weeks," she said. "And please give Grandma Sheila, Rick, and Grandma Joan big hugs for me."

"We will, Maddie," her mother replied.

"Let us know if you need anything," Steve added.

"I will, Daddy," she answered, suddenly feeling like a little girl. How she yearned to see them both, to just sit across the kitchen table from them and share a meal. It was almost too painful to picture.

"So, we'll talk to you again soon. Take care, honey," Steve added.

"We love you, sweetheart," her mom said, and Madison thought she heard Michelle's voice shaking a little.

"I love you, too," she replied before hanging up. Turning to Luke, she managed to hold back her tears, and she reached out and hugged him tightly. He was her lifeline. Not only to family but also to God. And right now, she needed him more than she ever had.

CHAPTER TWENTY-NINE

Luke lay awake, staring at the ceiling fan turning slowly overhead. Madison was sleeping, curled up next to him, but something was gnawing at his mind. He had a premonition that they were about to face a challenge that would test the two of them. What was it? Did it have something to do with his father and how tired he sounded? Or was it something about the orphanage?

What is it, Lord? Help me know how to pray here.

He waited in silence for an answer. Starting to go through the usual prayers for his wife, his family, and his ministry, he suddenly felt the presence of God fill the room.

Brace yourself. And know that I am with you always. I will carry you.

A strange combination of fear and faith surged through Luke's veins. What was he bracing himself for? He was thankful for the reminder of God's faithfulness, and an unusual sense of peace fell upon him. But he knew this tangible sensation of God's very close presence was not a random event. Something was about to happen, and he would need God to carry him through.

Luke awoke with a start. The jaws of a giant threatened to swallow the room as loud rumblings and shattering glass engulfed the two sleepers. Adrenaline jolted Luke out of bed as the place rocked violently, and Madison screamed in his ears.

Earthquake!

Jumping to his feet, and grabbing his wife's hand, he fled the room, narrowly missing a beam crashing to the floor. Pain shot through his bare foot as he stepped on a shard of glass from the broken window. Sweeping Madison up into his arms, he carried her out of the building. Loud voices and screaming children filled the air in the outside courtyard as they watched the structures around them sway and buckle under the powerful tremors.

"Lily!" Madison cried out, pushing away from him and starting to run toward the nursery.

Luke grabbed her and held her tightly. "You can't go in there! Wait for it to stop!"

They clutched each other through the final jolts, and then the earth rested. Loud cries continued to pour from the broken windows in the dormitory and the infirmary, and Luke saw Erick waving them over from across the yard. "We've got to get the kids out!" he called.

Every step brought searing pain to Luke, but he led Madison over to where they could join forces with Erick and the mission team.

"Are you two alright?" the senior director asked.

"We're fine," Luke replied, not wanting to impede the rescue by admitting his injury.

Sirens had begun to fill the air as they pried open the infirmary door. The place was a disaster, with broken glass, ceiling tiles scattered about, and doorjambs bent like straws. Kids were huddled under beds, while the night caregiver circulated throughout, evaluating the injuries. Thankfully they were all conscious and able to respond—most crying from pain and trauma, while some stared silently like deer caught in headlights.

"I need to go to Lily," Madison repeated.

Luke nodded. "Okay, but then come right back. We need to get over to the dormitory, too." He turned to the team members and began giving them instructions, silently thanking God for the extra hands to help in the crisis.

Madison found Lily whimpering in her crib, still wrapped securely in her swaddling blankets. Quickly unwrapping her and checking for injuries, Maddie converted the blanket into a sling and carried the infant in it back to the main infirmary. Luke was sitting on a bed with a little boy, who had his arm clutched to his chest.

"Better take a look at this," her husband said, gesturing to his charge.

Madison stooped down and gently pried the boy's hand from his arm. Bone protruded just under the flesh at an unnatural angle. Glancing up at Luke, she nodded, "It's broken. I'll need to try to set it or at least immobilize it in a sling until we can get him treatment."

"What can I do to help?" he asked.

Madison glanced around the room. Most of the kids were being ushered out of the building. "Should we get out of here? I know there could be aftershocks."

Luke nodded. "Good idea."

As Madison rose to her feet, she noticed the blood on the floor. "Where did this come from?" she asked, looking over the boy again for other injuries.

Luke lifted his foot to show her.

"Luke, why didn't you tell me? This is really deep. You'll need stitches."

"We can worry about that later. Let's get this little guy taken care of and see how the kids are in the dorm," he replied.

Out in the yard, Erick, Lian and the team members were getting kids settled into groups—those who needed medical care, and those who were only shaken. A separate area was set aside for the ones recovering from rubella, although that was the least of anyone's worries at this point. There were multiple cuts and abrasions that needed tending, as well as a few possible concussions Madison would need to evaluate for head trauma.

The only building that seemed unaffected for the most part was the cafeteria, which had been recently remodeled and retrofitted. Although the sun was beginning to peek over the horizon, the air was cool and damp, and Madison was concerned about all the kids who were shivering from both the shock and the drop in temperature.

"Would it be safe to move everyone into the dining area?" she asked Erick.

"Good idea, babe," Luke said in agreement.

After Erick had inspected the inside of the building, he gave them the thumbs up to begin bringing the kids in out of the cold. Madison discovered the little boy with the broken arm was named Chen. He stayed glued to Luke's side as the adults worked together to bring the children inside. A couple of aftershocks gave quick jolts, but none of them had the impact of the initial quake, and the dining hall structure seemed sound.

Since it was clear that little Chen needed Luke's presence, Madison handed Lily over to him as well, giving him strict warning to stay off his foot. Then she began circulating through the injured, triaging them for treatment and giving instructions to team members, while replaying in her mind the steps she'd observed for setting and splinting a broken bone when she was in her hospital rotation in nursing school.

Erick had tried to reach Dr. Su, but the phone lines were all jammed. It was likely she'd have to do the initial treatment herself, until he could get here.

Thankfully the equipment closet was located between the dining hall and the infirmary, so she was able to retrieve first aid supplies to hand out along with her instructions. Madison attended to the more difficult cases, often asking Lian to translate for the frightened kids so they would understand what she needed to do to treat their injuries.

Then she headed back over to Luke, who had somehow evoked a smile on Chen's face. Lily was sleeping peacefully in his arms, and Madison paused a moment, taking it all in. Her husband was such a natural with children. Guess it came from being the oldest in such a big family. He'd make a great father someday.

As she was about to explain to Chen what needed to be done for his arm, Dr. Su appeared in the doorway. "Thank you, Lord!" Madison exclaimed under her breath as she waved the doctor over.

Once Chen was settled with Dr. Su, Madison turned to Luke. "Your turn, honey," she said, gesturing to his foot. She handed Lily over to Lian and opened up her supply kit. Asking Dr. Su for a local anesthetic, Madison carefully injected the area around her husband's gash, cleaned it thoroughly, and began stitching the gaping hole closed. "This is going to hurt for awhile once that lidocaine wears off," she warned. "And you should stay off of it for a few days."

Because of the severity of the cut and the exposure to dirt and debris, Dr. Su recommended Luke take antibiotics as well as having frequent bandage changes and topical ointments.

"There's too much to do around here without worrying about a little cut," Luke scoffed.

"That 'little cut' took twelve stitches, sir," she replied firmly. "And an infection will only make you less available for longer."

"Yes, Nurse Ratchet," he replied with a grimace.

Giving him a gentle, playful shove, Madison turned to help Dr. Su with the sling for Chen.

That night, after all the kids were settled into makeshift beds of mattresses on the floor of the dining hall, Luke and Madison met with Erick to evaluate the damages and come up with a plan. Windows needed replacing in both the dorm and the infirmary, and ceilings needed repairs and some retrofitting. Luke and Madison's bedroom was uninhabitable until the beam could be replaced.

They learned from Dr. Su that many homes and structures outside the walls of Children's Garden were in shambles. Various temples and meeting halls were housing the displaced residents. It looked like it would take several weeks before they could hope to get replacement windows or any reconstruction done.

For the time being, their lives would revolve around the outdoor areas and the dining hall. Erick dragged their mattress in and set it in the corner of the big open room. Then he brought some bags of clothes from their closet as well as the essentials from their bathroom. Because of Madison's ongoing concerns about Lily and Chen's newfound attachment to Luke, they ended up with a ready made little family of four sleeping in their cordoned-off area.

Erick used the end of one of the dining tables as an office of sorts, and Dr. Su claimed another table as an examining bed for his patients. Each night, Erick and Luke would lead all the kids and adults in prayer, thanking God for their safety and asking for restoration of their orphanage.

CHAPTER THIRTY

With the help of the team, the housemothers, and Luke hobbling around on one crutch, they were able to clean up all the broken glass and clear out the debris in the various buildings. Erick got some plastic sheeting out of the outdoor storage shed that they kept on hand for leaking roofs during the rainy season. He helped the team replace the broken windows with the plastic, which allowed light into the rooms but limited the ventilation.

Both Luke and Madison's parents back home had heard about the earthquake, but with the cell towers in the Beijing area jammed, their only communication was the Internet, which thankfully allowed them to send email. Madison's homesickness was swallowed by her busyness as she attended to the injured and cared for Lily and for little Chen, who refused to be comforted apart from Luke's presence. Having only arrived at the orphanage a week before the quake, the little boy hadn't had a chance to bond with his housemother yet. And for some reason, Luke spelled security and safety.

Each night, their two little charges would sleep next to them, sometimes whimpering and needing attention before dawn.

One night as they were finishing their prayers as a couple, Luke said to Madison, "You know, Maddie, God gave me a warning about all this."

She propped herself up on her elbow beside him on their mattress. "Really?"

"Yeah. The night it happened, I couldn't fall asleep. And as I was praying for you and our families, I suddenly felt like God stepped into the room." He looked her in the eye and added, "It was really different than anything I've experienced before."

"Wow. So how did He warn you?"

"He impressed on my heart to brace myself and to pray for the kids. And He assured me that He would be with me and get me through what was coming." Luke paused and then added, "It wasn't like I heard an audible voice or anything. He spoke directly to my spirit."

"I've had that happen to me before, too," she replied with a nod.

"So have I. But I've never felt God's presence so strongly as I did that night." He studied her face as if to see if she understood. "I mean, it wasn't like the times I've cried out to Him about something, and then felt Him draw near. Instead, it was like *He* came to *me* with a distinct message of warning and reassurance in advance of the earthquake."

"That's amazing, honey," she said, snuggling her head down onto his chest. "We have a lot to be thankful for."

"Yeah, we do," he replied. And then he remembered something else from that night. God had also urged him to pray for his father. While Madison drifted off to sleep beside him, Luke stepped up his prayers for his dad, making a determination to call him the following day.

Michelle was hurrying back to her seventh-grade language arts class from lunch break when the school secretary intercepted her. "You had a call from the high school," she said. "It was the assistant principal. He'd like you to call back as soon as possible."

Oh, no. What now, Lord? "Okay, thanks for letting me know," she replied, taking the message slip from Elizabeth's outstretched hand. If she called now, she'd be late for her next class, but she hated to keep the assistant principal waiting. Poking her head into the counselor's office, she found Karen eating a salad at her desk.

"Would you do me a huge favor and watch my next class for a few minutes? I need to call the high school."

Karen smiled. "Sure, friend. No problem. Anything you want them to do until you get there?"

"There's a warm up on the board they can work on, and copying tonight's homework assignment." Starting to walk back to the main office, Michelle stopped herself and added, "Thanks, Karen. I really appreciate it."

"My pleasure. Hope everything's okay with your son."

"Me, too," Michelle admitted, taking a deep breath and heading off to make her call.

As she was connected to the assistant principal at Caleb's school, she shot up a quick prayer for wisdom. Their son had always been such a sweet, cooperative kid. Never any major issues. Now, he was a stick of dynamite, always one spark short of an explosion. Not only was it affecting him and his life, but it was taking a toll on Michelle and Steve as well. Michelle felt like she was constantly in the role of a referee—trying to keep the peace between her husband and their son.

Although she understood Steve's concerns and frustrations, she could see that Caleb was floundering emotionally and spiritually. Maybe her many years of teaching middle school teens helped her to look deeper into the hearts of broken kids. Wow, just thinking about that phrase, broken kids, brought tears to her eyes. How she wished she could have somehow spared Caleb all the heartache he was experiencing because of Adam's rejection.

"Mrs. Baron?" Tom Thorton's voice cut into her thoughts.

"Yes. I'm here," she replied. "Is Caleb okay?"

"Well, that depends on your definition of okay. He's sitting right here across from me. Physically, he's fine. But he picked a fight today with a classmate and it almost resulted in a slug out. Thankfully, the P.E. teacher intervened before anything beyond a shove occurred."

Michelle sucked in the air around her. "I'm sorry to hear that, Tom. That's not like Caleb."

"It caught me by surprise a little, too," he admitted. "You need to know that he's also missed his morning classes today."

"What? Really? Did he give any explanation?" she asked.

"Only that he wasn't feeling well," he replied.

Steve's going to blow a gasket on this one. "May I speak to him, please?" she asked, glancing at the clock on the wall. She'd already missed the first ten minutes of her class.

"I'll put him on."

"Mom?"

Michelle tried to calm herself before she replied. "You weren't feeling well this morning? You didn't say anything to me about that."

"I had a headache."

"A headache? So you decided to skip your morning classes? That's not like you, Caleb. What's going on with you? And what's this about you picking a fight?"

After a moment of silence, Caleb asked, "Can we talk about this later?"

"Definitely. We'll all three discuss this tonight after your dad gets home. Put Mr. Thornton back on the phone, please. And be sure you come straight home after school."

"Whatever."

Whatever? Really? Michelle felt her stomach clench. Before she could come back with a reply, the assistant principal was back on the line.

"I've assigned Caleb two detentions," he said. "He'll serve the first one today after school and the second tomorrow."

"Okay. And his father and I will talk to him as well. Again, I'm very sorry about all this." She thought for a second and then added, "I'd like to talk to you privately, Tom. I mean when Caleb's not in your office. Can I give you a call after school today?"

"Sure. I'll be here until five."

As soon as Michelle was off the phone, she hurried to her classroom. Karen had the class quiet, and students were either finishing their warm ups or reading silently. Michelle shot a quick smile to her friend and mouthed the word, "Thanks." Karen nodded and slipped out the back door.

"Your mother tells me she had a call today from the assistant principal at your school," Steve said to Caleb that evening as the three of them finished their dinner together. Caleb had been wordless the entire meal, staring at his plate rather than joining in any conversation.

Now he looked up at his dad defiantly. "Yeah, old man Thornton wouldn't listen to my explanation."

"Your explanation?" Steve replied. "How about if you give that to us?"

Caleb eyed them warily. "Some stupid jock said something about a girl I know—a friend of mine."

"Oh really?" Steve asked, not attempting to mask his skepticism.

"Really. But it sounds like you've already taken his side, so there's no point discussing it."

"I'm not taking any sides, son. And we are going to discuss it. So, go ahead and tell us what was said."

Caleb sighed and slumped into his seat. "He called her a hoe."

"A hoe?" Steve looked from Caleb to Michelle.

"It's slang for whore," she explained softly.

Propping his elbows on the table, Steve leaned toward Caleb. "Okay, I get that you'd be upset to hear someone say that about your friend. But starting a fight? How about ignoring the guy or just telling him to knock it off?"

"Right, Dad. Knock it off. Like that erases what he said. The guy's a total jerk. Just like Adam," he added under his breath.

Silence fell over the kitchen table. Steve sat back in his chair. *So that's what this is about.* "Caleb, we understand that you've been upset about the whole Adam thing, but you can't take that out on other people. What the kid at school said was wrong. Agreed. But you were just as wrong to try to pick a fight with him. I know you were trying to defend your friend's honor, and I respect that."

"We both do," Michelle added. "But your father is right. You can't go pushing and slugging to try to get someone to stop being a jerk."

"So what was I supposed to do? Just let him get away with it?" Caleb asked, his eyes brimming with challenge.

Michelle looked at Steve.

"You shake your head, turn the other cheek, and walk away. And you make sure you stand by your friend, encouraging her to ignore the foolish remarks of people like that jock."

"It wasn't like she was there, Dad."

"So she didn't hear it?"

"Nope."

"Then all the more reason to let it drop, son. I don't mind you saying something in defense of a friend. But fists are not the answer. They'll just land you in as much trouble or more than the other guy, especially if you're the one who starts it."

Caleb sat pensively staring at his empty plate. "Are we finished?" he asked quietly.

"Yes," Steve replied. "But I also don't want to hear about you skipping any other classes. Are we clear?"

"Clear."

More than five thousand miles away, Caleb's sister awoke in the early morning predawn hours to a strange sound of silence. Lily's labored breathing had stopped. Leaping from the bed, Madison lifted the tiny girl out of her crib and began CPR.

"Babe? Is she okay?" Luke asked, sitting up.

"We need an ambulance," she replied between puffs. "And call Dr. Su."

Luke was up and on the phone immediately. As Madison continued to work on Lily, he dressed quickly and opened the door, ready for the emergency response team. Soon Erick ran in, followed by the paramedics. Madison handed Lily over to the team and quickly changed into street clothes, racing after them as they headed out to the ambulance with one responder still breathing for Lily as he carried her body in his hands.

CHAPTER THIRTY-ONE

As the paramedics whisked Lily into the open doors of the hospital emergency room, Madison fought to follow but was blocked from entering the examination area. Erick and one of the aides ushered her and Luke over to the admission desk. After much discussion, the aide explained to them that policy forbids anyone in the examination area except immediate family.

"Tell her I'm a nurse," Madison urged.

The aide translated to the woman at the desk, who shook her head. "She's saying you must work at this hospital to be allowed back," the aide said.

"Erick, there must be something we can do," Luke said. "Since Lily doesn't have a family, can't we count as 'family' for her? I mean she lives with us, right?"

"I wish it worked like that," Erick replied. "But for now, I think all we can do is wait here."

The next fifty minutes, Madison paced and prayed. Luke sat hunched over in a plastic chair, his elbows on his knees and his head in his hands, while Erick and the aide spoke in soft tones to each other from time to time. People came and went in a blur, until finally, a voice spoke in English, "Who is here for the infant girl Lily?"

Immediately, they were all on their feet and clustered around a doctor. Before he could say a word, Madison's heart sank. The doctor's grim expression said it all. Leaning hard into her husband's side, she listened as the details unfolded. Lily had revived once for a few moments, but her heart was too weak to sustain her life. Although they'd done all that they could, Lily was gone.

Maddie could feel Luke's strong arm holding her up. Erick asked a few questions regarding the baby's remains as Luke led Madison over to a pair of chairs against the wall. Sinking into them together, they clasped hands and shared their grief.

Between sobs, Madison choked out what they were both thinking. "We could have saved her, Luke. We had the money from the church. She could have had the surgery."

As Erick made arrangements for Lily's burial, Luke took Madison outside. They sat on a wall, bowed their heads together and prayed.

When they finally arrived back at the Children's Garden, Chen was sitting alone on the playground. He spotted them and ran to their side, eyes clearly searching for Lily. Luke scooped him up in his arms, and the three of them walked back to their residence. Madison was exhausted, and Luke suggested she try to sleep a bit.

"What will we do with the surgery funds?" she asked quietly.

"I'll talk to my dad about it," he replied. "You just rest now. I'm going to see if I can get Chen to take a nap as well."

As Madison closed her eyes to go to sleep, her mind kept replaying what had happened. If she'd been watching more closely...if she'd gotten to Lily a few minutes sooner...surely there was something she could have done to save the little girl. Her thoughts circled in an endless loop as she struggled to find rest.

"I would have adopted her," she whispered in her spirit to God. "I would have made her my own."

And then a voice spoke to her heart. "Lily is Mine, Madison. She is home. And one day you will see her again."

"Did you hear Caleb leave this morning?" Michelle asked Steve as she packed her lunch for school.

"No. Why?"

"It's not like him not to say goodbye or anything," she replied, suddenly feeling her uneasiness grow. "I'd better go up and check on him and make sure he didn't oversleep."

When he didn't answer her knock on his bedroom door, she turned the handle and pushed it open. Caleb's bed was the way it had been the afternoon before when Michelle had put some clean laundry on it for him to put away. There was no sign of him. "Steve, come here!" she called from the landing at the top of the stairs.

"Are you calling me?" Steve replied as he walked into the living room.

"Yes. Caleb's gone."

Steve stared at her for a moment. "What do you mean, 'gone'?"

"I mean he didn't sleep here last night. His bed is still made and there are clothes stacked on it that I left there yesterday."

Joining her at the top of the stairs, Steve looked both worried and angry. "What is with that kid?" he muttered under his breath. Then he turned to Michelle and said, "Let's call and see if he stayed at the Johnsons."

"Good idea," she replied. "He was pretty upset last night. Maybe he just needed to talk with Logan." Michelle walked into the master bedroom and sat on the edge of the bed as she dialed the phone.

"Johnson residence, Liam speaking."

"Hi, Liam. It's Michelle. Is your mom there?"

"Just a second. I'll get her," he replied.

"Michelle? Is everything okay?" Kelly asked.

Michelle glanced at the alarm clock on the nightstand. She should already be on her way to work. "I'm worried about Caleb. Did he stay at your house last night?"

"No, why? What's happening?"

Michelle quickly explained and then added, "Would you ask Logan if he's talked to him? Maybe he'd know where Caleb stayed overnight."

While she was holding on the phone for Kelly's return, Steve said, "I'll go check out his laptop and see if I can spot anything in his emails."

"Good idea," Michelle agreed, looking at the clock again. If she didn't leave for school in the next fifteen minutes, she'd be late for her first-period class. Thankfully there were no teacher meetings before school today, and she didn't have any gate or bus duty assignments this month. But she'd already missed part of one class because of Caleb. She was about to call the office on her cell phone when Kelly came back on the line.

"Logan says he hasn't talked to Caleb. In fact, he said Caleb's been pretty much off his radar lately."

"That's weird. They're so close. Logan's like a brother to him," Michelle said, concern growing in her heart. "I've gotta run, Kel."

"Okay. Let me know if you find out anything. I'll be praying for you guys and for Caleb," Kelly replied.

"Would you see who's at the door please?" Amber called out to Will.

"Sure, babe."

Amber ran a brush through her hair and grabbed her backpack. She had a class in an hour. In contrast to her teen years when she did everything she could to avoid school, now she tried to arrive early for each of her college classes. What a difference a goal made! She could hardly wait to finish her credential and be a teacher like Michelle.

Walking out of her bedroom, she was startled to see Caleb standing in the entry hall with Will. "Caleb? What are you doing here?" she asked.

"I needed to get away," he replied, letting his backpack drop off of his shoulder. "Sorry about not calling first."

"Hey, man. You're welcome here anytime," Will said, patting Caleb on the back.

"How did you get here?" Amber asked.

"I took a bus."

Amber could tell something was wrong. She flashed back to the many times she'd tried to escape her foster homes growing up. "You took a bus? Do your parents know you're here?"

"Well...no...but, don't worry. They'll be fine. I just need some space," he replied.

Amber glanced at Will, who lifted his eyebrows and shrugged. "You should probably call home and let them know where you are, bud," he said to Caleb.

"I'll call later," Caleb answered. "Do you mind if I have something to eat? I'm starved."

"Caleb," Amber said, "you need to call your mom and dad right now, or I'm going to," adding in the next breath, "and then you can eat."

"Okay, okay," Caleb replied, throwing his hands up in surrender. Then he reached into his back pocket and pulled out his cell phone.

Amber knew she needed to get going to school, but she was determined to talk to Michelle after Caleb did. As he punched the button on his phone to call home, she let him know that.

"Yeah, it's me. I'm fine. I'm at Amber's," Caleb said into the phone. He glanced over at Amber and rolled his eyes. "Sorry. Sorry. I know. Okay. Yeah, hold on." Extending his phone to Amber, he handed it to her and then walked into the kitchen.

By the time Amber had explained to Michelle that she had no idea he was coming out, and Michelle had filled her in about Adam, Caleb had helped himself to a sweet roll and some milk and had crashed on the couch.

"I've gotta run, Michelle. I have a class this morning. Can we talk later?" Amber asked as she looked at the clock and then at Will. After promising to call her back that afternoon, Amber pushed the red button on the phone and placed it on the coffee table next to where Caleb was sleeping.

She scrawled a quick note to Caleb to stay in the apartment until she got home, and then she quickly took off for school.

After Michelle had filled him in on what she'd ascertained from Amber and then hurried off to school, Steve grabbed his briefcase and got in his car. He had a meeting that morning with one of his clients, and he needed to get to the office to go over his notes.

As he drove, he thought about their son. It seemed like Caleb's life was spinning out of control ever since he'd gotten the notion to find his biological father. Their usually happy and well-rounded teenager had become belligerent, disrespectful, and unpredictable.

"What am I going to do, Lord?" he asked aloud as he headed for the office. It seemed like nothing worked with Caleb these days. He rejected compassion and argued that no one could understand how he felt. Maybe that was true to some extent, but Steve was about out of ideas of how to reach the boy.

Maybe I'd better talk to this Adam fellow. If I can get through to him, maybe he can settle this whole mess with Caleb.

By the time Michelle got home from school, she was completely exhausted. Steve would be home in about an hour, and she needed to think through the situation with Caleb. But first, she'd just stretch out on the couch and close her eyes for a few minutes.

Michelle was just drifting off to sleep when the phone rang. Forcing herself up, she reached for her purse and dug through it until she found her cell. "Hello?" she answered groggily.

"Mom?" her daughter's voice came from a distant land.

Michelle jolted out of her stupor. "Madison! It's so great to hear your voice. How are you? Is everything okay?"

There was a pause on the other end, and then she thought she heard crying. "Maddie? Are you there? What's going on?"

"Oh, Mom," Maddie began, and Michelle could tell something was seriously wrong. "It's Lily."

"Lily? The little baby?"

"She's...she's gone. She died this morning." Madison sniffed, sounding very congested.

Michelle wished she could take her daughter in her arms and tell her everything would be all right. *How do I reach her through the air? Oh, God, please help sweet Maddie.* Taking a deep breath, she replied, "I'm so very sorry, honey. I know how you'd come to love her like your own."

"We had the money, Mom. It came a couple of days ago. But, with the entire earthquake clean up, we've been swamped here," she said. "Lily would still be alive if only I'd moved quicker on her surgery. I could have had it all scheduled before the funds even came through." She paused to catch her breath and sniffle again. "It's my fault she didn't make it."

"Oh, Maddie. Sweetheart, please don't think that. You and Luke have been so overloaded the past few weeks." Michelle hesitated as she searched for more words. "You know, Madison, you gave Lily something she needed. You gave her your love."

"It wasn't enough, Mom."

"You don't know that, honey. And there were no guarantees she would have survived the surgery anyway, right?"

Silence filled the airwaves broken only by a sigh. "Yeah. I guess," her daughter finally admitted. "It's just so...so hard. And you're right—I did love her like my own. I seriously would have adopted her in a heartbeat. I would have."

Michelle could picture her daughter's earnest expression in her mind. She'd actually thought the same thing herself—that Maddie and Luke would likely bring Lily home with them someday. "I believe you, honey."

They talked for a while as Madison described the events of the morning and the scene at the hospital. As Michelle listened, she could hear Maddie transition from a broken-hearted girl to a young and caring professional nurse.

Eventually, Madison asked, "How is everyone there, Mom? How's Caleb doing? I've been thinking about him and wondering how he's handling this whole Adam thing."

Michelle took a deep breath. "He's having a tough time. In fact, he ran away last night and caught a bus to Arizona to see Amber."

"What? Without telling you guys where he was going?"

"Yep."

"That's crazy! And it's not like Caleb. Oh, man, we'll be praying for all of you guys. What are you going to do?" Madison asked.

"I don't know yet. Your father and I are going to discuss it when he gets home from work."

"Mom?"

"Yeah?"

"It's not easy being a parent, is it?" she asked.

Michelle sighed and smiled a little. "No. It's not."

"Maybe Luke and I won't have any kids," Maddie said. "We can just work here and love the ones at the Children's Garden."

"Oh, sweetheart. I think you'll want your own children someday," Michelle replied.

"I don't know, Mom. I used to think so. But now I'm not so sure."

CHAPTER THIRTY-TWO

Michelle had just finished her conversation with Madison when she heard Steve's car pull into the driveway. She fluffed her hair with her fingers, folded the throw blanket she'd opened to use for her nap, and then greeted him at the door.

After kissing him hello, she wrapped her arms around his waist and leaned her head against his chest. They stood there pressed close together for a minute as if to draw strength from one another.

"What a day, huh?" Steve commented.

"Yeah, and you don't know the half of it," she replied. "I just got off the phone with Madison right before you pulled in."

"Is she okay?"

"Not really. Lily passed away. Maddie's pretty broken up about it," Michelle said.

Steve ran his hand down her arm and took her hand. "Let's sit down," he suggested, leading her over to the couch. As they settled next to each other, he tugged on the knot of his tie and pulled until it slipped out from under his collar. Unbuttoning the top button of his shirt, he said, "Tell me everything. What did she say?"

Michelle turned sideways on the cushion and bent her knee so she could face him. Retelling the events Madison had relayed to her, she felt her own heart breaking for their daughter and the little infant that she and Steve had never even met. Reaching for a tissue on the end table, she dabbed her eyes and finished sharing the details Madison had given her.

"Come here, you," he said, pulling her into his arms. As Michelle rested against him, he asked, "So, were you able to comfort and reassure Maddie a little before you hung up?"

"I think so," she replied. "We ended up talking about Caleb, too. She asked how he was doing, and one thing led to another."

"So she knows he's at Amber's?"

"Yeah."

"Maybe that's a good thing. Hopefully, those two are still communicating through emails. Even though Caleb argues with her, I think at some level he respects and listens to Madison. And to Luke," he added.

Michelle nodded. "I don't know if either of them will have time to email Caleb right now, but at least Maddie knows what's happening with him."

"And speaking of that," Steve said, "what are we going to do about this? Do you think I should fly out there and get him?"

"I don't think that's necessary. But I do think we should get him a flight home and have Amber and Will make sure he gets on it," she replied. "His attendance is already sketchy this year without missing more days."

"Okay, I'll get on the computer and secure a ticket for tomorrow."

"Sounds good, honey. And I'll heat up some dinner for us," she added, standing to her feet. "And Steve?"

"Yeah?"

"Thanks."

"For what?" he asked.

"For everything," she replied with a weary smile.

By the time they crawled into bed together that night, both of them were dead tired. Caleb's ticket was secured for the following afternoon. He'd arrive home in time for a late dinner.

As Michelle nestled into his arms, Steve thought about their son and Adam. The more he thought about the situation, the more he realized it would not be a good idea to talk to Adam himself. At least not yet. Hopefully, Caleb was ready to let go of the idea of having a relationship with the man. And, even though Steve would like to give the guy a piece of his mind, he knew it wouldn't accomplish anything.

After Caleb told Amber everything about Adam—the karate lessons, confronting him about being his dad, and the things Adam had said in response, Amber was livid. It was bad enough that Adam had abandoned her when she was pregnant with Caleb. Now for him to slander her and blatantly reject their son was more than she could forgive. Making a mental note of the name of the karate studio, she decided she'd call the following day.

Will took Caleb to work with him in the morning, and Amber didn't have any classes, so the timing was perfect for her call.

"Martial Arts Studio," a cheerful young female's voice chirped into the phone.

"Yes, I'm looking for someone who works there. His name is Adam," Amber said.

"Hold on. He just finished a class," the girl replied.

A moment later a voice from Amber's past said, "This is Adam."

She felt her stomach leap into her throat and she was unable to speak for a second.

"Hello?" Adam said.

"Uh hello," she stammered. "I'm glad I caught you there."

"Who is this?" he asked, an edge to his voice.

She took a deep breath. *Help me, Lord.* "It's Amber. Amber Gamble."

Silence hung in the air for a moment, and then Adam said, "What do you want?"

"I need to talk to you," she replied.

"If it's about that kid, you can forget about getting me involved. I don't want to have anything to do with your baggage from the past. Understand?"

"Caleb isn't 'baggage,' Adam. He's a great kid, and you really hurt him. And what's this about you telling him that I was with a bunch of guys? You know that wasn't true. Why would you say something like that?"

"Hey, I don't know what you were doing when we weren't together," he replied.

"What do you mean 'when we weren't together'? You make it sound like we hardly ever saw each other."

"Whatever. Listen, Amber. I can't do this right now."

"Fine. I'm really glad I put Caleb up for adoption. To think that I actually thought you and I might make a go of it—what a joke. Well, for your information, Caleb *is* your biological son, but he's got parents that are much better people than you'll ever be."

"Is that so?" he asked sarcastically.

"Yeah. His dad's a very successful attorney, and his mom's a teacher."

"Well, good for him," he replied, and then added, "Are we done here?"

"You're such a jerk, Adam. I hope Caleb stays far away from you," she said, her heart aching with regret about ever having loved this guy.

"Nothing would make me happier," he replied before hanging up on her.

Amber's call stuck with Adam as he prepared for his next class. She sure was a feisty thing—just like when they were dating. He could still remember that sweet body of hers. Allowing himself to replay some of their physical encounters in his mind, he felt a familiar arousal. Yeah, Amber had been good in the sack. And, he had to admit, he'd kind of fallen for her.

But that was before she threw a kink in their relationship. Flashing back to the day she'd told him she was pregnant, his stomach clenched. She'd had some pipe dream about them getting married and raising the baby together. What a crazy idea! He was still in high school, and she was only fourteen. Like they could really be parents!

He'd tried to talk her into an abortion. And she almost went along with him, too. But that stupid social worker and Amber's teacher had interfered and told her she had 'choices.' Really? What a crock.

Thinking about the phone conversation, he replayed what Amber had said about Caleb's adoptive parents. It sounded like they were probably loaded with dough. Well, good for Caleb. The kid ended up with a silver spoon in his mouth.

Hey, wait a minute. Maybe this could be the answer to my financial problems. What if I could become friends with the kid? Maybe he'd be able to channel some of that wealth toward his old man. I mean, hey, why not? It would be worth whatever time I had to spend with him.

A plan began to take shape in Adam's mind—one that he'd try to implement as soon as he could. Maybe even this week.

Caleb leaned back against the workbench as Will slid out on a dolly from underneath the car he was working on. "I don't see why I can't stay out here with you and Amber for a while," Caleb said.

Looking up at him, Will said, "Well, for one thing, you've got school."

Caleb rolled his eyes. "I could probably pass the GED right now and be done with high school."

"Come on, Caleb, you don't want to do that. Senior year is the best year of all. You'll have senior prom, grad night, graduation parties—all kinds of fun stuff."

"Well, what if I transfer and finish out here?"

"Without your friends? Really? Think about it, man. You wouldn't know anyone at the high school here," Will said. "It wouldn't be the same. You gotta finish school there in Sandy Cove. You can come back here next summer if you want. You know you're always welcome at our place."

Caleb thought about it and nodded. "I guess you're right."

"Have you thought about college and what you want to do?" Will asked.

He shook his head. "Nah. I'm not even sure I want to go to college." Caleb paused and then added, "Hey, maybe I could move out here and work with you at the shop after I graduate."

Will sat up on the dolly and gave Caleb a look that said he was crazy. "You're too smart for this kind of work, Caleb. You should get a degree and make something of yourself." Studying Caleb's face, he added, "I'm not a book guy myself, but from what I've heard about you and school, you're a good student."

Caleb shrugged.

"Hear me out, Caleb. Take advantage of all the opportunities your parents give you to get a good education now, while you can. Look at Amber. She's just now getting back into her studies. She'd already be a teacher if she'd been able to finish high school and go straight to college."

"Yeah, I guess," Caleb agreed.

"Amber's smart, too. She just had some hard knocks growing up. You've got her brains, Caleb. Don't waste them."

Caleb sighed and then nodded.

"Now hand me that five-eighths wrench, okay?" he asked as he gestured to a tool on the bench.

Handing it to him, Caleb asked, "So do you think I was crazy to want to find Adam?"

"Crazy? No, not at all."

"Really? Everyone else seems to think so," Caleb said. "I mean, he did turn out to be a jerk."

"Yeah, I guess," Will agreed. "But I kinda see both sides of this thing."

"You do?"

"Well, yeah. I mean…I think about what I would do if some kid suddenly showed up and told me he was my love child from some former relationship. I'm not sure how I'd respond myself."

"You wouldn't act like Adam did," Caleb said. "You're a good guy. I'm glad you and Amber got together."

"Thanks. I'm pretty glad, too," he added with a smile and a wink. "And I hope you're right about how I'd respond in that situation." He paused and then added, "I guess the main thing is, Caleb, I wouldn't take it too personally how Adam reacted to you telling him. It had to be a big shock for him."

Caleb nodded. "Yeah."

Will rolled back under the car, and as Caleb listened to him tinkering around under there, he thought about Adam again. Maybe he should give him another chance.

CHAPTER THIRTY-THREE

Although the Chinese tradition did not allow for any special ceremony for Lily because showing respect for those younger than oneself was not acceptable, Erick held a Christian memorial service for her back at the Children's Garden after her simple and silent funeral.

While the image of her tiny coffin being lowered into the ground was replaying in Madison's mind, she listened to Erick speak of Lily's sweet spirit and contagious smile. Luke hugged Madison to his side as Erick prayed that Jesus would receive Lily unto Himself and that they would see her again one day, healthy and whole.

All the children seemed to sense the soberness of the adults, and many were more sensitive and needy throughout the next few days. Madison tried to focus on them and their needs for any types of medical care or even just emotional support.

Meanwhile, Chen was silent, never smiling and always watching Luke's every move. He continued to stay with them in their residence, dividing Luke's attention between Madison and the little boy. Although Madison understood Chen's need for Luke, she felt equally needy when they finally escaped to their apartment at the end of each day.

By the time Chen was bathed and asleep, Luke was also beginning to doze off. One night, after they'd been asleep for several hours, Madison awakened from another dream of Lily. Tears seeped out of her eyes and down onto her pillow. Although she didn't want to awaken Luke, he reached for her in the dark, and she collapsed into his arms sobbing softly so as not to disturb Chen, asleep across the room.

Luke turned her face toward his, wiped her tears with his thumbs, and then cradled her to his bare chest. After all her tears were spent, she scooted up and kissed him. As they kissed and held each other, they began to make love in a way that was sweeter and deeper than ever before. They were learning to share more than their bodies. This time they shared their very souls.

As they finally drifted off to sleep again, Madison felt peace in her heart and an awareness that something had shifted in their marriage and lives. An unexplainable hope rose up within her, replacing the overwhelming grief over the loss of Lily.

Caleb's parents grounded him from after school time with his friends, requiring him to come directly home and work on his homework and chores. If he had a work shift at the Coffee Stop, he'd ride his bike there. Until he earned enough money to pay for his traffic violation and his return flight from Arizona, he was restricted to work, work, work.

As he was walking out to his bike after school one afternoon, he heard someone call his name. Turning, he spotted Adam heading in his direction. *Wonder what he wants?*

"Hey, Caleb. I'm glad I caught you," Adam said as he approached.

Caleb could feel his defenses rising. Their last encounter had been so bad. But this time the guy was actually smiling. "Hey," Caleb replied.

"I got a call from Amber," he said, "and I've been rethinking what I said at the studio. You've gotta admit, you caught me off guard with all this," he added.

"What did Amber say?" Caleb asked.

"She was pretty ticked. Can't say I blame her. But how was I to know that she wasn't with anyone but me?"

Caleb stared at him.

"Anyway, we talked for a while, and she convinced me that it's true—about you and me, I mean."

"So?"

"So, I thought maybe we could start over. Like forget everything that happened at the studio and get to know each other a little," Adam offered.

Caleb hesitated, studying the man's face. He looked sincere enough. Maybe he really meant it when he said he wanted to get to know him better. "You picked a lousy time. I'm pretty much grounded from life right now."

"Really? Why?"

"I got a speeding ticket, and I kind of went out to Amber's without telling my parents I was leaving."

Adam laughed. "Yeah, you sound like my kid, alright." He paused for a moment and then said, "What if I offered to teach you private karate lessons again? Think your folks would go for that?"

"I doubt it."

"Where are you headed right now?" Adam asked.

"I've gotta shift at the Coffee Stop."

"Why don't I give you a lift? I can put your bike in the back of my truck," he suggested. "Besides, I could use a cup of coffee."

"Okay, sure. Sounds good," Caleb replied.

Adam led him out to a beat up pick up truck parked across the street from the high school. Caleb hoisted his bike into the bed of the truck, and they took off for the Coffee Stop.

After Caleb had changed into his work shirt with the restaurant logo on it, he clocked in and took Adam's order. The place was pretty busy. A lot of the high school crowd hung out there for about the first half hour after class let out.

Adam didn't seem in any hurry to leave. Whenever Caleb passed by his spot at the counter, he'd say something casual but friendly.

By three-thirty, the crowd had thinned to a few stragglers. Usually, the ones who remained were more the loners from school. They'd hunker down on the couches or easy chairs with earphones isolating them from the sounds of the coffee shop as they either worked on homework or played a video game on a handheld device.

"Want a refill?" Caleb asked Adam.

"Nah. I'm good. But thanks," he replied. "So, I've been thinking, and I wonder if your parents would let me teach you private lessons if I go and talk to them myself." He gave Caleb a moment and then asked, "What do you think?"

"Uh…I don't know. Maybe."

Adam slapped his hands onto his knees, "Okay, settled. I'll talk to them. Want me to come by when you get off and give you a lift home? That way I could meet your folks."

"Sure. Sounds good. I'll be off at six," Caleb replied.

Standing up, Adam pulled a couple of bucks out of his pocket and dropped them on the counter. "For you," he said with a smile. "I'll see you at six."

Caleb scooped up the tip and crammed it into his jeans. Maybe he and Adam would become friends after all.

Michelle was stirring the spaghetti sauce when she heard Caleb come in. He was talking to someone, as the two of them approached the kitchen.

"Hey, Mom," her son said. "I'd like you to meet someone."

A man stood beside her son, and just by looking at him, she knew in an instant who it was. The resemblance was uncanny.

"This is Adam, my...uh...karate instructor," Caleb said.

Michelle's throat tightened as fingers of anxiety wrapped around it and threatened to squeeze the breath out of her. All she could manage was an acknowledgment. "Adam," she said.

"Ma'am," he replied, extending his hand toward her.

She hesitated for a second and then reached out and grasped it. His handshake was firm but moist. So he felt nervous, too. Good to know. Next, she shot Caleb a questioning look.

As if reading her mind, her son explained, "Adam came by school today and gave me a lift to work."

"Oh really?" she asked. Why the sudden friendliness? And why would Caleb accept a ride from the guy?

"Yeah. Then we hung out while I worked."

"I see," she replied.

"I thought maybe he could stay for dinner so you and Dad could get to know him," Caleb added.

Adam jumped in with, "I don't want to impose or anything. Sure smells great, but it's fine if this isn't a good time. The dinner idea was Caleb's."

Michelle studied him for a moment. He seemed to be really trying, maybe even too hard. Might be a good idea to let him stay and see if she and Steve could get a feel for what was going on between him and Caleb. He'd clearly crushed their son not long ago. Now he was all smiles and friendliness. Something didn't jibe. "It's no problem," she said. Then turning to Caleb, she added, "Your father will be home in about ten minutes, and we'll eat soon after that."

"Okay, cool," he replied. "Adam and I will be up in my room."

As Adam brushed past her, Michelle gave him a warning look. He tipped his head in acknowledgment and then followed Caleb out of the kitchen.

Michelle was adding a place setting to the table when Steve walked in. He looked beat. Not the best night for a guest. Especially Adam.

"Hi, hon," he said as he set his briefcase down and tugged at the knot of his tie. Leaning over and giving her a kiss, he added, "Smells delicious in here."

"Thanks. How was your day?" she asked.

"One headache after another. But I think I've resolved most of the issues with that merger, so hopefully, the worst is over." He pulled out a chair and started to sit down. "Four placemats? Did I forget something?"

Michelle touched his shoulder lightly and then sat down beside him. "No. We have a surprise guest."

Steve's eyebrows rose.

"Caleb brought Adam over and invited him for dinner."

"What? You're kidding right?" Steve looked more than troubled.

Cringing, Michelle shook her head. "Sorry, babe. I'm not kidding. They're up in his room as we speak."

"But I thought Caleb was finished with the guy," Steve said, raising his voice a bit.

Michelle reached over and put her hand on his. "I'm really sorry about springing this on you, especially after the day you've had today. But they just showed up here. And before I knew it, I was agreeing to let him stay for dinner." She explained how Adam had come to the high school and found Caleb and that they'd spent the afternoon at the Coffee Stop together talking between customers. "Caleb thought it would be good for us to get to know him."

"Really," Steve said sarcastically. Scrubbing his hands over his face, he pushed away from the table and stood up. "I'm going to change clothes before dinner. What time are we eating?"

"It's ready whenever you are. Maybe you can tell the guys to come downstairs after you're finished changing," she suggested.

He just nodded and walked out of the room.

By the end of dinner, two things were clear to Steve. Adam's complete turn around with Caleb was masking a hidden agenda. And Caleb was completely deceived by his charm. After Adam had left, Steve decided to have a chat with his son.

"So, I was surprised you brought Adam home. I thought you'd called it quits with him," he said.

"Yeah, well, maybe I was too hasty," Caleb replied. "After all, I did spring the news about me on him. Wouldn't you kind of freak out if some high school guy showed up and did that to you?"

"I understand about his surprise, son, but he said some slanderous and inappropriate things about Amber, too. And he made it very clear he didn't want to have anything to do with you." He paused to let his words sink in, and then he asked, "What changed all that?"

Caleb shrugged. "I don't know, Dad. He just seemed so different today. And he apologized for what he'd said."

Steve didn't want to upset him, but he didn't want his son to be hurt more down the line. "I hate to say this, but here's what I think, Caleb. I think Adam has some kind of motive here. Something's not right."

Caleb glared at him. "You always think the worst about people. Besides it probably bugs you that he wants to get to know me. You can at least give him a chance. I'm going to." He stood up and walked out of the room.

Steve winced inwardly. Maybe he was a little uneasy about what it might mean if Caleb developed a close relationship with his biological father. But that didn't stop the feeling in his gut that something was off. Maybe it was the attorney in him, but he'd learned to read people pretty well. And this guy did not add up.

CHAPTER THIRTY-FOUR

True to his word, Caleb did give Adam a chance. In fact, Caleb poured himself into private lessons with Adam, draining much of his wallet in the process. It bothered him a little that he had to pay to have his own biological father teach him martial arts, but the guy did have bills to pay like anyone else, right? And this was his bread and butter.

Besides, the more time Caleb invested in their relationship, the more certain he was that Adam was softening to the idea of attending church with Caleb and his family. Then maybe Caleb's parents wouldn't be so judgmental about Adam.

Sometime during each week of lessons, Caleb would find an opportunity to say something casual about church. Often he would add a subtle invitation. But Adam didn't seem to pick up on it.

Finally, one Friday as they were walking out to the parking lot after his lesson, Caleb decided to ask Adam point blank if he'd like to join them on Sunday.

"Sure, kid. That sounds interesting," Adam replied.

Caleb cringed inwardly about the 'kid' reference, but he went ahead and set up a meeting time and place for right before the second service. "So I'll see you by the walkway at the north end of the parking lot at quarter 'til ten?"

"Yep. I'll be there," Adam replied.

When Caleb got home, he quickly tracked down his father in his study. "Guess what, Dad?"

"What?" Steve asked, looking up from his paperwork.

"Adam's going to meet us at church on Sunday. Pretty cool, huh?"

His father hesitated, looking at him with raised eyebrows. "I guess."

"You guess? What's that mean?" Anger coursed through Caleb's veins, and he wanted to shake his dad. "Aren't we supposed to share our faith? Isn't that the most important commandment?"

"Well, now if memory serves me correctly, the most important commandment is to love the Lord your God with all your heart, soul, and mind," Steve replied, his voice softening some.

"And love your neighbor as yourself, right?" Caleb challenged. "So this is my way of loving my neighbor— inviting him to church."

Steve nodded. "That's fine, son. And I hope he comes."

Caleb bristled. "He will."

That Sunday, Caleb was the first one ready for church. He urged his parents to hurry up, so he wouldn't be late to meet Adam. With Christmas around the corner, he was hoping for a miracle that would draw his biological father into their faith and bridge the gap between Caleb's parents and Adam.

As they were about to walk out the door, Michelle remembered that she'd promised to bring a book to her mom, and she headed back into the house to find it.

"Great," Caleb muttered. "Now I'll be late."

"I'm sure Adam will wait for you," Steve replied, starting the car so they could pull out as soon as Michelle returned.

When they pulled into the parking lot, Caleb asked his dad to drop him off at the north end of the lot. "We'll meet you guys inside," he added as he climbed out of the back seat.

After his parents had pulled away, Caleb searched for Adam. Maybe he'd wandered toward the entrance of the sanctuary looking for Caleb since they were running a little late. Approaching the front door, Caleb spotted Logan. "Hey!" he called out.

"Hey," Logan replied. "What's up?"

"I'm looking for Adam. He was going to meet me here today."

"Adam? You mean Adam as in your martial arts teacher?" Logan asked, clearly groping for the right title.

"Yeah. Have you seen him?"

Logan shook his head. "Hope he shows," he added, giving Caleb a pat on the shoulder before walking away.

Turning toward the parking lot again, Caleb could see his parents approaching. Wouldn't his dad be thrilled if Adam didn't show up? Caleb felt his defenses rising. Surely Adam would be here any minute, right?

Plastering a smile on his face, he waved to his folks. Steve seemed to be looking over Caleb's shoulder, as if checking for Adam's arrival, while Michelle returned his wave and smiled back. "Any sign of him?" Steve asked a moment later.

"Not yet. I'll just wait for him out here. Save us a couple of seats, okay?" Caleb replied.

His father nodded. "Okay, son. But don't wait too long."

Michelle gave Caleb a sympathetic smile and took Steve's hand as they entered the sanctuary.

Gazing out to the lot, Caleb could see that most of the activity of parking and walking had subsided. The lot was full, except a couple of places in the far back corner, so he kept his eye on those.

The praise and worship team started singing, and the music wafted out through the open windows and door. Caleb began to feel a little funny standing out there alone staring at the parked cars. After about ten minutes and two late-arriving families hurrying past him, he sighed and turned to go inside, disappointment and frustration battling for his heart.

Pastor Ben's teaching that morning was on the prodigal son. As Caleb listened, he thought about Adam and how much he needed to know the love of God, represented as the father in the story, who eagerly awaited the return of his wayward son. Certain that Adam would give his life over to God if he just heard the message, Caleb's frustration grew.

What was happening here? He'd prayed and asked God to make Himself real to Adam, and he'd finally persuaded the man to come to church. The message was perfect for his biological father, and yet he was nowhere to be seen.

Although Caleb was mostly disappointed in Adam, he was also upset with God. Surely God could have gotten Adam to church that morning, right? And didn't scripture say that He was not willing that any should perish, but that all would come to repentance? So why hadn't He made sure Adam was there to hear the sermon?

Steve glanced over at his son. He could see how upset Caleb was feeling, and it made Steve angry with Adam for once again bailing on the boy. He hoped Caleb had picked up on the message of the teaching—the love of a father for his son—a love that Steve had for him.

Michelle squeezed his hand, and Steve glanced over. She mouthed the words, "Don't bring up Adam," as they stood for the final hymn before leaving.

He nodded. There would be no point in upsetting Caleb more by focusing their conversation on Adam's failure to show.

As Caleb approached the martial arts studio, he practiced in his mind what he would say to Adam. He wanted to keep it light and casual, not letting on how upset he'd been when Adam had failed to show up at church on Sunday.

Glancing around the parking lot, he noticed that Adam's truck was not there. *Great! Now he's bailing on my lesson, too.*

As he opened the door, he immediately spotted Adam on his cell phone. He appeared to be in a heated discussion with someone, mentioning something about money and that he'd come up with the amount somehow. After ending the call, he turned to Caleb, dropped his scowl and smiled. "Hey, kid. How's it going?"

'Kid' again. Does everyone think I'm twelve, or what? "Fine. How about you?" Caleb asked, tipping his head toward the cell phone in Adam's hand.

Adam glanced down at the phone. "Oh, that. It's no big deal. My truck's busted, and I've got to come up with some cash."

"Is that why you didn't show on Sunday?" Caleb asked, hoping his tone sounded unaffected.

Adam looked puzzled for a second. "Oh, that," he said. "Sorry about church. Yeah, my transmission gave out Saturday night. I should have called you."

"No problem," Caleb replied nonchalantly.

"Got any ideas where I could get a loan?" Adam asked, his voice sounding a bit defeated to Caleb. "I'm going to need a chunk of change to get that old clunker back on the road."

"Wish I could help you out, but my job doesn't pay much," Caleb replied.

Adam laughed and shook his head. "I was only kidding, Caleb. I wouldn't take a loan from you anyway."

As they worked on the lesson together, thoughts swirled in Caleb's head. *I wonder if I should offer to pick him up next Sunday if he still wants to come to church. Or maybe I should ask Dad if he'd be willing to loan Adam the money.*

Before leaving the studio, Caleb casually mentioned that he'd be happy to give Adam a ride to church if he'd like.

"Thanks, but I think I'll wait until I get the truck fixed. I may have to try to do it myself this weekend if I can figure out a way to afford the parts," Adam replied.

He sounded like he was still interested in giving church a try, so Caleb decided he'd approach his dad and see if Steve would be willing to loan Adam the money, at least to buy the parts.

After dinner that night, Caleb said, "Hey, Dad. Can we talk?"

"Sure," Steve replied.

Michelle stood and cleared the table, and then told them she'd be grading papers in the living room if they needed her.

"So what's up, bud?" Steve asked.

"I talked to Adam about Sunday," Caleb began.

"And?"

"And he explained that the transmission in his truck broke down on Saturday," Caleb explained.

"It would have been nice if he would have called to let you know," his father said.

"Yeah. He apologized for that."

Steve just nodded, but Caleb could tell he was skeptical.

"So anyway, he still wants to come to church after he gets his truck fixed, and I was wondering if maybe you'd be willing to loan him a little money for parts." Caleb held his breath as he waited for the reply.

Clearing his throat before answering, Steve finally asked, "Did Adam ask you to ask me this?"

"No. It was my idea. He doesn't even know I'm asking you."

Steve sat back in his chair and rubbed his chin. "Let me think about it, Caleb."

"Really? Okay, great! Thanks, Dad." What a surprise that his father didn't just say 'no' right out of the gate. Hopefully, he'd see things the way Caleb did and agree to help Adam out.

"Don't thank me yet. I just said I'd think about it."

"Sure," Caleb nodded agreeably. "No pressure. I just appreciate you considering it."

"What do you say we surprise your mom and get the dishes done?" his father asked.

"Good idea," Caleb replied with a smile.

CHAPTER THIRTY-FIVE

"He asked you what?" Michelle said as Steve relayed to her his conversation with Caleb while they were getting ready for bed.

"He wondered if I'd loan Adam money for parts to repair his truck's transmission."

Michelle studied his face. "What did you say?"

"That I'd think about it."

"And? What *do* you think?" she asked.

Steve sank onto the bed beside her and took her hand in his. "I'm torn. Adam doesn't have a good track record, and my gut is telling me I'll never see the money again if I do loan it to him."

"But?"

"But I know how important this is to Caleb. And I don't want to be the bad guy here." He paused and looked her in the eye. "Know what I mean?"

"Yeah."

"So what do you think?" he asked.

"I think either Adam will surprise us all and pay you back, or Caleb will learn a hard lesson about the guy," she replied. "Maybe that's the best way."

He nodded. "Yeah. I guess I'll loan it to him." Slapping his hands on his knees decisively, he stood and walked toward the door. "If he's still awake, I'll let Caleb know."

A couple of weeks later, Steve began to seriously question his decision to loan Adam the money. Not only had the guy failed to show up at church both of the subsequent Sundays, giving vague excuses instead, but he'd also turned down Caleb's invitation to Thanksgiving dinner.

Every time Steve started to say something to Caleb about it, a voice in his spirit stopped him. God's mandate seemed to be to simply wait, pray, and trust Him with the results. So, in spite of the agitation and frustration he could see in his son, Steve bit his tongue and prayed.

The second weekend in December, Madison and Luke arrived home for their vacation with family. Michelle spent a month fixing up Madison's room for their stay. "I want it to be a cozy place for them," she told Steve. Pulling the side of the bed away from the wall, she flanked it with two new nightstands. And Madison's girlie bedding set was replaced with a quilt Joan and Phil had used in their guest room. Shades of soft greens and cranberry gave it a Christmassy look. It had always been a favorite of Michelle's whenever she'd stay at her grandparents' home.

At the last minute, she put fresh flowers in a vase on the dresser along with a few water bottles and some granola bars in a basket.

"Wow, are you opening a B & B?" Steve teased as he surveyed the room.

Michelle stood back and smiled. "I want it to be perfect for the kids."

He grinned and pulled her into his arms. "You're pretty special. You know that?"

Before she could reply, Caleb called out from downstairs, "Maddie's home!"

As they hurried down and joined their son at the open front door, they could see Madison and Luke unloading their luggage from Ben's car. Michelle ran out and embraced her daughter, trying to control the tears that threatened to spill. "Oh Maddie, I have missed you so much," she said, holding her tight.

"I've missed you, too, Mom," she said. And as they pulled back, Michelle could see that her daughter's eyes were also a sea of tears.

"My turn," Steve said, pulling Madison into his arms.

"Hey, there, bro," Caleb said, giving Luke an awkward hug.

Glancing over at Ben and Kelly standing off to the side and smiling, Michelle offered, "Let's all go inside. I've got fresh coffee brewing and some homemade muffins."

That night, before turning in, Madison stopped by Caleb's room and knocked.

"Come in," he said.

Opening the door, she saw that he was sitting at his desk on his computer. It looked like he was in the middle of an email. "Is this a bad time?" she asked.

"No." He reached over and pulled his backpack and sweatshirt off the bed and said, "Sit down." Then he closed the laptop and turned to face her. "You must be pretty tired after all that traveling."

"A little. But I wanted to check in and see how things are going with you and Adam," she said. "I didn't want to ask in front of Mom and Dad, but I haven't heard anything from you in a few weeks."

"Yeah, well, there's not much to say. You knew that Dad loaned him the money to fix his truck, right?"

She nodded. "Yep. You told me that. So did he end up coming to church?"

"No."

Madison could see the hurt in her brother's eyes. "Maybe he's afraid," she offered.

"Afraid of what?"

"Afraid he won't know how to act. Or maybe afraid of what he'll hear and how it will affect his life," she said.

"Yeah. Maybe," Caleb replied, but his tone was skeptical.

After a moment of silence, Madison stood up. "Don't give up. He may still come around."

Caleb nodded.

"Guess I'll go to bed," she said, starting for the door.

"Hey, Mad?"

"Yeah?"

"I'm really sorry about Lily," he said, standing to his feet as well.

"Thanks," she replied, trying not to cry. Would her heart ever stop hurting? Every time Lily's name was mentioned, the pain resurfaced. Glancing at Caleb, she saw his arms wide open. As she walked into his hug, a few stray tears escaped. It seemed strange to her that her 'little brother' was much taller than her now. And as they embraced, she realized that he was becoming a man—a man with a boy's heart that was still very vulnerable.

Before she and Luke got into bed, they sat on the edge of the mattress and held hands to pray. "Let's say a special prayer for Caleb and Adam," she said.

"So how are you doing, Maddie? You've been through a lot lately," Michelle said.

Trying to be strong and hold her emotions at bay, Madison replied, "I think about Lily every day, and I try to remember that she is happy and is with Jesus. But sometimes it's really hard, Mom."

Michelle nodded. "I wish I could have been there for you."

"You were. I could feel all the prayers from everyone here," she said. "You know, we were seriously considering adopting her. It was like she'd already become part of our family."

Michelle sighed. "Oh, baby, I wish that would have worked out. You and Luke are going to be great parents someday."

"Thanks, Mom," Madison replied, smiling through her tears.

"What about the little boy—Chen? How is he doing?"

"It was tough when we left. He was clinging to Luke and crying. Erick had to pull him off and distract him while we got into the van to go to the airport."

"Do you think he'll be okay while you're gone?"

"One of the aides is going to stay in our room with him. He's gotten so used to sleeping there, and we're hoping that will help," Madison explained.

"I hope I can meet the little guy someday," Michelle said. "Your Dad and I would like to come out during my spring break if we can work it out with his caseload."

"That would be great, Mom! We'd love to have you," she replied, her sorrow lightened by the joyful anticipation of their possible visit.

"There you are," Luke said, as he walked into the kitchen. "We have a meeting at church, remember?"

Madison glanced at the clock. "Oh yeah! We'd better go." Turning, she gave her mom a hug. "See you this afternoon at Grams," she said, remembering the annual Christmas tea party she and her mom, grandmother, and great grandmother enjoyed together at the beginning of each December.

As the four generations of women sat around Joan's festive little table, Madison noticed how frail her great grandmother was looking. Not having seen her in months, it was even more obvious. She couldn't help but wonder if this was their last Christmas tea as a foursome.

Madison's mom and grandmother seemed to take extra care with Joan, gently reminding her of events that slipped her mind. "And we'll be having Christmas dinner together at Michelle's house, Mom," Sheila said for the second time that afternoon.

"Oh, okay. Thanks for telling me. And you'll pick me up and take me there, right?" Joan asked.

"That's right," Sheila replied, smiling patiently at a question she'd already answered just ten minutes earlier.

"How's the devotional coming?" Madison asked.

"Devotional?" Joan said, looking puzzled.

"The one you were working on from Gramps' sermon notes," Maddie replied.

"Oh yes. That one. I think I've finished that." She glanced over at Sheila.

"That's right, Mom," her daughter replied. "I gave it to Michelle to edit."

Joan turned to Michelle who nodded her head. "I'm working on it, Grandma. You did a great job. Grandpa would be proud."

When the subject of Lily came up, Joan's countenance changed, and she turned to Madison with a clear expression of compassion. "The loss of a child is never easy, sweetheart."

Maddie nodded.

"But over time, God will give you peace. And you'll learn to rest in the knowledge that Lily is in heaven." She paused and gazed off into space. Then clearing her throat, she turned back to her great granddaughter. "When you have your own children, your heart will be whole again." She reached over and squeezed Madison's hand. "Just wait and see."

Two weeks later, Madison made a discovery that confirmed God was indeed at work to do that healing work. But first an unexpected crisis would rock their world.

CHAPTER THIRTY-SIX

Luke's cell phone rang, awakening him and Madison in the predawn hours of the rainy mid-December morning. Propping himself up on his elbow and flipping on the lamp by the bed, Luke saw his mom's name on the screen of the phone. "Hello?"

"Luke, it's Mom. You need to get over here right away. It's your father. The paramedics are here, and they're taking him to the hospital. I need someone here with the kids."

"What happened? Is he okay?" Luke asked, his pulse racing as he shot a concerned look in Madison's direction.

"They think he's had a heart attack. I've gotta go. Can you come right now?"

Sitting up and swinging his legs over the edge of the bed, he replied, "We'll get dressed and be there in a few minutes."

After hanging up, he explained the situation to Madison. They both quickly dressed, and Madison knocked on her parents' bedroom door. "Mom?"

"Madison?" her mother's voice came from the darkened room. "Is something wrong?"

"We need to borrow the car. Luke's dad is going to the hospital. They think he's had a heart attack, and Luke and I need to go over there."

Michelle was up in a flash, followed by Steve. "Go ahead and take the van," she said. "The keys are hanging by the door out to the garage. Your father and I will be over as soon as we can get dressed."

Maddie and Luke took off, driving as quickly as possible through the pouring rain, and praying aloud together. They got to Luke's parents' house just as the paramedics were closing the back doors of the ambulance.

"I'm going to follow them in my car," Kelly said, her face giving away her concern.

"Why don't you drive her," Madison said to Luke. "I can stay here with the kids. And my parents will be here to help any minute."

Luke didn't hesitate. "Thanks, babe. I'll call as soon as we know anything." He wrapped his arm around his mother's shoulders and led her to the car, both getting drenched in the process.

As Madison sat in the living room praying, she heard footsteps overhead. Someone was up. Glancing at the clock, she saw that it was only five-thirty. Whoever it was must have heard some of the commotion.

A minute later, a very groggy Logan ambled down the stairs. "Mad? Is that you?" he asked.

"Yeah. Is anyone else awake up there?"

"No. What's going on? Why are you here?"

What should she say? Madison searched for the right words. "It's your dad. He...well...I guess he wasn't feeling right...and...anyway, the paramedics came. They think he might have had a heart attack, but we don't know anything yet," she added quickly, hoping she sounded reassuring. "They're taking him to the hospital just in case."

"So he's okay?"

"I think he'll be fine. I'm waiting to hear from Luke as soon as they know anything. He drove your mom over there."

"Oh…" Logan sank down onto the couch across from her. "Who's that?" he asked as a car drove into the driveway.

"That'll be my parents. They wanted to come over, too. In case they could help," she explained.

Logan nodded. "I guess I should call Lucy."

"I think your mom probably already did." Madison walked over and opened the front door. She was a little surprised to see Caleb with her folks. "I'm glad you came," she said to him, tipping her head toward Logan.

Caleb went and sat by his friend, trying to make small talk to distract him. After Steve and Michelle had taken off their wet coats and shoes, they joined the three of them. "Let's pray," Steve suggested. Everyone nodded, and they formed a circle, linking hands as Steve interceded for his best friend.

In the middle of their prayer, Madison's cell phone began to buzz. She released her brother's hand and pulled it out of her purse. It was Luke.

"Sorry," she said, glancing around the circle. Then she turned her attention to the phone. "Luke! How's he doing?"

All eyes were on her as she pressed the phone to her ear.

"He's stable. They've admitted him and gotten him into a room. There are a bunch of tests they want to run, and I think I'll hang out here with Mom if everything is okay over there."

"Sure. That's a good idea. I'll pass along the news. Logan's up and my parents and Caleb are here. We were just praying for your dad," she said.

"Thanks, babe. I'll keep you posted."

Madison turned her attention back to the loved ones around her and shared the update.

"Sounds like he's going to be okay," Steve said.

"That's what I was thinking, too," she replied. "Luke seemed pretty upbeat."

Glancing at the Christmas tree in the corner of the room, she wondered to herself how this upcoming holiday would unfold.

When it was clear that Ben was out of the woods for now, and that he had indeed had a heart attack, but they'd caught it in time, Kelly and Luke returned home. By this time everyone was awake, and Michelle and Madison were fixing breakfast for all of them.

Madison could feel fatigue settling on her like a heavy blanket. She'd noticed she was more tired than usual lately. Probably a combination of jetlag, recovering from her grief over Lily's death, and all the hubbub of the holidays. When they got back to her parents' house, she decided to go up and lie down for a while.

Awakening an hour later to cramps, she said softly to herself, "Great. Now my period, too." Pulling her phone off the nightstand, she flipped to her calendar. *Wait a second. This can't be right.* Her period was overdue by two weeks. How had she lost track of it?

Over the next few hours, her cramps subsided, but her period did not start. "It's just stress," she told herself. But by the end of the day, she'd made a decision. She'd go and pick up a pregnancy test to make sure.

When she saw the positive results the next morning, she was stunned. Although she wanted a family with Luke, and they'd talked about having kids, this was not a good time. With Luke's father in the hospital, and the orphanage expecting them back in a few weeks, their

276

plates were full. She didn't know how she could spring this on Luke right now. *I won't tell anyone yet.*

Sitting on the edge of her bed, she prayed for wisdom and God's timing. Her tears began to flow freely as she opened her heart to Jesus, pouring out her sorrow about Lily, her concerns for Luke's dad, her worries about her great grandmother, and her qualms about Caleb and Adam. Burden after burden slipped off her shoulders and into the Lord's able hands, and by the time she was finished praying she had a word from God.

This child is My gift. Do not fear. All is well.

"Babe? Are you okay?" Luke stood in the doorway looking at her. She hadn't even heard him come up.

Nodding, she patted the bed beside her, and he came over and sat down. "Any news on your dad?" she asked.

"No," he replied, draping his arm over her shoulders and pulling her close to kiss the top of her head. "But I believe he's going to be fine. Really." He paused and then pulled back and looked her in the eye. "What about you? Are you feeling okay?"

She smiled. "I've got some news for you."

Luke cocked his head with a curious expression. "Okay. Fire away. Is it something big?"

"Well, it's actually something small right now. But it'll be getting bigger," she said with a twinkle in her eye.

"You've got me. Spit it out," he said.

"So, it turns out I'm pregnant," she said, laughing.

He laughed back. "Funny."

"I'm serious," she replied, taking his hand in hers and placing it on her abdomen. "You've got a baby cooking in there."

"Are you sure? I mean we've been pretty busy these past few weeks…"

"Apparently not too busy for this," she said with a wink.

"Wow. I mean, wow." His expression was a combination of confusion and elation.

"Sorry to spring it on you like this, with everything else that's going on with your dad and everything," she said.

"You're kidding, right? This is the best news ever. My parents will be thrilled, and so will yours," he replied, pulling her to her feet and hugging her close. Then he bent down and kissed her tenderly. "I love you, Mrs. Johnson."

"Feeling's mutual," she replied, kissing him back more passionately.

"There you go again," he warned with a wink. "But I'd better get going. I'm meeting my mom at the hospital. Save that kiss for tonight."

"Oh, I will, Mr. Johnson. I most definitely will."

"Do you want to come with me? We could tell my folks," he suggested. "Or do you want to tell yours first?"

"Let's wait and tell everyone at Christmas. Hopefully, your dad will be home by then, too," she said, giving him one more kiss before he left.

CHAPTER THIRTY-SEVEN

Turning from his patient to Kelly, Ben's doctor reiterated his warning. "I'm really serious about this, Mrs. Johnson. If your husband continues to push himself, his heart will not hold out. You're both very fortunate that he had this warning. Although no heart attack is a good one, his was mild, and we were able to treat it in time to prevent any serious permanent damage. Next time, he won't be so lucky. Of that, I can almost guarantee."

She nodded and thanked him. "I'll be sure to keep tabs on him. And we'll be modifying our diet and getting more exercise. Right, honey?" she asked, glancing at her husband.

"Right."

"I also recommend a modified work schedule, as we discussed earlier," the doctor added. "You'll be no good to your parishioners if you're dead."

Ben winced and tried to smile. "Got it."

As the nurse wheeled him out to the parking lot in a wheelchair—"hospital procedure," she explained above his protests, Ben thought about what the doctor had said. *How do I cut back my hours? Especially now with the holidays upon us?* How he wished the life of a pastor was as simple and free as many believed. More than once, he'd heard the comment, "Must be nice to only have to work on Wednesday nights and Sunday mornings."

If only they knew the countless hours of counseling, the late night hospital visits, the grieving spouses and parents, as well as the demands of running the practical business side of keeping a church going. Now he'd have to figure out some way to cut back. *Give me wisdom, Lord. Show me the way.*

As they left the hospital building and the sun peeked out from the cloudy sky, they spotted Luke pulling the car up to the curb. And almost as if Ben could audibly hear God's voice, a whisper in his spirit told him *Luke is your way.*

Trying to shake it off, Ben immediately thought about Luke's commitment to the Children's Garden. There was no way he could ask his son to stay here and help with the church.

No, he must have heard God wrong.

"So, Dad," Luke began, later that evening. "I've been thinking about the Christmas Eve service, and I was wondering how you'd feel about me speaking that night. God's been putting a message on my heart to share. Besides, it would do you good to rest and recuperate."

Ben studied his face. Had Kelly prompted their son to do this?

"What? You don't think I'm ready?" Luke asked teasingly. "I think I can handle a forty-five-minute message," he added.

Ben smiled. "Okay, buddy. You're on." As soon as the words were out, relief swept over him. His heart attack seemed to have muddled his mind a bit, and he'd been struggling to come up with a message of his own.

Maybe God was right. Maybe Luke could help him out. At least until it was time for him to return to China.

Christmas Eve was upon them so quickly that Kelly barely had time to wrap the gifts and get them under the tree. As the church service began, and the worship team asked the congregation to stand and sing "Oh Come All Ye Faithful," a wave of thankfulness washed over her. This Christmas could have been very different. Reaching for her husband's hand as they stood together and sang, she pushed away images of widowhood and single parenting and praised God for preserving Ben's life.

Each Christmas song held even more depth of meaning to her as she pondered the words and the amazing gift of God's only Son. She glanced across at their children standing and singing along, too, and she knew that her heart would never be the same if she lost any one of them. Yet God had willingly allowed Himself to be separated from His one and only begotten Son and had allowed Him to die on the cross to redeem the lost.

Tears clouded her eyes. Such amazing love. It was unfathomable.

And then it was time for the sermon. Kelly's heart swelled with pride as Luke took to the pulpit, standing tall and steady as he greeted the congregation. "Let's pray," he said, and a hush fell over the room.

"Heavenly Father, we've come tonight to celebrate the greatest gift of all—the gift of Your love and mercy, poured upon us through the touch of your Son. In the midst of the holiday feasts and family gatherings, may we not forget the purpose of Jesus' incarnation, His brief life on earth, and His crucifixion and resurrection. Without

Him, we would have no Christmas. But worse yet, we would have no hope. So lift our eyes tonight and always, to the Giver of the Greatest Gift ever. In the precious name of Jesus, we pray. Amen."

"Amen," echoed the congregation.

"Tonight I've chosen to focus on the wonder of new life. Those of you who are parents know the overwhelming emotions that stir your heart when you first see and hold your new baby. It is an experience that reminds us of the very real presence of God in our lives.

"Many of you know about little Lily, the infant at the Children's Garden Orphanage who needed heart surgery. She had found her way into our hearts and lives, and we were so thankful that you, in this body of believers, rallied to provide funds for her surgery.

"We loved that precious baby and were so eager to share a successful surgery and a healthy outcome with you." He paused and took a deep breath, momentarily making eye contact with Madison. Kelly could see the pain in his expression, and she prayed for him to have strength and peace as he shared.

Clearing his throat and looking around the sanctuary again, he smiled sadly and said, "But God had other plans for Lily. He took her home to spend this Christmas with Jesus."

He looked back at Madison and said, "When I think of Mary, a young mother with a newborn baby, I picture the same love in her eyes that I saw in my wife's eyes whenever she held Lily. There's something about the bond between a woman and the child she holds dear that can give us a new layer of understanding to the Nativity narrative.

"God chose Mary to be that woman for His Son." Glancing around the sanctuary, he smiled and added, "And He's chosen many of you to fulfill that role in the lives of other children—some through birth and some through adoption. He's crafted a woman's heart to have such tenderness and love, that even the youngest, most helpless babe can find security and rest." This time his eyes lit on Kelly, and he gave her a smile that warmed her heart and even made her blush a little.

How often she'd taken her role as a mother for granted. Yet, here was her oldest son communicating with his eyes and a loving smile just how much she meant to him. Again the tears welled in her eyes.

As Luke continued his message about Mary and the special bond she had with Jesus, Kelly glanced over at Madison. She was wiping tears from her own eyes. *She must still be so tender over the loss of Lily. Dear Lord, please comfort her and give her peace.*

The service ended with one of the high school girls singing a solo of the song, "Mary, Did You Know?" As the words spoke of all the awe and heartache that Mary would experience through the life of her Son, Kelly could hear sniffling and see that there wasn't a dry eye in the sanctuary. She squeezed Ben's hand, and he looked over at her, nodded and smiled through tears of his own.

CHAPTER THIRTY-EIGHT

Caleb arose Christmas morning with an empty feeling in the pit of his stomach. Amber and Will had canceled their annual holiday trip to Sandy Cove, and Adam made it clear he was not interested in participating in any of Caleb's family's celebrations. "It's just not my thing," he'd explained. "I've never been much for holidays. But I'm making a New Year's resolution to get to your church," he'd added, giving Caleb a playful shove.

Everyone was so happy to have Madison and Luke home, and now with Luke's dad out of the hospital, Caleb knew there'd be a huge family dinner together that night. He knew he should be in the spirit of things. But ever since he'd started looking for his biological father, he felt a wedge of sorts between himself and his family.

Sighing deeply, he pushed out of bed, half-heartedly pulled up the comforter, and grabbed his jeans from the floor. After he was dressed, he glanced in the mirror to find his hair was shooting out in all directions and his face was looking a little scruffy. "Better shave," he muttered to himself, wanting to avoid the usual comments from Steve. No need to ruffle any feathers today. He'd just force a smile and do his best to get through the day.

As he walked past Maddie's bedroom door, he could hear them getting ready. Picturing Madison married was still a bit of a stretch, but at least she'd chosen well.

Heading down the stairs, he could smell the fragrance of their traditional Christmas coffee cake. In spite of his mood, his stomach responded with a hearty appetite. "Morning, Mom," he said as he walked into the kitchen.

She turned and smiled. "Merry Christmas, honey."

"Yeah. Merry Christmas," he replied, trying to sound upbeat. "Where's Dad?"

"In the study wrapping something," she said.

Caleb smiled and shook his head. "True to form. The Christmas Eve shopper lives on."

Soon the five of them were settled around the breakfast table feasting on egg casserole and coffee cake. It seemed a little weird to have Luke there. Usually, it was the four of them. But hey, Luke was a welcome addition as far as Caleb was concerned. Now there were two of them at the table who had been 'added' to the family, so to speak.

After eating and opening gifts, Madison and Luke headed over to Luke's family's house for their Christmas gift exchange and lunch. Then they'd all congregate together again here for dinner, along with Grandma Sheila and Rick as well as Great Grandma Joan. Caleb knew his mom would be swamped throughout the afternoon preparing food for all those people, and she'd likely recruit his dad to help out.

Perfect opportunity for Caleb to disappear for a while and get a break from his happy façade. He ended up in his room playing video games and taking a snooze.

At five o'clock, the families came together for supper. As they sat down around the enlarged dining room table together, Ben asked to speak for a moment.

"I just want all of you to know how very thankful I am for each and every one of you. This past month has been a real wakeup call for me and a reminder to never take family for granted."

"Amen," Steve replied. "And we're all more than thankful for you and that God has given us more time together." Then he turned to Luke, "Would you do the honors?"

Luke glanced at Madison, sitting beside him, and they exchanged smiles. "I'd be happy to. But first, Maddie and I have an announcement." He stood up and pulled her to her feet, amidst her protests. She was blushing, and Caleb could tell that she was happy but also embarrassed to be the object of everyone's focus.

"We'd like to share with all of you that there'll be an extra place at the table next Christmas," he said, draping his arm over Madison's shoulder and giving her a squeeze.

Everyone's eyes were riveted on Maddie. "So, it turns out I'm pregnant," she said with a grin.

"That's wonderful!" Michelle blurted, jumping to her feet and rushing over to hug Madison.

Soon everyone was surrounding them, hugging and kissing them and sharing their excitement.

The empty feeling from the morning hit Caleb again and pierced his heart. Madison truly belonged to this family, and now so did Luke. And their baby would never know the hollow feeling Caleb was experiencing. He or she would belong to Luke and Maddie in every way.

As Madison turned to face him, Caleb wanted to be happy for her. He forced a smile and fought back his tears. "So what do you think, little brother?" she asked.

"Uh, it's great. Really. I'm totally happy for you," he replied. Reaching over, he gave her a hug. "Be right back," he added as he walked out of the room, leaving behind all the chatter and celebration.

Erick called Luke the next morning. "Chen is really struggling. He's refusing food and keeps asking for you. Do you think you could cut your vacation short and head back? I'm concerned about him."

"How long's this been going on?" Luke asked.

"For the past week. I didn't want to upset your Christmas, so I held off calling. But I think you'd better try to get back."

"Let me talk it over with Madison, and I'll let you know," Luke promised. "It's probably not the best way to tell you this, but we just discovered we're going to have a baby."

"Really? Wow, that's great, Luke. So hey, you guys do what you need to do. Your own family has to come first," he said. "How's your dad doing?"

"Great. He's been home for a few days, and he's starting to get his strength back."

"Well, that's good news," Erick replied.

After they hung up, Luke sat on the bed and thought about Chen. The boy's sweet little face was etched in Luke's memory, and he suddenly felt compelled to go back. But he knew because of Madison's von Willebrand's condition, her pregnancy would be a higher risk one. Plus he felt pressed to help his father with all his responsibilities at church.

Take Caleb and go a voice spoke into his spirit. Caleb? Really? Luke dropped to his knees beside the bed and prayed fervently for wisdom. By the time he arose, his marching orders were clear. He was to return to Children's Garden for a short stay and see what he could do about Chen. And he was to take Caleb along.

The next morning, Caleb was out back shooting hoops when Luke approached him.

"Can I join in?" his brother-in-law asked.

"Sure," Caleb replied, tossing the ball to him.

They played one-on-one for about fifteen minutes. Luke was a pretty good match for him, but Caleb was able to take him with a few extra baskets.

"Guess I need to practice more," Luke said with a grin as he launched the ball back to Caleb. "Hey, can we talk for a minute?" he asked.

"Okay," Caleb replied, resting the ball on his hip. "What's up?"

"Maddie and I have been talking, and we've decided I need to make a trip back to the orphanage. Chen—the kid who kind of adopted us while we were there—isn't doing so well. Plus, I need to talk to Erick about us needing to stay here in the states at least through the pregnancy. With my dad's health issues and Maddie's higher risk pregnancy, we both feel we need to be here in Sandy Cove right now."

Caleb nodded. "Anything you want me to do for you while you're gone?"

Luke looked him in the eye. "Actually, I was wondering if you'd consider going with me."

The idea caught Caleb completely off guard. Why would Luke want him to go along?

Before he could gather his thoughts to answer, Luke added, "I know things have been a little rough here with you and your dad. Maybe it would be good for you to get away for a while."

He *did* have a point there. It would be cool to get out from under his dad's thumb. "What about school?" Caleb asked, knowing his parents would never let him slack off there.

"Yeah, I thought about that. But you're off for winter break now, so the timing might be perfect," Luke replied.

"Yeah, but just for another two weeks."

"So, what if we could be back by then? I'm thinking maybe a week to ten days would be enough time for me to work things out with Erick and help Chen get settled into a routine."

The next thought that popped into Caleb's head was his job. "I'd have to check with work," he said. "But maybe I could get a couple of the other servers to cover. Most of them are off right now, too."

"Okay, what if I talk to your parents about it, and you see what you can do about scheduling people to cover your shifts?" Luke suggested.

Caleb hesitated for a moment. Did he really want to throw away the rest of his vacation to go to some orphanage in China? Plus he'd be losing some income. On the other hand, Luke was right—it would be great to get away. He bounced the ball a few times, and then looked over at his brother-in-law. "Sounds good. If you can get my parents to agree to me going, I'll make some calls, to see who's available to work."

That evening, after discussing his idea with Madison, Luke sat down with Steve and Michelle. He explained his plan to return to the orphanage for a brief stay and proposed his idea of taking Caleb with him.

After he'd assured them that it would be a short visit, and that he'd have Caleb back in time for the end of winter break, Steve asked, "Are you sure you want the responsibility of him along with everything else you'll need to accomplish while you're there?"

"I believe this is what God wants me to do," Luke replied. "And for that reason, I'm not concerned about any added responsibility weighing me down."

"So you've prayed about this?" Michelle asked.

"Yes. In fact, I was praying about the whole trip, when I suddenly felt God put it on my heart to take Caleb along."

"Have you mentioned it to him?" she asked.

"I did. I hope you don't mind, but I wanted to see if he'd even be open to the idea before I approached you," Luke replied. "Of course, I told him you'd have to agree to it."

"How did he respond?" Steve asked.

"At first he was reluctant, but the more we talked about it, the more he seemed interested," Luke said.

"It might be good for him to see a world that's very different from the one he's used to here," Michelle said to Steve. "I mean it's easy to take for granted everything we have. It might open his eyes and make him thankful for what he's got."

"I'm for that," Steve replied. "Lately it's pretty clear there's nothing I can say or do to reach him." He paused and then turned to Luke. "We'll discuss it between the two of us and pray about it. Then we'll give you an answer in the morning. I'm sure you're eager to book your flight."

By morning, Luke had his answer. Caleb would be allowed to go with him. He immediately checked back with his brother-in-law and learned that Caleb found some replacements to cover his work shifts. Within an hour, their tickets were purchased, and the packing began.

CHAPTER THIRTY-NINE

Snow blanketed the city as Luke and Caleb's flight landed in Beijing. Erick met them at the airport, greeting Luke with a warm embrace. "And this must be Madison's brother, Caleb," he said.

"And now my brother, too," Luke added, giving Caleb a pat on the back.

"Hey," Caleb said as he clasped Erick's hand in his.

While Luke and Erick talked in the front seat, Caleb checked out the views of the city and countryside. Everything looked gray and dreary with heavy clouds and dirty snow. *Great. Ten days of gloom.*

Finally approaching the Children's Garden, Caleb was relieved to be finished traveling. He'd been hungry for over an hour but didn't want to say anything to Luke. Taking another swig of water from his bottle, he hoped they'd be eating soon.

The place looked pretty desolate until they entered the recreation center. Children of all ages were occupied in various activities, and a cacophony of noises from their voices and the televisions and toys took a minute to get used to. Then a small boy came barreling their way.

"Mr. Luke! Mr. Luke!" he called as he charged into Luke's arms.

"Chen!" Luke replied, lifting the boy and swinging him in a circle in his arms.

As Chen nestled into Luke's neck and hugged him tightly, Caleb felt awkward and out of place. He'd watched Luke play with his little brothers and sisters, but that seemed perfectly normal. This bond with Chen was different. Something in the boys' eyes haunted Caleb. It was like the joy of a son who'd finally been reunited with his father. The joy Caleb had lost with his own father and had sought with Adam.

Turning to Luke, Erick said softly under his breath, "Amazing. Those are his first words since you left." Then directing his attention to the boy, he said, "We'd better let Mr. Luke get settled back into his residence, Chen," as he tried to peel him out of Luke's arms. But Chen just clung tighter to Luke's neck.

"It's okay, Erick. He can come along," Luke said. "We'll see you at dinner."

"Okay, let me know if you guys need anything. I put some extra blankets in your room. It's been falling below zero at night."

"Thanks," Luke replied. Then turning to Caleb, he added, "This way," as he headed out of another door and into a long hallway.

While Caleb followed, he saw Chen watching him over Luke's shoulder. He gave the boy a half-hearted smile. But Chen just buried his face. Caleb shook his head and looked away. *What am I doing here?*

Once they were inside the residence, Luke sat down on a chair and gently removed Chen's arms from around his neck. As the boy got settled onto his lap, Luke said, "Chen, I want you to meet Caleb."

Chen eyed him warily. "Where Miss Maddie?"

"She couldn't come. This is her brother." Luke explained.

Chen scowled a little at Caleb. "You no go away again, Mr. Luke," he said firmly.

Caleb could see the emotion in Luke's eyes. Leaving again in a week and a half was going to be as difficult for Luke as it was for the boy. *Wish I would have stayed home. I don't need Luke's problems on top of my own.*

Caleb was starving by the time they had dinner. The dining hall was crammed with children and the aides who cared for them. A ringing bell hushed the room, and Erick stood to ask a blessing on their meal. Then serving began.

As Caleb inhaled his food, he listened to Erick and Luke discussing the events of the past few weeks. Chen remained glued to Luke's side, watching his every move as he silently ate.

After dinner, Erick asked Caleb if he'd mind taking Chen back to the residence while he and Luke had a meeting. "Okay," Caleb replied reluctantly. Holding his hand out to the boy, he couldn't help thinking, *Wow, now I'm a babysitter.*

As if reading his thoughts, Chen grasped Luke's hand instead.

"It's okay, Chen," Luke said reassuringly. "You go with Caleb. I'll be there soon."

Chen studied his face with furrowed brow.

"I promise," Luke added.

Shifting his gaze to the floor, Chen slid off of his seat and silently took Caleb's hand. As they walked, Caleb made a stab at a conversation, but Chen was unresponsive. He marched along beside Caleb like a little soldier headed to battle with a determined courage but lacking any joy. *You and me both, kid,* Caleb thought to himself as he escorted the boy back to the room.

Once they were in the residence, Chen released Caleb's hand and went over to a small box of toys in the corner. Pulling them out, he began playing with two trucks, moving them over the wood floor and making engine sounds.

Caleb pulled out his cell phone and checked for messages. He was just getting into a Facebook post when he felt a tap on his shoulder. It was Chen, handing him a fire truck. The boy looked so serious and almost sad that Caleb felt guilty ignoring him. Sighing and putting his phone back in his pocket, he sat on the floor and began making the sounds of a siren, as he drove the truck around in a circle.

Taking the engine from Caleb, the boy imitated what he'd seen. Soon they were taking turns driving the fire engine, while Caleb hoped to himself that Luke would return and take over.

"Are you serious?" Luke asked. "When did this come about?"

"A few days ago, we got the call. She claims she is his father's sister. She and her husband were living in the states, but work has brought them back to Beijing. They just found out about Chen, and she sounds like she's interested in possibly adopting him."

"But they haven't even met him," Luke said.

"True. But they've seen pictures on our website," Erick explained, adding, "They seem like sincere people."

"Are they believers?" Luke asked.

"I don't know. We didn't discuss that. But they're coming out here this week. I wanted you to be here to meet them."

Luke sat back in his chair. "Wow… I guess this could be good," he said adding softly, "all things considered."

Erick nodded. "I know you're pretty attached to Chen, Luke. And he's definitely bonded with you. But your life is taking a new turn now with Madison having a baby. And it sounds like you're going to be needed back in Sandy Cove to help with your father's church, too. This could be the answer for both Chen and you."

Luke looked up at him and nodded. "Yeah," he replied, trying to smile, but his heart felt heavy.

When he got back to the residence, Chen immediately left what he was doing with Caleb and raced into Luke's arms. "Whoa, there," Luke said.

"We've been playing with the trucks," Caleb offered.

"You play, Mr. Luke," Chen added, taking Luke's hand and pulling him along.

Caleb stood and took a seat on the bed, whipping out his phone, and Luke and Chen pushed cars around the small apartment, while Luke tried to imagine Chen living with the other family.

After finally setting his phone aside, Caleb turned to Luke. "You okay?" he asked.

"Yeah. Why?"

"You look like you're upset about something," he replied.

Luke deflected by changing the subject. "Time for this little guy to get ready for bed," he said.

Chen sighed and obediently began collecting the vehicles and putting them away. Luke knew that the next few days would be a challenge as he prepared the boy for a possible adoption that would change his life forever.

Once Chen was settled for the night, Luke turned to Caleb. "I've gotta call Madison. I'll be back in a little while," he added.

"No problem. I'm going to bed myself," Caleb replied. "Been a long day."

Luke walked out into the courtyard. He could see his breath as the cold air nipped at his face. *I need to be alone to talk to her. But where?* Then he remembered the office next to the infirmary. That would be perfect.

Pulling his key ring out of his pocket, he flipped to the correct key and hurried over to unlock the door. It was cold inside, but not as cold as the courtyard. Quickly, Luke cranked up the wall heater a bit and settled down at the desk.

As soon as he heard Madison's voice on the other end, he realized how acutely he needed and wanted her by his side. "Everything okay out there?" she asked.

How should he respond? And why wasn't he happy and hopeful about the possibility that Chen could have a forever family in his near future?

"I miss you," he said, swallowing hard to push down the emotions that threatened to overtake him.

"We miss you, too," she replied.

"We?"

"Me and the little peanut," she said with a sigh.

"But you're feeling okay, right?"

"Yep," she replied. "Good as gold. I saw the doctor today, and she said I'll need to be cautious because of the VWS, but I'm feeling excited and...okay...maybe a little bit nervous, but that's to be expected."

"No morning sickness or anything like that?" he asked, trying to focus on her and the addition of a baby into their lives, while he pushed away thoughts of Chen.

"Not really. A little bit now and then throughout the day when I go too long between eating, but nothing horrible."

"That's great," he replied.

"How's Chen?" she asked, and his emotions surged again. "I'll bet he was happy to see you."

"Yeah. So there's some news about him," he added.

"Really? Tell me."

"Apparently his father had a sister, and she and her husband are coming to meet Chen. They may want to adopt him."

"Seriously? That's great!"

"I guess. In fact, they're coming to meet him in a few days."

"You don't sound happy about that," she commented.

"I'm trying to get used to the idea," he replied. "When I saw Chen…it was like…" Luke sighed and searched for words. "It was like a missing piece was found." He paused and then added, "I can't really explain it, Maddie. There's just something about that little guy…"

The phone line was silent.

"Are you still there?" he asked.

"Yeah. I'm just thinking," she answered. "Luke, I know you and Chen are super close, and I totally get it if you are wanting to bring him home with you."

"But?"

"But it just seems like there are so many changes going on in our lives right now—with the baby, and your dad, and moving back to Sandy Cove."

"Yeah. You're right. It's probably not the best thing for us or Chen," he admitted. "Maybe this other couple is the answer."

"Just see what they are like. Give them a chance, okay? And see how Chen responds to them," she said. "I think you'll be able to tell if it's a good match or not."

"Okay," he replied. "Thanks, babe."

"For?"

"Just for understanding and helping me get some perspective," he said.

"I'll be praying for you to have wisdom and discernment when you meet them," she promised.

Before they hung up, they prayed together for all the orphans at Children's Garden, for God to use this trip in Caleb's life as well as Luke's and Chen's, for Madison and the baby, and for Luke's father.

"I love you, Luke," Madison said after their amens.

"Feeling's mutual," he quipped, his heart a bit lighter after laying their burdens at the feet of Jesus.

CHAPTER FORTY

The next day, Luke introduced Caleb to a group of boys from the four-and-five-year-old class. Although he felt a little awkward at first, Caleb managed to break the ice by offering one boy a piggyback ride around the playroom. Soon they were all begging for a turn. For the first time in quite a while, Caleb felt kind of good about himself. The kids really seemed to like him.

When their break time was over, he noticed one little boy sitting off to the side by himself. When Caleb approached him, the boy fixed his focus on the ground, refusing to make eye contact. Glancing over at Luke, Caleb shrugged his shoulders in a questioning gesture.

"He's new," Erick interjected, walking over to them. "Reminds me of how Chen was when he first arrived and while you were on vacation," he added to Luke.

A teacher's assistant walked over and ushered the boy back to their classroom.

"Man, it must be hard on these kids to suddenly be thrown into a strange place," Caleb commented. "Not that there's anything wrong with Children's Garden," he added hastily.

Erick smiled and nodded, patting Caleb on the back. "We try to make it as easy as possible, but many of our kids come from a place of tragedy and loss," he said. "Like that little guy. He was living with his grandmother, and she passed away last week. A neighbor found him alone in the house with her lifeless body, and brought him here."

Caleb winced. He felt really bad for the little guy. "Tough break," he said. "What happened to his parents?"

"No one knows," Erick replied. "The neighbor said he'd been living with the grandmother since he was a baby."

"So she was all he ever knew," Caleb said. "Too bad." Then he looked Erick squarely in the eye. "How do you do it?" he asked. "I mean doesn't all this get to you after a while?"

Erick nodded. "Sometimes. But there are some good days here, too. Like tomorrow, for instance. One of the little girls in Chen's group is going home to her 'forever family' tomorrow afternoon. They've been working on her adoption for quite some time and have visited her on several trips from the states, so she knows them, and as much as a preschooler can understand, she knows they will be her family soon."

Caleb nodded. "How long has she been here?"

"Two years, right?" Luke asked.

"Uh huh. She was a baby when we got her. Just barely walking," Erick replied.

"So tomorrow they just come and pick her up, and that's it?" Caleb asked.

"Yes and no. First, we will be having a big celebration. There will be banners and balloons, songs and games, and lots of hugs and photos with all of us as well as with her new parents and big sister," Erick replied.

"It's sort of like a birthday party," Luke explained. "It's the beginning of her new life, and we all want to celebrate with her."

Caleb nodded. "Cool," he said. Doubt if there was a big celebration when I was adopted.

As they were walking through the courtyard a few minutes later, Caleb spotted an older boy bouncing a basketball over by a hoop. He was all alone and looked pretty bummed.

Erick broke into Caleb's thoughts. "That's Tan. He's had a rough week."

"No luck, huh?" Luke asked.

Erick shook his head. "His birthday was yesterday."

"Tan just turned fourteen, Caleb," Luke explained. "Chinese adoption policy states that he is no longer eligible for adoption."

"What?" Caleb asked. "You mean he can never get out of here?"

"Nope," Erick replied. "He's a great kid, too. It's a real shame. He's been here for seven years. But finding homes for the older kids is more difficult, and we've had plenty of youngsters under five that are available, so most couples gravitate to them."

"Does he have any friends here?" Caleb asked. "I mean anyone else who's too old to be adopted?"

"There's another boy with Down Syndrome. But they don't spend much time together because he prefers the younger boys who are more at his developmental level," Erick explained. "He had a younger sister here, but she was adopted last year. His best buddy was a couple of years younger than Tan, but he was adopted two months ago."

"Wow. That's a bummer," Caleb replied.

"Why don't you go shoot some hoops with him, Caleb," Luke suggested. "He could use a friend right about now."

Although he felt awkward, Caleb nodded and walked over to the boy. "Hi," he said, lifting his hand in greeting. "Wanna shoot hoops together?"

It was clear that Tan didn't know much English. Caleb gestured to the ball and then to himself and Tan, throwing an imaginary ball toward the hoop.

Tan's face lit up a bit, and he nodded. Bouncing the ball toward Caleb, the two boys began interacting through the game.

"We'll be in the infirmary," Erick called out to Caleb. "Take your time."

Caleb waved without taking his eye off of Tan or the ball. "See you in a while."

Tan was quite a good shooter, and Caleb had a great time on the court with him. By the time they wrapped up their game for lunch, Tan was relaxed and smiling. Although they couldn't communicate much through words, Caleb could see that Tan was thankful for their time together.

That evening, after Chen was settled for the night, Caleb turned to Luke and said, "Don't you wonder where God is sometimes? I mean, look at all these kids here. None of them have families. It doesn't seem right. Sure some of them may get adopted, but they'll never know their real parents." He paused and then added, "And Tan—he seems like such a nice guy. What will happen to him?"

"He'll stay here through school. Then Erick, or whoever is running the orphanage at that time, will try to help him find a job. But he'll be on his own from about your age on. He won't have a family to turn to when he needs something. No holiday gatherings or anything like that."

Caleb shook his head. "It's a rotten deal."

Luke put his hand on Caleb's shoulder. "It would be great if we could place all of them. But sometimes it doesn't work out."

302

Caleb nodded and sank into a chair. "You know something, Luke? I wish, in a way, that I'd never even found out I was adopted. It's messed with my mind lately—all the stuff about Adam."

Luke, who was now sitting across the table from him, leaned in. "I can imagine. The other day, I was wondering what I would think and feel if I found out my parents had adopted me. I honestly tried to put myself in your shoes, and I think I probably would have done the same thing you did—I mean trying to find Adam. I'd definitely be curious about what my biological parents were like."

"So you get it?" Caleb asked.

"Yeah," Luke replied. "I mean, I think everybody pretty much gets it, Caleb. It's just that none of us, especially your parents, wants you to get hurt." He paused and seemed to be choosing his words carefully. "I know you're already aware of this, but there's a lot more to being a dad than...well..."

"Than getting someone pregnant?" Caleb said.

"Right," Luke said. "Just look at Steve or my dad. They've invested their lives in us. I'm talking about a lot more than money here. I've seen my father wrestle in prayer late at night for one of us. Or attend countless games even when he's exhausted. I'm sure you have, too."

Caleb hesitated and then nodded. "Yeah, I guess."

"Being a real father is a lifelong commitment, one that I'm trying to wrap my head around, now that Madison and I are expecting. Sometimes it scares me a little," he admitted.

"Really? You? I think you'll be a great dad. You've had plenty of experience with kids," Caleb said, referring to all of Luke's younger siblings. "Besides, you and Madison are ready."

"I'm not sure anyone's ever completely ready," Luke replied. "But the thing is that no one *has* or *is* the perfect dad, Caleb. As much as any of us try, we're all going to fail at times along the way."

Caleb nodded. "Some more than others," he muttered. Then he flashed for a moment on Tan and felt a little bad. Still, even though his father had given him a home, he'd also made it pretty uncomfortable living there sometimes.

"Caleb, you need to cut your dad some slack," Luke said. "He loves you, and he's doing the best he can."

"Right."

"You don't think so?" Luke asked.

"I think he used to," Caleb replied, thinking back to his childhood and all the good times he and his dad had shared. "But now, I'm not so sure."

"Why do you say that?"

Caleb stared at the floor. "Because he's changed."

Luke paused and then replied, "Ever thought about the possibility that you may have changed, too?"

Looking up, Caleb locked eyes with him. "How do you mean?"

"I mean in the way you treat him," Luke replied, "and in some of the choices you've made."

Caleb shrugged, feeling defensive. "Like what?"

"Like school stuff, the tickets, tracking down Adam," Luke replied. "You've gotta know that's all been on your dad's mind."

"I guess." Caleb could feel himself pulling back a little.

As if sensing his withdrawal, Luke said, "Part of that's normal stuff, bro. I mean I had my share of bad choices in high school. And my dad blew his stack a few times, too."

Caleb tried to picture it, but he wasn't convinced. There was a definite difference between him and Luke. "At least you knew he was your real father."

Luke paused. "In the physical sense, yes. But truthfully, the way I see it, Caleb, the main question all of us need to keep asking ourselves, whether we are adopted or live with our biological parents or are orphans like Tan, is this—who's our real Father?"

Caleb studied his face. What was he talking about?

"Your dad's not perfect. Neither is mine. But we both know we have a heavenly Father who is. You might look around here and think that God's missing in this picture at Children's Garden. And in a way, I get that. It's a bummer these kids were separated from their families. But trust me, Caleb, God's doing some amazing things in their lives."

"Like?"

"Like putting them into new families that will give them opportunities they would never have had, as well as a chance to know God personally."

"And Tan?" Caleb asked.

"I don't know what God will do for Tan, Caleb. None of us do. But we're called to live by faith and to stand on God's promises and trust in His character. Whatever His plan is for Tan, I believe it will be a good one, and that someday Tan's testimony will include the love and care he was shown here at Children's Garden."

Caleb nodded. He could see Luke's point. Even in his own life, he knew deep down inside that his mom and dad had given him a life that Adam and Amber never could have. Growing up, he'd believed that God had a part in that. But lately, with all the hassles from his dad and the rejection from Adam, it seemed like God wasn't even around.

As he thought about all of it, Caleb's eyes began to fill. He yearned to be close to God again and to put aside his animosity toward his dad. But how? It seemed like at every turn he made the wrong move. And now that Adam was part of his life, would things ever be the same?

Fighting back his emotions, he turned away and stood up. Then clearing his throat, he said, "Thanks for the talk, Luke. Think I'll go to bed."

That night, Caleb dreamed about his dad. A smattering of images from his childhood were woven through the dream. In each scene his dad seemed to further away. Or was it Caleb who was pulling back? At one point, he saw himself as a little boy alone in a room. A man came in and said someone was there to take him home. In walked Adam. He grabbed Caleb and pulled him out the door.

Caleb awoke in a sweat. It was still dark outside, but he slipped out of bed, pulled on his jeans and a sweatshirt, and left the residence. He found a bench in the hallway that led to the recreation room and sat down to get his bearings. Anxiety, confusion, and a sense of desperation gripped him.

In the quiet of the hallway, with his heart pounding in his chest, he began to pray, begging God to calm the storm that was raging inside. As he prayed, the images of his dream and the sad face of Tan kept replaying in his mind, and he found himself yearning for hope and for his dad—the man who had invested a lifetime raising him. *Will it ever be right again between us?* He wondered.

Pouring himself out in prayer, he began to sense something he'd missed for a long time—the very real presence of God. It was something he'd often felt as a child but had lost somehow this year. Then a verse from scripture popped into his mind.

I will never leave you nor forsake you.

Tears fell as Caleb yielded to the love of his heavenly Father. He didn't know how long he sat there, but eventually, a peace settled over him. Then Caleb's prayers shifted from himself to his dad as he asked God to somehow rebuild the bridge between them. And he prayed for Adam—that one day his biological father would know the love of God as well.

Finally, Caleb pled for Tan, someone he'd only known for one day, but whose life had permanently affected Caleb's perspective. As he interceded for the teen, a voice spoke into his spirit—*I have a plan for you. A plan to impact lives like Tan's.* And in that moment, Caleb realized that his trip to China was just the beginning of his life's call. Although he didn't know all the details, he knew he would never be the same.

As the sun began to rise, Caleb snuck back into the residence and stretched out on his bed, slipping into a deep and dreamless sleep.

He awoke to the sound of Chen playing and chattering with Luke, who was trying to shush him. "Shhh…Caleb is sleeping," his brother-in-law said in a whisper.

Sitting up, Caleb said, "It's okay, Luke. I'm awake."

After he had greeted little Chen, Caleb locked eyes with Luke for a minute.

"What?" Luke asked with a nervous smile.

"Thanks," he began. "Thanks for bringing me here."

"Sure. Thanks for coming." Luke replied.

Then watching Luke get Chen ready for breakfast, Caleb noticed the tenderness in his brother-in-law. He was going to make a great dad. "You're a pretty cool brother, you know that?" he said, relaxing into a smile. "I'm glad Maddie chose you and not some jerk."

Laughing, Luke replied, "Thanks. Me, too."

The adoption celebration went well the following day, and little Sun Li was exhausted but smiling as her new parents led her out of the dining hall to leave Children's Garden behind and begin her new life. "Tomorrow, Chen's aunt and uncle will be here in the morning," Erick said. "Perhaps we'll be planning another celebration soon."

Luke nodded.

As if on cue, Chen piped up, "Chen with Mr. Luke. Yes?"

Wisely, Luke turned the question to the immediate, replying, "Yes, Chen, tonight you stay with Caleb and me." Then, taking the boy's hand, he led him back to the residence.

After breakfast the next morning, Cami and Kai Thâm showed up at Erick's office, ready to meet Chen, with a wrapped gift in Cami's hand for the boy. Luke was waiting with Erick, and after the introductions had gone full circle, he said, "I'll go get Chen. He's playing in the recreation room with Caleb."

As he walked the boy back to the office, he reminded Chen of their conversation earlier that morning. "Your aunt and uncle are excited to meet you," he said, hoping his voice sounded upbeat and would put Chen's mind at ease.

"Mr. Luke stay with Chen," the boy replied adamantly, squeezing Luke's hand tightly.

"Yes, I will stay," Luke replied, glancing over at Caleb, who's face mirrored the worry Luke felt in his heart.

The initial introductions found Chen staring at his feet. "Can you say 'hello' to your visitors, Chen?" Erick asked.

Without a glance, Chen muttered, "Hello," but kept a death grip on Luke.

"Luke and Caleb are going to sit right over there," Erick said, pointing to a bench along the wall, "while we get to know your aunt and uncle."

Chen looked in the direction Erick was pointing, and then up at Luke.

"It's okay, Chen. I'm not leaving," Luke reassured the boy.

Reluctantly, Chen released his hand, and Luke and Caleb walked over and sat down.

"We are so happy to meet you," Cami said with a smile. Luke could see that she was nervous, and her husband seemed a bit guarded. "Would you like to come over and sit with us?" she asked, gesturing to the chairs that had been set up in a circle.

Chen obediently walked over and sat down between Erick and Cami. He seemed a bit scared of Kai.

As Cami tried to engage Chen in conversation, he limited his answers to one-word responses. Kai crossed his arms and sat back in his chair with a skeptical expression on his face. Cami glanced over and silently pled with her eyes, but Kai remained stiff as a statue.

"Would you like to show us around where you live and play, Chen?" Cami asked.

Chen looked at Luke. "Mr. Luke come?" he asked.

Luke glanced at Erick, who said, "Mr. Luke has some work to do. I'll go with you," he offered.

"No Mr. Luke, no Chen," the boy replied firmly.

Luke took a deep breath and was about to say something when Cami changed the subject. "Would you like to see what we brought you?" she asked, indicating the wrapped package.

Chen looked at Luke for approval and then nodded.

"Here. Open it," Cami said, handing him the small box.

Chen carefully unwrapped it and removed the lid. Then he lifted out a little statue.

"Do you know who that is?" Cami asked.

He shook his head.

"That is Buddha," she replied. "Do you see his big belly?"

Chen nodded.

"You can rub that for good luck," she instructed with a smile as she leaned over and demonstrated.

Chen stood and carried the statue to Luke, extending his hand to show it to him.

Luke looked in the boy's eyes. He seemed to be waiting for Luke's approval. *What do I say, Lord? How do I show respect here without sending the wrong message?* Clearly, Cami and Kai were not Christians. Their intention would be to raise Chen in the faith of so many Chinese—Buddhism.

"It was very nice of your aunt and uncle to bring you a gift, Chen," Luke said. He gave the boy a warm smile.

"Buddha is very special to us," Kai interjected firmly. "We can teach you about him and how to pray to him, Chen."

Now Chen looked very confused. Luke wanted to sweep him into his arms and carry him out of the room. He glanced over at Erick, who cleared his throat and said, "How about if we get on with showing Miss Cami and Mr. Kai around Children's Garden?" he asked Chen.

"Here," Cami said, handing Chen the box. "You can keep him in here for now."

Chen dutifully placed the Buddha statue back into the box.

"We'll be coming back here," Erick said. "You can leave the box on the table."

As they stood, Cami rested her hand on Chen's shoulder. The boy jerked away a bit and took Erick's hand, looking forlornly over his shoulder at Luke as they walked out of the room.

Once they were gone, Caleb turned to Luke. "A Buddha? Really?"

"It's understandable," Luke replied. "And Buddhism was likely the religion of Chen's biological parents," he added.

Caleb shook his head. "No way can you let that little guy grow up thinking that rubbing that statue's belly or praying to it will bring him answers."

Luke slumped into his seat. "I know. I'm just not sure I have a choice here."

CHAPTER FORTY-ONE

Luke gazed at Madison's face on the screen of his laptop. He wasn't sure if Skype was a blessing or a curse. Her smile lifted his spirits, but more than anything else, seeing her made him want to be home by her side.

"You look troubled, babe," she said.

He took a deep breath and forced a smile. "I'm fine."

"No you're not. What is it? Is Chen okay?" she asked.

What do I say, Lord? Luke cleared his throat, stalling for wisdom.

"Hey, tell me," she pressed.

Luke looked into her eyes. She'd been through a lot lately with the death of Lily and now an unexpected pregnancy. He didn't want to put anything else onto his bride.

As if she could read his mind, Madison said, "Whatever it is, I can take it." She locked eyes with him and asked, "Are you wanting to stay at Children's Garden? Because if you are, I understand. And I'll be okay. Really."

He smiled. "No, honey. It's not that."

"Then what is it? Is Caleb okay?"

"He's fine. In fact, we had a really good talk. This trip has been an eye-opener for your brother. I can see God really using it," Luke replied, happy to change the subject.

"That's great. I've been praying for him. He's been in such a funk for a long time."

"Well, I'd say your prayers are being answered," Luke said.

"So back to what we were saying. Is this about Chen's meeting with his aunt and uncle? Is that why you're looking so troubled?"

Luke smiled. "You can read me like a book," he said.

"What happened? Did Chen like them?"

"Not exactly. The aunt—Cami is her name—was nice, but her husband was really stoic. I could tell Chen was uncomfortable with him."

"It'll take him time to get used to someone new," she said. "Especially after bonding so well with you."

Luke nodded. "So, Cami brought him a gift," he said, Madison's eyebrows lifted questioningly.

"It was a statue of Buddha. She told him he could rub the statue's belly for good luck and pray to it."

Her face fell. "Really? Wow."

"Yeah. Wow."

"So what are you going to do?" she asked.

"What *can* I do?"

"Talk to Erick," she suggested.

"And say?"

"And say that Chen already believes in Jesus—that we've talked to him and prayed with him," she replied.

"But if they decide to adopt him, it's Erick's responsibility to help Chen have a family of his own," Luke countered. "And that family will determine the faith under which they want to raise him."

Madison's face revealed her frustration. "We've got to really step up prayers for him," she said.

"I agree."

"God will work this out, Luke. I just know it. And if you need to stay longer, just put Caleb on his flight back and stay as long as you need to. I'm serious. Mom and Dad are taking good care of me and the baby. We'll be fine."

"Okay," he replied hesitantly.

"Promise?" she asked.

"Promise."

Luke fell asleep that night interceding on Chen's behalf, knowing that his very soul was at stake. He awoke in the predawn darkness to a strange pounding sound. Flipping on a lamp, he could see Chen convulsing in his bed. "Caleb! Wake up!" he said.

"What? What's wrong?" Caleb asked, as he sat up from a deep sleep.

"Get Erick. Tell him to call the doctor," Luke ordered as he scooped Chen's quaking body into his arms. Wrapping a blanket around the boy, he headed for the infirmary.

By the time Erick arrived, Chen had stopped seizing. "Dr. Su is on the way," he told Luke.

"Is there anything I can do?" Caleb asked.

Luke glanced at his watch. It was about noon in Sandy Cove. "Would you call Madison?" he asked. "Tell her Chen had a seizure and we're waiting for the doctor. She'll want to know so she can pray for him. Oh, and have her call the church office and put him on the prayer chain."

"Will do," Caleb replied, heading out the door to go back to the residence and phone his sister.

Chen was awake but a bit delirious. Burying his head into Luke's chest, he curled into a ball, and Luke held him close. Soon Dr. Su arrived and examined the boy. "He has a bit of a fever, but not enough to explain a seizure like that," he said. "We'll need to keep him under surveillance for the next twenty-four hours. If it doesn't recur, it may be an isolated incident. Either way, we should run some tests. I'll set up an EEG for tomorrow."

After the doctor left, Luke held Chen in his arms until well after sun up. He seemed to be sleeping deeply with the exception of one incident where he pushed away and muttered, "Chen no go."

Once the nurse and Dr. Su arrived to run their tests, Luke took the opportunity to call Madison.

"Luke, how is he? I've been praying like crazy. We all have," she said.

"He's okay right now. The doctor and nurse are doing an EEG and running some tests," he replied.

"Oh, I wish I was there!" she said with a moan. "The poor thing. How long did the seizure last?"

"About five minutes," he said. "It seemed like forever, though."

"Yeah, I'll bet you were pretty scared."

"It all happened so fast. We were sleeping, and all of a sudden a strange noise woke me up. Chen was really thrashing in his bed," he said, adding, "It's a good thing he didn't fall out."

"Yeah. Then he could have other injuries as well," she agreed.

A knock on Luke's door interrupted their conversation. "The doctor has an update for us," Erick said as he popped his head into the room.

"I've gotta go, Maddie. Dr. Su wants to talk to us."

"Can you ask him to call me?" she asked.

"Yeah. I'm sure he'll be glad to talk to you again anyway. Everyone misses you here," he added before they said goodbye.

Chen was sleeping peacefully as they entered the infirmary. The doctor led them into his side office and gestured to the seats facing his desk. After they were settled, he began, "Chen's EEG is showing some mild abnormalities. We've contacted his aunt to find out if there is a family history of epilepsy, but she is unaware of any. And although Chen had a slight fever, it was pretty low to trigger a grand mal seizure. I'd like to run a CT scan to check for abnormal masses or lesions, but my initial inclination is that this will either be an isolated incident or possibly the beginning of idiopathic seizure disorder. Most children outgrow that in adolescence, although not all of them."

"What can we do to facilitate the CT scan?" Erick asked.

"I'll put through an order at the hospital. We should be able to get it approved, but the government is known for dragging its heels with these kids," he said, indicating the orphan status of Chen.

"What if I took him back to the states?" Luke asked. "Is there any way to arrange that? Then we could have him evaluated by a pediatric neurologist. I'm sure the church would help with the funding."

Erick sat back in his chair and pressed his fingertips together. "It's not impossible, but it would require a lot of red tape."

"Or," Dr. Su inserted, "if Chen's relatives decide to adopt him, they could seek the medical care he needs."

Erick glanced at Luke and stood up. "Thanks so much, doctor. And thanks for the middle-of-the-night house call," he added.

As the three men stood and shook hands, Luke remembered Madison's request. "Doctor, would you mind calling my wife? She'd really like to discuss Chen's condition with you."

The doctor glanced at Erick, who nodded affirmatively. "She's still considered one of the staff for now," he said.

"Of course," Dr. Su replied, taking down her number.

Two days later, Chen had another seizure, this time on the playground. He fell and bumped his head and bruised his body in the process. Whisked back to the infirmary, Luke paced the floor with Caleb as they awaited the doctor's evaluation.

"I'm going to try to push through his CT scan," he told them. "In the meantime, I'm placing Chen on a mild anti-seizure medication, and he'll need to be watched carefully. He was on a soft surface on the playground this time, but he could get hurt even worse if he falls to the ground in the courtyard or on some other hard surface."

When Erick called to report the second seizure to Chen's aunt and uncle, Kai came onto the phone and told Erick they were sorry to hear about the boy but would no longer be able to consider adopting him. "We are not prepared to take on the responsibility of a child with such an impairment," he stated in no uncertain terms. "We wish the boy the best, and we're happy he's in a place where he can get the help he needs."

"I understand," Erick replied, and a sense of relief washed over him.

"They what?" Luke asked.

"They withdrew their adoption application," Erick said. "They claim they're 'not prepared to take on the responsibility of a child with an impairment' or something along those lines."

"Wow. Good thing we found out now rather than later."

"Yep," Erick agreed. "So you and Caleb are scheduled to leave in a few more days. We'll need to start preparing Chen for the transition."

Luke's heart sank as he thought about everything Chen was going through. How could he leave the boy right now? "Let me talk to Madison," he said. "I may stay longer."

Erick nodded. "I was hoping you'd say that," he replied.

"Any news on the scan?" Luke asked.

"Not yet. Dr. Su says it could take weeks or even months to get the approval."

As Chen slept that night, Luke stayed close by, watching his rhythmic breathing and praying for an answer. How could a man feel so tethered to two homes across the globe from each other? And how was he going to ever leave Chen behind?

"I'm going to hit the sack," Caleb said, collapsing onto the couch. "See you in the morning."

Luke nodded. "Thanks for all your help today," he said.

"No problem. I'm glad Chen's doing okay tonight," Caleb replied.

After Caleb was out, Luke fell to his knees beside his bed, bent over the mattress with his hands clasped tightly together, and silently prayed. *Lord, show me what to do. I feel like I have two callings that are as far apart as possible. I know Madison and our baby are my first and foremost responsibility. But Chen...oh, Lord, he's so fragile and so dependent on me. Please help me know what to do.*

Finally, he got into bed. Drifting off to sleep, he dreamed of Chen blocking the door so he couldn't leave. "No go, Mr. Luke," the child's voice echoed in his mind.

Luke awoke to a gentle nudge on his shoulder. It was still dark but he could see Chen standing beside his bed. The boy patted his own chest and then the mattress beside Luke.

"Sure, buddy, hop in," Luke said, scooting over so Chen could stretch out beside him. Luke draped his arm over the boy's tiny frame, nestled under the covers beside him, and they drifted off to sleep once more.

A buzzing sound awakened Luke the following morning. It was his cell phone vibrating on the bed beside him. Carefully easing out of bed without waking Chen, he padded into the bathroom and answered the call.

"Madison," he said softly. "Is everything okay?"

"Yeah. Did I wake you?" she asked.

"No…well…yes, but it's okay."

"You sound so quiet," she observed. "Everyone else still sleeping?"

"Yeah. In fact, Chen ended up climbing into bed with me sometime during the night. Poor guy is pretty scared these days."

"Awww. He needed his baba," she said, using the Chinese term of affection for a father.

An arrow pierced Luke's heart. He loved that little boy so much that it hurt.

"Luke, are you there?" Madison asked.

"Yeah." He wanted so badly to talk to Madison in person. He needed to see her and hold her and get his bearings.

"Honey, listen to me. I've been really thinking about Chen a lot. And I've been praying about what we should do," she said. "He needs us, Luke. He really does. And I think we need him, too."

"What do you mean?" Luke asked, a flicker of hope stirring within.

"I mean, let's face it. Chen's already part of us. He's been a member of our family ever since he moved into the residence there. I just don't see how you can come home and leave him behind." She paused for a moment, as if to let her words sink in, and then she said, "I want to adopt him, Luke. We need to do this."

"But the timing, babe, with you pregnant and all the stuff going on with my dad and church. Are you sure you're up to such a huge commitment and all that it entails?" he asked, trying to be realistic.

"Who better than us? We've already made room for him in our hearts. Why not in our home?" she asked. "There would be a hole in our family without him. We both know that."

Luke was silent, letting the whole idea sink into his heart and mind.

"You're the one who always says God will equip us for what's ahead, right?" she challenged him.

"Yeah, that's right," he admitted. "I just don't want to see you overloaded, especially since you have a higher risk pregnancy."

"If you think for one minute your family or mine are going to let that happen, you're crazy. Besides, we have our church, too. There are so many people in our lives to help us out, honey. But Chen…he only has us, when it gets right down to it. I mean, I know everyone there would do their best to take care of him. But we could do better. Between my experience in pediatric nursing and your calling as a pastor, we can meet his physical and spiritual needs right here in Sandy Cove."

"Wow. You're something else. You know that?" Luke said, his voice full of love and affection. "Chen and I are pretty blessed to have you."

"And don't ever forget that either," she added with a laugh. "Talk to Erick, honey," she added. "Do it this morning. And then let me know what I need to do on this end to get the ball rolling on making Chen an official Johnson."

When Luke told Erick about their decision, he was noticeably relieved. "I've been praying God would open that door for you," he said. They sat down together and began going over all the steps Luke and Madison would need to follow to process Chen's adoption. "Because of the medical situation, I think we can expedite things on this end," he said. "So the sooner you can set up your home visits back in Sandy Cove, the better."

Next Luke shared his news with Caleb. "So what do you think?" he asked.

Smiling, Caleb replied, "I think Chen just scored a homerun!"

"You know something," Luke added, "I'm really glad Chen will have you for his uncle. God may give you two a special bond and use your adoption as something that really blesses Chen's life, Caleb."

Caleb looked pleased. "Yeah. That would be cool. And maybe I can keep him from making some of the same mistakes I did," he added with a note of regret.

"God's got some great plans for you, Caleb. I can just feel it," Luke replied.

CHAPTER FORTY-TWO

Once Chen understood that he would be going to live with Luke and Madison soon, he came to terms with Luke accompanying Caleb back to Sandy Cove. With the knowledge that the boy's adoption could be expedited and completed within a couple of months after they completed a home study with a social worker in Sandy Cove, Luke and Maddie had to quickly do some house hunting.

The Frasers, an older couple from their church had two residences on their property, and they offered the main house as a rental for the family. With their kids grown and moved away, they had decided to live in the granny unit and use the front residence as an income property. Having moved out the prior month, it seemed as if God had prepared the place just for Luke and Madison.

The address was on a quiet cul-de-sac a few miles from Michelle and Steve's home. "You'll be able to use the yard as well," the owners explained. "We have a little patio off the back of our unit, and that's all the outdoor space we need."

"It's perfect," Madison said, as they walked through the house. "With three bedrooms and a den, Chen will have his own room, and so will the baby. The den can be your office," she added with a smile.

"How soon could we move in?" Luke asked.

"As soon as you'd like," Ted Fraser said.

Within a week, they'd gathered together enough second-hand furniture and family donations to make the house their home. And although it was a bit sparse, the social worker approved the space.

"You know that I was instrumental in your brother's adoption, right?" Bonnie Blackwell asked Madison.

She nodded. "Yes, my mom told me all about how you helped her with Amber."

"Your mom is an exceptional person, and I'm so glad she and your father decided to adopt Caleb. From what I hear, he's turned out to be a great young man."

"He has," Luke piped in. "And I think he'll make the perfect uncle for Chen."

Smiling, Bonnie nodded in agreement.

As they wrapped up their visit, she explained the steps she'd follow to communicate their home study to Erick at the Children's Garden. "He'll have everything he needs by tomorrow afternoon," she said.

Six weeks later, Luke and Madison were on their way to China to finish the last of the paperwork and bring Chen home.

After Steve dropped his daughter and son-in-law off at the airport, he came home to find Caleb waiting for him.

"Dad, can we talk?" he asked.

Steve nodded. "Sure, son." He gestured to the empty couch and the two of them sat down, one at each end.

"Pretty exciting about Chen, huh?" Caleb said. "You should have seen his face when Luke told him he'd be coming to live with him here."

"I'm glad you got to see that," Steve remarked. *Hope that doesn't bring a defensive reaction. I've gotta watch what I say with him.* But the expression on Caleb's face was anything but defensive. In fact, he looked pretty nervous and vulnerable.

"So, while I was in China with Luke, I realized how great I've had it here, with you and Mom, I mean. I know I've made it hard for you guys with all the Adam stuff. But it was something I just felt like I had to do," he explained, looking at Steve earnestly. "Anyway, I wanted to say that I'm sorry for causing you any grief in the process."

Steve smiled and reached over and patted his knee. "Apology accepted," he said. "Besides, it was never about my feelings. All of my concerns were about you and yours." He paused and then added, "I know I haven't been a perfect father, Caleb. And if I could go back in time, I'd do some things very differently. But I've never intentionally hurt you, and I didn't want to see Adam do that."

Caleb nodded, and the two of them sat silently for a moment. "You know, Luke and I had a really good talk one night at the orphanage."

"Oh, yeah?"

"We were talking about dads and what it means to be a dad."

Steve leaned in closer. "I'll bet that's on Luke's mind a lot now, what with adopting Chen and he and Madison having a baby, too."

"Yeah. He was saying the same stuff like you were—about not being able to be a perfect dad."

"I have a feeling Luke will be a great father," Steve said.

"Me, too," Caleb replied. "But he made a good point of talking about how God is the only perfect Father."

Steve could see how much that truth was sinking into his son's mind and spirit. Then Steve felt God nudge him to share the first moment Caleb had taken a hold of his heart. "I want to tell you something, Caleb. Something I've wanted to share with you ever since we told you that you were adopted. But the timing never felt right."

This time it was Caleb who leaned in. "Yeah?"

"Yeah. It's partly about you and me, but it's also about me and God," Steve began. He leaned back on the arm of the couch and looked away for a moment, searching for just the right words. The scene he wanted to share was clear in his mind, but he needed to communicate it in a way that Caleb would fully grasp.

"So, here's the thing. When your mom first told me about Amber and her pregnancy, I thought about what a shame it was. Then, when she told me that Amber wanted us to adopt you, a list of reservations immediately formed in my mind. Wouldn't this get pretty messy with Amber knowing us personally? Could I love you with the same kind of love that I had for Madison? And finally, how would your mother take it if Amber changed her mind?

"We've never shared this with you or with Madison, but Maddie was a miracle baby, Caleb. There were some medical issues on my part that made it nearly impossible for us to have kids. In fact, we almost adopted another little baby that we'd planned to name Caleb."

"Really?"

"Yep. We had the nursery all set up and everything. Your mother was walking on air. And then we got the call that the birth mother changed her mind."

"Bummer," Caleb said.

"It was really tough. But then we did artificial insemination, and your sister was conceived. There was a slight chance that she'd be biologically mine. But the likelihood was slim."

Caleb's eyebrows rose. "Wow."

"I really wrestled with it more than I thought I would, to be honest with you. And by the time she was born, I just had to know for certain one way or the other."

"Kind of like how I needed to know about Adam," Caleb interjected.

That caught Steve off guard. He paused for a second and then replied. "Yeah. Kind of like that."

"So what did you do?" his son asked.

"I did a DNA paternity test, much to your mother's chagrin," Steve replied. "But before I could even get the results, I had a talk with your Great Grandpa Phil, and he gave me a totally different perspective on Madison and the whole biological father thing."

"Really? What did he say?"

"He reminded me of something really important in the Bible—that Joseph wasn't Jesus' biological father, and yet he played an important role in Jesus' life as Mary's husband and Jesus' dad."

"Oh yeah. I never really thought about that," Caleb said with a grin.

"Me neither," Steve replied. "So anyway, before we even opened the lab results on the DNA test, I realized that I'd still be Maddie's dad either way."

"So are you?" Caleb asked. "I mean are you her biological father?"

"Actually, yes. I am. Like I said, it was a miracle. But God didn't allow me to find that out until I was already at peace about the alternative."

"Did you think about that when you were considering adopting me?"

"I did. But I'll tell you something, Caleb, God taught me something even more important through my becoming your father." Steve looked deeply into Caleb's eyes before he continued. In an instant he was transported back in time to the first time he'd been alone with that tiny baby boy in his arms.

"The first two weeks after we brought you home from the hospital were a blur, just like when Madison was a newborn, only more so. Now, we not only had a tiny baby keeping us up on and off all night, but we also had a little girl who needed our attention throughout the day."

Caleb grinned nervously. "Sorry about that, Dad."

Steve smiled in return. "Anyway, after a couple of weeks, your mom wanted to go to school for her eighth graders' graduation ceremony. And she left you with me.

"You were a little fussy that day, and I ended up in the rocking chair with you, trying to get you to settle down and fall asleep. Finally, you stopped crying and looked up at me with the biggest eyes as if you were studying my face. Your body relaxed into my arms and a wave of love came over me. It was so powerful. I'll never forget that moment. It was when I knew that you were mine, and that I was yours," Steve said, his voice shaking a bit as he tried to compose himself.

Caleb's eyes filled with tears. But he didn't say anything. He just watched as Steve took a deep breath and continued.

"God spoke to me in that moment, son. It wasn't audible, but it was clear as clear can be. 'That love you feel is the same love I have for you,' He explained. 'And although you are *adopted* into My family, My love for you is as deep as the love I have for My only begotten Son. Always remember that, above all else."

Now both men's eyes were brimming with tears.

"So, you see, Caleb, God has used the gift of our adoption of *you* to help *me* understand the amazing gift of His love. Although I was a believer for a number of years before you came into our lives, I never completely grasped the heart of God and the depth of His vast and endless love for me until that moment with you in my arms."

Caleb's heart swelled in his chest with a renewed feeling of deep connection with his dad. And then he considered what kind of life lessons he might be hearing tonight if he were being raised by Adam, instead, who'd only been a teen in high school when Caleb was born.

In that moment, Caleb realized that God had provided a much better dad than the one through whom Amber had conceived. And as an image of Tan swept through his mind, he also realized how very much he had to be thankful for. Turning to face Steve, tears threatening to embarrass him, he reached out and welcomed his dad's embrace. "I love you, Dad," he said.

"I love you, too, son," Steve replied, as they clung tightly to each other.

Later that night, as a storm brought wind and rain to Sandy Cove, Caleb fell to his knees beside his bed and prayed to his heavenly Father in ways he'd never done before, thanking Him for the parents who'd raised him and for Amber's courage to give him up at birth. And once again, he prayed for Adam—that he would one day come to know God himself. Before ending his prayer, he also asked God to watch over Tan. *Show me how I can help kids like him someday,* he prayed in earnest.

And then a scripture his mom had shared with him many times popped into his mind. "For I know the plans I have for you," declares the Lord. "plans to prosper you and not to harm you, plans to give you hope and a future."

The next day, after the storm had subsided, Michelle ran to the market for her grandmother. As she was unloading the groceries at Gram's house, she was able to share Steve's conversation with Caleb from the night before.

"I'd almost forgotten about Grandpa's conversation with Steve," Michelle remarked.

Joan smiled and nodded. "Your grandpa was a smart fellow. He sure did know how to bring the Bible right into our lives." She stared off into space for a moment and then added wistfully, "I miss that man."

"Me too, Grams," Michelle replied, wrapping her arms around Joan's frail form.

The two clung to each other, and Michelle silently thanked God for both of her grandparents and the legacy of faith they'd instilled in her. It had been so difficult for her to let go of Grandpa Phil. He'd been such a spiritual anchor.

Lately God was teaching Michelle that her grandfather was a foreshadow of her direct relationship with her heavenly Father. In her quiet times of prayer and Bible study, He kept opening her eyes to the depth of His love for her as His very treasured daughter. With both her earthly father and grandfather gone, God Himself was becoming so much more personal and important to her.

Watching Grandma Joan grow more and more frail and forgetful reminded Michelle that soon another spiritual leader of their family would cross over into Jesus' waiting arms. She determined to spend as much time with Joan as possible, while she continued to deepen her relationship with God.

"Grandma?" she asked.

"Yes, dear?"

"Do you talk to God more now that Grandpa's been gone for a while?" Michelle paused and then added, "I mean, does God seem even closer to you?"

Her grandmother smiled and nodded. "He sure does, sweetheart. Why, when I'm all alone at night, I sometimes just sit here and talk to Him right out loud." She laughed to herself and then looked a little embarrassed. "I suppose I'm turning into a senile old coot."

"No, Grams. I don't think so at all," Michelle replied. "I do the same thing myself, just not out loud as often because there's usually someone around. But I'm learning to go straight to God these days more and more. It seems like He's teaching me to depend less on other people and more on Him to meet all my needs."

Joan patted her on the arm. "Your grandpa would be so proud of you, Michelle." She smiled and then added, "Whew wee—you gave us a run for our money when you were a youngster and got yourself going with all that New Age stuff. But look at you now! God's done some mighty work in you and your family, sweetheart. And I've got a feeling He's not finished yet."

NOTE FROM THE AUTHOR

Dear Reader,

When I sat down to write this story, I was coming from a place of brokenness. Having been rejected by some people very close to me, I was in the process of examining my pain and my past, and how those factors influenced my relationships today.

As my journey and the story in this novel unfolded, I began to see the immense impact a father has on his children and their lives. And I knew there were two important messages God wanted to communicate through this book.

The first is the overriding importance of knowing God as the only perfect Father.

The second is the sacred responsibility of earthly fathers to influence their children's lives in positive ways—giving them a taste of the love of their heavenly Father while also pointing them to Him as their ultimate source of fulfillment of their deepest needs.

Through my own journey of soul-searching brokenness, I've come to discover a much deeper understanding of the heart of God our Father. He is teaching me to let His love be the fuel that energizes me, the river of Life that fills and fulfills me, the strong tower that protects me, the balm that heals me, the calm in my storm, my resting place at night, my anchor to Truth, and my unending fount of wisdom.

I believe God gave us the example of His Son to demonstrate the unique bond between a father and his children. And then He took it a step further by inviting us to join His family through spiritual adoption.

When a child is placed in foster care, he is afforded the basic necessities of life in the home of someone who is legally obligated to be his temporary guardian. But when a child is adopted, he becomes an heir alongside any siblings that may be in his new family.

Fostering can be motivated by a number of factors, but adoption is a lifelong choice based on the desire to forge a family tie that cannot be broken. This process is perhaps one of the most profound gifts exchanged between any people. For the parents, they are gifted with a child, an heir, a focal point for their love. For the child, he receives the gift of belonging to his very own family.

Here's the most important truth I hope to communicate through this story—to those who were raised by godly fathers and to those who were not—you have access to a heavenly Father who is more than godly. He is God.

His love is limitless, His grace is bountiful, His judgment is fair, and His salvation is eternal.

And if you are a father, trying to raise your children to know and love God, understand it's not all on your shoulders. No matter how much you love your children and try to be the perfect father, you will make mistakes. You will let them down many times. You will fail to keep some of your promises. And you will react in the flesh at times in ways that are far from godly.

God is not calling you to be Him. He's calling you to point your children to Him.

The most important lesson you can teach them is to look to God as their ultimate source of love—a love that will give them strength when they are weary, that will fill and fulfill them when they are empty, that will guard and protect them from the darkness, that will heal their broken hearts and the wounds of the world, that will be a source of calm in any storm, provide a safe resting place in the night, be their anchor to truth, and provide them with wisdom.

As their earthly father, you have more power than anyone else to connect them to their Heavenly Father.

In this story, Madison faced feelings of inadequacy and fear. She needed to learn to trust God with her calling as Luke's wife. She did this by learning to listen to her heavenly Father, who spoke to her through her prayers, her parents, her counselor, her great grandmother, Joan.

Meanwhile, her brother Caleb had to struggle to come to terms with the inadequacies of both his adopted father and his biological father to meet some deep inner needs he had. In the end, only his heavenly Father could provide that. He did it for Caleb, He's done it for me, and He can do it for you.

If you've never accepted God's invitation to join His family, now's the perfect time. The adoption papers have been drawn up with your name on them, signed in the precious blood of Jesus, who redeemed you on the cross.

Do you want in? Into the heart of God? Into His unending provisions, His boundless love, and His eternal mercy and grace? It's only a prayer away. You don't need any magical words. Just tell Him you know you aren't perfect—that, in fact, you've fallen far short. Ask Him to forgive you and to make you one of His own. Thank Him for the cross and the forgiveness made possible by Christ's death there, where He paid the price for every sin you or I have ever committed. And then trust Him to begin guiding you from this point on.

If you are already a member of the family of God (or even if you just became one!) thank Him for being the Father no human ever could. Thank Him for His promises, His faithfulness, His loving kindness, and His unending grace.

Then go tell someone else, who needs that kind of Father.

If the story of Chen touched your heart, and you feel moved to reach out to orphans who need both earthly parents and a Heavenly One, a good place to start would be Shepherd's Field. The Children's Garden was based loosely on information about that orphanage. You can learn more here: http://chinaorphans.org

Thanks for taking this journey with me. I believe there are more stories to come. I'd love to hear your stories as well, and how this book impacted you. You can email me at rosemary.w.hines@gmail.com. If you would like to receive updates about special offers and future releases, you can email me with the simple message of "Add me" and you'll be added to my personal contacts list. You'll be the first to know about upcoming releases and special offers, as well as opportunities to participate in launch teams. As a special thanks, I'm creating a digital gift for all of my subscribers that will be sent out soon.

You are a blessing to me! Let's keep in touch. You can visit me on the web at www.RosemaryHines.com and keep up with my blogs and news on my Facebook author page: https://www.facebook.com/RosemaryHinesAuthorPage.

And don't forget to visit my Amazon author page, where you'll find all the titles in the Sandy Cove Series.

If you enjoyed this story, please take a moment to post a review. Here is the Amazon link for its page: https://www.amazon.com/dp/B01N9B59GL
In Christ,
Rosemary Hines
Rosemary.w.hines@gmail.com
www.facebook.com/RosemaryHinesAuthorPage
www.rosemaryhines.com

ACKNOWLEDGMENTS

I am so very thankful for the many people God brings into my life, as I write each book. From my faithful readers, who encourage me to press on, to consultants who bring authenticity and accuracy to my story, to the technical workers who create a cover, edit my writing, and format my manuscript—it requires a team to bring each tale to fruition.

In the crafting of this particular story, I had the blessing of consulting with a good friend, Gretchen Hill, who has adopted a sweet boy from China. She was able to share with me many details that helped in the portrayal of life in an orphanage in that country, as well as giving me insights into the process of overseas adoption.

After praying, outlining and months of typing, I handed my manuscript to my dear friend and editor, Nancy Tumbas, who did a complete content edit for me, finding any inconsistencies, suggesting changes in the beginning, and helping me solidify the message of the story. Then she painstakingly edited for spelling, grammar, and other technical errors.

Next, the corrected manuscript was sent to another sweet friend and sister-in-the-Lord, Bonnie VanderPlate. Line-by-line, she proofed it one more time to catch any lingering mistakes.

Meanwhile I sat down with my cover designer and son, Benjamin Hines, as we began the process of designing a cover. Every time we do this, I'm delighted and blessed by the work he is able to produce to catch the eye of readers and give a glimpse into the story, and this book cover was no exception.

Then, my formatter, Daniel Mawhinney at 40 Day Publishing went to work creating the ebook and print book files for publication. With an eye to perfection and consistency, he makes the interior of my books look great!

Although all of these people were so very helpful in the process of moving *Above All Else* from a concept to a book, many heartfelt thanks also go to all of *you* who have taken the time to email me and nudge me to continue this journey of message-driven fiction. Your letters reveal the power of God, by showing how He uses these simple stories to bring His love and truth into hearts and minds. Your emails inspire and encourage me in ways that go beyond measure.

Finally, special thanks go to the readers on my launch team, whose role it is to read and review the story before helping me spread the word of its release.

To all of the above and to you, my reader, I owe my deepest gratitude. You are a blessing to me!

BOOKS BY ROSEMARY HINES

Sandy Cove Series Book 1

Out of a Dream

Sandy Cove Series Book 2

Through the Tears

Sandy Cove Series Book 3

Into Magnolia

Sandy Cove Series Book 4

Around the Bend

Sandy Cove Series Book 5

From the Heart

Sandy Cove Series Book 6

Behind Her Smile

Sandy Cove Series Book 7

Above All Else

Made in the USA
Columbia, SC
17 January 2019